Lyndon Publishing

Run ... You Can't Hide

Janice Olson

Lyndon Publishing

Run ... You Can't Hide
Copyright © 2015 by Janice Olson

Requests for information should be addressed to:
Lyndon Publishing
2200 S. Smith Berry Rd., Suite 200
Pantego, Texas 76013
Website: www.LyndonPublishing.com

ISBN: 978-0-9764915-6-9

For more information about Janice Olson, please access the author's Website at: www.JaniceOlson.com, or email her at Janice@JaniceOlson.com.

Cover image, original photograph manipulated by Harry Olson, all rights reserved.

Lyndon Publishing Mission Statement:
To the best of our ability we publish, and distribute inspirational products that offer exceptional value and Biblical encouragement to the world while honoring God.

Dedication

This book is dedicated to all the women who struggle to be free as my protagonist in the story.

May God grant you the courage to overcome, the determination to persevere in the face of adversity, and the fortitude to make the necessary changes.

Blessings,

Janice Olson

Run ... You Can't Hide

"When I am afraid, I put my trust in you."
Psalms 56:3 NIV

Chapter 1

Aimee Hamilton's '57 pickup sprayed a rooster tail of brown dust into the air as her truck barreled down the country road. So far, she'd managed to hit every rut and pothole left behind by the last downpour as she drove at a faster-than-normal rate of speed.

And for what? To catch a man.

Whew! What a change. She hadn't wanted anything to do with a man since she'd run from one over two years ago. Now she was racing to catch her reclusive neighbor, Tom Branigan, an odd one at that.

Knowing the mailman delivered mail between eleven and one to the mailboxes lining FM 279 at the corner of the County Road 4614, Aimee figured Branigan would wait until after one to drive out to get his mail. She hoped her assumption was correct. If not, she'd be here at eleven tomorrow and stay until she caught the man.

Seeing her quarry standing alongside the mailboxes, thumbing through his mail, she applied her brakes. It wouldn't do to pelt him with dirt or choke him with dust when she wanted his cooperation. That is, if he stayed long enough for her to ask.

Branigan must have heard her coming. *Duh!* The man would've had to been blind, deaf, and barely breathing not to know she was heading in his direction.

Glancing up from his mail, even with his aviator glasses shielding his eyes, she knew he saw her, but he skittered off toward his Silverado. One of her neighbor's traits, a barely perceptible limping gait, was even more pronounced today.

Gaze locked on her prey, Aimee aimed her truck in his direction. She wasn't about to let him get away.

Branigan climbed inside the cab and shut the door quick-like.

Before Aimee could stop her pickup, she heard his diesel engine chug to life.

Land's sake alive! The man was trying his best to avoid her. She was just as determined he wasn't leaving until she had her say.

Angling her old beat up army-green truck in front of Branigan's new, fully-loaded grey one, she blocked his retreat.

You have to get up pretty early, buster, to escape me.

When he shoved his cap up, she saw his puckered brow and figured he was doing his best to stare her down. He reminded her of a bull, head down, ready to charge, with her being the red flag.

Smiling, she hustled out of her truck, or at least she tried to hustle. The cantankerous door wouldn't open without putting her full 110 pounds behind a good arm-shoulder slam to the door. When it flew open, she nearly fell out on the ground.

More than likely, she'd have a good bruise on that arm come morning.

In disbelief, he watched as she righted herself and then headed in his direction. She noticed a slight curve of his lips before they went rigid again.

Did the man ever smile?

Come to think of it, she didn't smile much when she first arrived in Ben Wheeler, Texas.

Branigan didn't talk much either.

Then again, Aimee didn't talk much until she became acquainted with Leah, at the art gallery. Her change of attitude was a good year in the making before she could smile, talk, or even laugh over the simplest of things.

Looking less than elegant in her paint splattered Stars 'n' Strips t-shirt, her seen-better-days Ropers, and faded blue jeans with miscellaneous holes—not the designer kind, but honest-to-goodness holes that came from hard work and being plain worn out—she headed for his truck.

She was having second thoughts. Maybe she should have taken some time to dress a little better. Fix her unruly, curly hair. Maybe put on some mascara.

To be honest, if she had taken the time, she wouldn't have dressed any differently. She wasn't here to impress the man, just get him to agree to her proposition.

She approached the driver's side of the truck and stood there smiling until she thought her face would crack.

Was Mr. Personality gonna roll down the window, or just sit there and stare at her like she was some kind of aberration?

Branigan must have seen the stubborn set to her jaw and figured she wouldn't move until he complied.

You're right on that score, buster.

Before another second ticked by, she heard the little whining noise of the electric window as the glass moved with smooth, effortless precision downward, unlike hers that took serious arm power to achieve. The cool air from inside the cab escaped and fanned her overheated face. Though it was late spring, it was hotter than blazes out.

For a brief moment, forgetting why she was there, Aimee stood luxuriating in the cool air before the south wind blew a warm breeze across her cheeks. The memory of effortless power windows and the luxury of a late model automobile with AC had her practically drooling. But she wasn't here to drool.

"Hi. We've never been formally introduced. I'm Aimee Hamilton, your neighbor." She gave her somber neighbor her best smile.

The firm set of his jaw and the irritated glare, for that's what she bet was hidden behind his dark shades, didn't faze her in the least — *well, maybe a little.*

"My land butts up to yours on the west side." She gave hand signals in the general direction, still offering him a huge smile hoping to soften him up. When he didn't nod or answer, she continued, "You know" — this time using her head as a directional signal — "if you take the Y to the left instead of to the right, you'll end up on my property?"

He was looking at her like she was some kind of nutcase.

Having dealt with Branigan's kind and a whole lot worse in her former life, she wasn't put off by his lack of cordiality.

More determined than ever, she pressed on.

"I have a proposition that will serve both our needs. And since we are neighbors, we can easily accomplish it without anyone being the wiser. In fact, I'd prefer it that way — keep it just between the two of us — private like, if you know what I mean."

His brows shot up quicker than the old tomcat could spring for a mouse. Two thick wrinkles appeared at the bridge of his nose. Though she couldn't see behind his shades, she could feel his hot glare.

She couldn't fathom what she'd said to tick the man off. Maybe he didn't like women. Or maybe she was the one he didn't like. They weren't acquainted so that couldn't be the reason.

"I'm not interested in your *proposition*, Ms. Hamilton. Now if you'll excuse me. Good day." He nodded toward her truck blocking his way.

Concerned she wouldn't have another chance, yet knowing he had taken offense to something she'd said, she forged on. "Mr. Branigan, I'm sorry if I've offended you. But how can you say you're not interested? You haven't heard what I'm prepared to do for you if you will in turn service my needs?"

His hot, stern features caused her to quake in her boots.

"Lady, let me make myself perfectly clear. Nothing you have to say or offer could induce me to *service your needs*. Good day."

"Mr. Branigan, please ..."

Cut off by the soft whine of his window being rolled up in her face, he had effectively shut off all further conversation.

Aimee wanted to stomp her foot and yell loud enough for him to hear her through the glass. She thought better of it, not wanting Branigan to view her as some silly woman throwing a tantrum.

Of all the insufferable men. You just think we're through? Well, think again. You haven't heard the last from me.

Crossing her arms to keep from pounding on his window and telling him what she thought of his rude behavior, she huffed and gave him a mean-eyed squint, for all the good it did her.

Branigan wasn't looking in her direction. Instead, his arm resting on the seat back, he glanced out the rear window, before proceeding to back up almost into the ditch.

It'd serve you right if you got stuck. I'd leave you right ... No. That was a pack of lies. She would never leave anyone stranded, not even her irritating neighbor.

Without giving her another glance, Branigan cramped the steering wheel a hard right, shifted the gears, and tromped the gas pedal.

Aimee stepped back for fear he'd run over her toes. As it was, he barely skirted her old truck before he took off down the road, unconcerned about the dust and dirt he was flinging in her face.

"Of all the ill-mannered, insufferable, uncouth old goats, you're certainly one."

Several more choice words came to mind but Aimee clamped her mouth shut. She refused to stoop to name-calling.

Knowing he couldn't see her, she kicked a rock, gaining little satisfaction.

"You aren't getting rid of me that easily. You don't know it, Mr. Branigan, but you've just met your match."

Chapter 2

Aimee Hamilton's image in Tom's rearview mirror soon faded and became obscured by the dust but not erased from his mind. Her perfume lingered inside his cab—*flowers*. She, in her raggedy clothes showed curves in all the right places, and those coffee-colored eyes with specks of gold that ignited with fire when he rolled up his window, were hard to forget. And her full lips ...

Enough!

That little woman spelled trouble, something he didn't need nor want, especially now when he was beginning to get his life back together again.

To say she had her nerve propositioning him right out in broad daylight was putting it mildly. She may be a beauty in her own ragtag way, but he wasn't that lonely. In fact, he never would be *that* lonely.

Some guys would have said he was plum stupid for passing up such a sweet setup. To his way of thinking, sex outside of marriage was like playing Russian roulette. He wasn't about to go down that bullet-riddled trail.

He'd had a lifetime of trouble and he wasn't looking for more, even if this particular problem came wrapped in a pretty little package. She was one person he'd steer clear of regardless how appealing she might be.

Avoiding Aimee Hamilton might prove to be a full-time job. In a town the size of Ben Wheeler, Texas, trying to avoid anyone was like avoiding an inmate in a POW camp. Near impossible.

When he approached the Y dividing his road from Aimee's, he shook his head. To say he was shocked at her tenacity was putting it mildly. The fact she didn't seem ashamed or the least bit put off by his rude behavior, made him pity her all the more.

Next time, *if there were a next time*, he'd tell her straight out he wasn't interested in what she was peddling. If she knew what was good for her, she'd leave him alone. Otherwise, he would feel obliged to alert the sheriff.

Tom did his best to think of something other than his disgusting but provocative neighbor. Yet, her image kept popping up, as if seared into his brain. And it wasn't just today either. Those few times he'd seen her at the mailbox or in town, the memory of her had a way of lingering for hours.

His wrought iron gate opened and he pulled through, heading up the road to his house. As tenacious as Aimee was, if it weren't for his gate barring her way, he figured she would have stormed his house instead of waylaying him at the mailboxes.

The sharp pain that had been building all morning long, latched onto his leg with intensity. A cramp grabbed hold of his thigh, drawing up and twisting the muscle. The excruciating torture shot down the length of his leg practically doubling him over. He managed to slam on the brakes and park in the middle of his drive, leaving the engine to idle while he massaged the old wound.

Gritting his teeth, he continued to pound and knead his leg. The spasm gave no sign of letting up. Fortunate for him the cramp didn't start while he was at the mailbox. What a pretty sight that would have been—him on the ground with a hormonal chick all over him wanting to help relieve what ailed him.

Chuckling in spite of the pain, he rubbed the spot where the shrapnel had torn through flesh and muscle and lodged in his bone, the remnants of Afghanistan. The medics said it was a miracle they were able to save his leg, let alone his life. He should have been dead.

The memory of friends blown up in front of him flashed across his mind. The nightmares still continued to wake him, heaving for breath, drenched in sweat.

Tom didn't remember much about that day, only the initial blast. Much later he learned he was the lone survivor, left with a shell of the man he'd been. He blamed God, if there was a God, for what happened. The why still begged to be answered.

Continuing to knead his leg, he shoved the anger aside. The torture eased up by small degrees until it was manageable enough for him to drive on up to the house. He knew he'd be wiped out for the rest of the day. Thankfully, the pain was coming less frequently due to exercise, knowing his limitations, and what to do for the attacks.

Pulling into the clearing, he took in the sight of his two-story log cabin.

What on earth possessed him to build such a monstrosity? Must have been one of his weaker moments when he still hoped for a wife and kids. Thankfully, he'd worked through that phase. He'd never be fit company until he was free of the demons of the war—something that might never happen.

For him, being a loner was best.

He hobbled down from the truck, irritated by his lack of control. Clyde's bark came from somewhere deep in the woods. By the time Tom labored up the porch steps and had the front door open, the Redbone Coonhound was by his side, tail thumping his good leg.

"How ya' doing, ol' boy."

The hound woofed then nuzzled his hand.

Tom gave Clyde a good scratch behind the ears before entering the house. The sound of his boots and the dog's nails clacking on the hand-scraped oak planking continued to drive home his lonely existence.

Fortunately, he had Clyde. Somehow a coonhound didn't quite take the place of human conversation or companionship, even if the dog was a better listener than most.

Switching on the stereo to drown out the silence, Tom moved to the kitchen to fill Clyde's water bowl. After grabbing the ice pack for his leg along with a glass of iced tea and a couple of dog treats, he scooted back in his recliner, eased his bad leg up, relieving the pressure.

Clyde laid his head on Tom's good leg and whined, his eyes sorrowful. The dog always knew when he was having a bad day.

"You must think I have a treat." For the first time since he'd left this morning, Tom actually smiled. He gave the dog's head a good, sound rubbing. "Sit."

Clyde sat up with an expectant look in his huge black eyes, tail thumping the floor.

"Good boy. Here."

The dog gently took the biscuit from his fingers before settling down beside the recliner. Tom ran his hand over the dog's coat, his fingers trailing through the short, stiff hair.

Maybe he should think about selling this place and moving into Tyler where his sister lived.

The thought made him grimace. He loved his sister but she would smother him with sympathy, and her kids would drive him crazy. His brother-in-law Bob, on the other hand, was a nice sort of guy.

"Well, Clyde."

The dog dropped the treat, his ears perked up, eyes alert.

"There'll be no going to town tonight for supper. A can of soup and a few slices of cheese will have to do."

The dog whined, cocking his head to one side before settling back down again.

Leaning his head back, Tom closed his eyes. The dull pain throbbed, reminding him why he'd moved here in the first place. This time he was assaulted with pain of a different kind, one that couldn't be eased by hands or ice.

Clyde nudged his good leg and whined, resting his chin on Tom's knee, watching.

"It's OK boy." He gave Clyde the last treat. "Just feeling sorry for myself with no good reason."

The music soothed as his thoughts wandered and the ice pack numbed his leg.

Wild, reddish-brown hair, large dancing brown-eyes, and a smile that could snatch a man's breath from his very soul, slipped in and captivated his thoughts. Aimee …

Maybe she would make a good masseuse.

He chuckled, then sobered. He'd live with the pain.

Chapter 3

Frank Thornton entered Rick Stanley's plush corner office. His windows overlooked the State Capitol and a good bit of Austin's downtown real estate.

Stanley, an official smile in place, moved from behind his desk. Late thirties, he looked every inch the lawyer slash politician. Stanley exuded the epitome of wealth. Suit coat off, sleeves buttoned at the wrist, Frank figured the man's tie alone cost a couple hundred bucks.

As a rule, no one called Frank for a meeting unless they wanted to hire him for his PI abilities. Stanley was no different, even if the cause for him being there hadn't been stated beforehand.

"Frank, nice to finally meet you. And thanks for coming to Austin." Stanley motioned him to one of the club chairs.

"You have an impressive view." Frank nodded in the direction of the picture window.

A slight tick appeared in Rick's jaw before he smiled again. "I chose this office specifically for the view." He sat in the chair opposite. "I'm sure you're curious why I asked you to come."

"I'd be lying if I said I wasn't."

"You came highly recommended by Phillip Bradley, and at present I'm in need of your services for a personal matter."

"I'll be happy to consider the job. What is it?" Frank crossed his leg, his boot resting on his knee. He wondered why Rick hadn't called a PI in Austin, since his own Thornton PI firm was in Dallas.

"I'm not sure if you follow politics or not, but a few years back I ran for Senate and lost."

"I read something about it." With Frank's preliminary research before this meeting, he knew just about all there was to know about Stanley and his family. At least, the part that was public and easily accessible by the Web. Before he decided on the job, he'd do a more in-depth research.

"The loss of my race can be attributed to one thing. My ex-wife, Jennifer." The lawyer paused. His gaze narrowed, as he reflectively gnawed at his bottom lip before offering a humorless smile.

"Like a lot of men, I was fooled by a pair of lovely eyes and a body … well let's just say, Jennifer was beautiful. I learned too late she married me for the sole purpose of snagging a rich husband." A sarcastic laugh rolled off his tongue. "What I didn't realize, Jennifer was incapable of loving anyone but herself. Sorry, I don't mean to sound like sour grapes." He shrugged. "However, if you take this case, you must know the truth that few know."

Frank offered a noncommittal nod. Stanley, the candidate, wouldn't have received his vote, but Frank wasn't here for the candidate.

As was Frank's habit, he'd reserve judgment of what he thought of the man until he researched more.

"I learned too late that Jennifer was unstable. For two years, I tried to save our marriage. She had bouts of depression and would harm herself while in a fit of rage. I often wondered if she wasn't bi-polar." He waved his hand as if dismissing the memory.

"Long story short, she refused to get help. When I finally had enough, I asked for a divorce. That's when Jennifer threatened to ruin me. And I'm afraid she's come close to accomplishing her goal."

Frank Thornton knew spousal abuse wasn't a respecter of class or gender. He also knew the insidious crime was too often hidden behind closed doors in some of the best of families. But …

"Were her accusations that you beat her founded?"

"No!"

His passionate answer didn't mean a thing to Frank. Many men could hide facts and their behavior well.

"That's the crux of the matter. The Jennifer the public saw was everyone's little darling—pleasant, well mannered, and loving. However, the Jennifer behind closed doors could be normal and sweet, but more often than not, hateful and vindictive.

"The people who don't know me believe Jennifer's lies that I beat her. However, if you ask any of the people who know me, they'll tell you I wouldn't harm one hair on her head. The sad part ... I loved her, worshipped the ground she walked on."

Rick's face turned red and he offered a miserable smile. "Not many people know, and I'm ashamed to admit it, but I was the one who was being abused, not her."

Rick glanced away.

Frank couldn't reconcile the beautiful woman he'd seen in the news photos with the picture Stanley painted. Yet, he knew without meds, bipolar disease could cause huge mood swings and often make the person lash out verbally and physically.

"You see, I married her straight out of college. When the abuse first started, I thought with maturity she'd grow out of her rages. That didn't happen. Eventually it got to the point that I couldn't live with her self-destructive ways or the shame of me being abused any longer. When I filed for divorce, Jennifer began her campaign to assassinate my character."

"If, as you say, the abuse was a lie, where did the pictures of Jennifer's injuries come from, or the hospital reports that she was admitted several times with broken bones and contusions?"

Rick offering a humorless laugh. "I see you've done your homework." He shook his head. "Phillip said you were good and thorough."

"I'm a private eye. You wouldn't want to hire me if I hadn't looked into your background."

"You're right. I'm glad you did." He raked a hand through his dark wavy hair.

"At one time, I tried to protect her by being silent. Now I keep no secrets where Jennifer is concerned. To answer your question, the reports came from Jennifer.

She found a dupe in John Radican. The scandal sheet he works for was more than willing to print the lies."

Rick rolled up his right sleeve. His forearm bore a long, red, jagged scar from elbow to wrist. "This was one of many souvenirs Jennifer left behind. She tried to grind the jagged end of a broken wine bottle into my face. I deflected the bottle with my arm."

Disgusted, Rick shoved his sleeve down and buttoned it again. "When Jennifer didn't get her way she'd go into uncontrollable rages. She'd throw things, hit me, do and do whatever she could to get even with me. One time, when her self-inflicted injuries landed her in the hospital, she accused me of throwing her down the stairs, then recanted."

"How many incidents are you talking about?"

"Total?"

Frank nodded.

Stanley paused to reflect. "Six, maybe seven times I'd classify as over the top behavior which could have ended badly. Each time the abuse got progressively worse."

Having dealt with spousal abuse in the relocation of abused women over the past five years, this was a first for Frank. He'd never worked with a man where the woman was the abuser.

"Did you file a police report on any of the incidents?"

"No, Jennifer begged me to forgive her and not shame her by revealing her problem. She always promised she'd change, even get counseling, but never did. Each time I agreed, she'd be better for a while until something ticked her off again."

He stared at Frank. "Call it pride or stupidity, but I didn't want to appear weak or unable to control my own wife, especially when I was running for Senator."

Rick rubbed a hand over his eyes expelling a breath. "But you see where that landed me. I wish things were different, but they're not. And now it's my word against Jennifer's and Radican's."

The lawyer looked Frank straight in the eyes. "I swear I didn't abuse Jennifer."

"What do you want from me?"

"I need you to locate Jennifer."

Rick stood, pulled a picture from his desk drawer and then handed it to Frank. "This is Jennifer. Once I know where she is, I'll give the information to Radican so he can print a retraction that she's alive and I had nothing to do with her disappearance. I want my name cleared of all wrong doing."

If what Stanley said proved true, Jennifer had inflicted a great deal of pain on the man.

"What makes you think Jennifer is alive and hasn't met with foul play?"

"My gut. Regardless what Radican writes, I know Jennifer is alive and hiding. Where? ... I haven't a clue. That's why I called you."

Frank knew he had some serious research to do before he'd even consider taking the case.

Countenance troubled, Rick shook his head. "Regardless of our troubled past, if she met with foul play, she didn't deserve to die that way. However, knowing Jennifer as I do, hiding is the sort of thing she would use to get even with me."

"Why? What's her motive?"

"In her small, twisted mind, she believes hiding and making others believe I killed her is payback for our divorce." He shrugged. "Even her family doesn't believe she's dead."

"And you know this how?"

"I'm still on good terms with her parents. Fortunately, they didn't believe her pack of lies. But they're worried something dreadful has happened. They haven't received letters, calls, texts, nothing. It's as if she disappeared off the face of the earth."

Frank was surprised the man had kept in touch with Jennifer's parents.

"Can you trust them to tell you the truth?"

"Yes, I believe I can. With their blessings, I hope to marry their daughter, Melissa."

"I see." Frank didn't see. This case was getting more bizarre by the minute. There was something drastically wrong with these people.

"Before Melissa will marry me, she made me promise I would do everything within my power to find Jennifer. That's a promise I mean to keep. But I also need to prove to the world I'm not the monster Radican and Jennifer have painted me to be."

Moving to the window, Stanley stared out at the city. "I'm sorry, but everything that went down over two years ago still affects me. At one time, I loved Jennifer deeply." He turned and let out a heavy breath, looking like a defeated man. "Will you help me find her?"

Frank lowered his foot to the floor and scooted forward in the chair.

"I'll do some research, and if it proves to be what you say, I'll take the case. But in the meantime, I'll send some preliminary questions for you to answer to help in locating Jennifer. You'll need to be completely honest in your answers. The more information, down to the smallest detail, the better chance of locating her."

"Certainly." Rick moved to his desk and retrieved a business card.

"Is that the latest photo of her?" Frank pointed at the picture of Jennifer.

"Yes, it's a good likeness. It was taken a few months before her disappearance."

"I'll need a copy."

"You can have that one. I don't need or want it any longer."

Giving Stanley an odd look, Frank asked. "I'm curious. If Jennifer is the type person you say she is, why would you want to marry her sister?"

Stanley chuckled. "It's not what you're thinking. Melissa is Jennifer's stepsister and her complete opposite. They have little in common. Melissa has all the sweetness Jennifer lacked and none of the devious nature. Melissa may not be the beauty Jennifer is, but she has an inner beauty her sister lacked."

Rick walked Frank to the door.

"If you decide to take the job, all I need from you is to take a picture to prove Jennifer is alive and supply the address where she may be found. Once I have that, you're job is done. Radican has agreed to check the information and print a retraction."

He opened the door and stood back so Frank could pass.

"I want nothing more than to get on with my life, marry Melissa, and become Senator in the next election." He smiled and then hesitated.

"Frank, I believe there's something you should know if you take this assignment."

Frank raised his brow in question.

"If you find Jennifer, be on guard. She isn't what she appears to be. In fact, I believe she's unstable enough to try to kill anyone who comes looking for her."

Chapter 4

"Aimee, what did the man say? Will he do it?" Maggie Dunn came out of the house wiping her hands on her apron, the screen door banged shut behind her. Her expectant brown eyes held hope. As always, a portion of her straight, light brown hair hanging around her shoulders fell across her right cheek to shield the ugly, jagged scar—a memento from her ex-husband.

Today at twenty-eight, Aimee felt older than Maggie at forty-five. The weight of her own failure sat heavy on her shoulders. She couldn't bear to see Maggie's or the others' disappointment.

"He wouldn't talk to me." Witnessing a hint of alarm in Maggie's face, she hastened to say, "But that doesn't mean he won't. I swear ... Well, I really don't." She crinkled her nose. "But you know what I mean."

When she heard Maggie chuckle, Aimee knew the woman still held out hope.

"That man is downright infuriating. But don't you worry. I'll go back tomorrow and the next day, and every day after if I have to, until I wear him down and he says yes. Even if I have to go to his house and hog-tie him to get him to agree, he will.

Aimee paused. "I'm not sure how I'll get through that eight-foot fence of his — wire cutters maybe?" She laughed at the silly thought, then shuddered. "He'd probably get his gun and shoot me on the spot if he found me snipping away at his fence."

"And he'd have every right to." Maggie shook her head smiling before turning to go back inside the house. "But if anyone can get him to agree, it'll be you."

She waved at Aimee. "C'mon inside. I've got a Chocolate Sheet Cake inside. I had a notion 'bout now we might want a piece, but I thought it would be more as a celebration, not as a pick-me-up. No matter. C'mon. You can tell me all about it over cake."

Maggie stopped, then looked at her. "You might want to keep the meeting to yourself around the others. No use of upsetting 'em further."

"You may be right, but they're bound to ask. Since Leah mentioned a stranger has been asking around town about his missing sister, they've been a bit skittish. They know as well as we do, the man asking questions could be here for any one of us."

"Well, no use borrowin' trouble." Maggie held the backdoor open and motioned for Aimee to follow. "Cake's awaitin'. You'll feel a whole lot better once you've taken your boots off and had a piece."

It never failed. When she felt down in spirit like now, one of the women of Paradise Found, or even one of the children, would say or do something to perk her up. Her life had been miserable and without purpose before they had arrived. Aimee couldn't imagine what it would be like without them.

She recalled her terror filled nights, afraid she'd one day have to face her ex and fight for her life again. Today, her main focus was keeping the others safe and alive.

In the mudroom, she removed her boots. The smell of chocolate and pot roast mingled in the air, causing Aimee's mouth to water. Her house—once a pigsty—was beautiful inside and out. Just like the many friends who had come and gone through her doors over the last year and a half.

Thankfully, when she'd bought her property, the existing farmhouse had good bones. Everything else in the house had been worn out like she'd felt when she landed in Ben Wheeler. Rooming with Leah Franklin in her little apartment above her art gallery was good for her and had given her hope. Now Aimee and Paradise Found were full of expectations and promise.

Maybe one day soon she'd be able to contact her dad and see if it might be safe to return home for a visit. Or maybe he and her stepmother could come here to see all she had accomplished. She prayed for that day.

Dad and Sarah wouldn't recognize their former debutant daughter as this hard working woman running a halfway house for abused women. Overwhelmed with the loss of her family, she snuffed the pity party out. No use dwelling on what can't or might never be.

Aimee, in stocking feet, moved from the back entrance into the great room. She loved the open concept she'd been able to achieve when she remodeled the place. The kitchen, dining, and living room were all open, giving the space the look of one huge room. The upstairs housed Maggie and one other person if need be. Aimee's bedroom was on the bottom floor next to her office.

Two plates of chocolate sheet cake were on the long dining table making Aimee's mouth water.

This wasn't the first time Aimee silently thanked God for her friend and the loving atmosphere that reigned in her home. Now if only Branigan would agree to her plan, maybe then she could begin to feel safe again.

Her bent-out-of-shape attitude dissolved as she sat down and took the fork Maggie handed her.

"What did the old codger have to say?"

Aimee laughed at the far from factual image of Branigan that *old codger* conjured up.

"Well, believe it or not, the *old codger* had little to say. He's a man of few words." She pulled her plate closer.

"*Old codger* he isn't. Branigan isn't bad looking if one looks beyond the hard ridges of his face and the brooding brown eyes that are always covered by dark sunglasses. Definitely not my type, if I had a type." She chuckled.

Aimee knew his eyes were dark brown and brooding because she'd seen him once in town at the diner when he wasn't wearing his shades. His eyes reminded her of her own eyes when they looked haunted and alone.

Maggie snorted. "And what is your type?"

"It sure isn't him."

With more force than necessary, Aimee's fork sliced through the thick fudge topping to the soft chocolate layer below, her fork clinked loudly on the plate.

"Eat the cake. Don't break the plate." Maggie cackled. "The man must've been plumb downright mean. I don't ever remember seeing you this upset before."

"Let's just say, I'm not a happy camper." Aimee breathed out heavily.

"Well, spill the beans and tell me what happened."

She didn't want to rehash the meeting but knew Maggie wouldn't let it rest till she'd heard at least most of what took place.

"I introduced myself, which seemed to go well enough. But when I said I had a proposition that would serve both of our personal needs, he cut me off" — she snapped her fingers — "just like that."

Aimee slipped the bite of chocolaty goodness into her mouth, her anger seething. The rich, chocolate exploded on her tongue soothing her ruffled feathers some.

Maggie's chuckle started slow and then built into uncontrollable laughter that bordered on the ridiculous.

Aimee swallowed. "What? What's so funny?"

"Did you tell Branigan you had a proposition?" The woman scrunched her brows together in disbelief.

Puzzled by Maggie's reaction, she said, "Yes. I told him I had a proposition that he'd be interested in.

And since we were neighbors, we could accomplish it easily without anyone having to know."

Laughter filled the kitchen again.

"I don't see what's so funny?"

Maggie calmed down some, took a deep breath as she wiped her cheeks with her apron. She gave Aimee a *you poor child* look that didn't ease Aimee's mind.

"Lands sake, Aimee, didn't you mention anything about him training us?"

"He cut me off before I had a chance."

"Honey, with a man the likes of Branigan, he probably thought you were propositioning him for sexual favors, not his skills as a Special Ops."

"How could he?" She glanced down at her ragged clothes. "Look at how I'm dressed. What man in his right mind could construe my words to mean … oh … no. Surely he didn't."

Maggie nodded, doing a miserable job at holding back her laughter. "*Ohhh*, yes, I believe he did. And even dressed as you are, the man would have to be completely blind to miss seeing your womanly assets."

Branigan's actions and Maggie's reasoning all began to make sense.

"Just shoot me now and put me out of my misery." A slow burn crept up Aimee's neck into her cheeks. Elbows on the table, she buried her face in her hands, wishing she could roll up and die.

Her humiliation knew no bounds. How would she ever face the man again? Living in a town the size of Ben Wheeler there would be no way to avoid bumping into him. Worse yet, how could she approach him again to ask for his help?

When Aimee looked up, Maggie was doing her best to keep a straight face.

"What have I done?" Aimee wished she could erase the last hour from her mind.

"Nothing that can't be undone with a little plain talk, sweetie." Maggie patted Aimee's back, soothing her as a mother would a child.

"Tomorrow, you'll meet Branigan at the mailboxes. This time, you'll tell him plain out what you want. No beatin' around the bush." Maggie chuckled. "That is if the man'll stop long enough to listen."

"But that's what I thought I was doing—plain talking."

"Sweetie, a man like Tom Branigan won't understand or construe *a proposition* as anything other than the use of a woman's body."

"*My, goodness.* What have I done? There's no way I can go back and face him, let alone ask for his help. Maybe someone else could go."

"You know the others are too scared to talk to him. You're the only one. You'll have to do it." Maggie looked thoughtful. "After all, let's look on the bright side. I could be wrong. Maybe it's his nature to be rude and surly."

Shaking her head, she knew Maggie was right. Branigan thought she was ...

"Aimee, listen to me." The older woman patted her hand. "We have something he wants. The cantankerous man just doesn't know it yet. He has all the skills to survive the jungles of Africa, the Afghani desert, and to get through enemy lines, but I doubt he knows how to cook or clean a house properly. We do.

"Tomorrow, just tell him plain out—cleaning and meals in exchange for him teaching us self-defense. What man in his right mind would turn down that kind of deal? He'd be a fool if he did."

"You haven't seen him. Just knowing he's glaring at me from behind those dark shades of his unnerves me."

Aimee shivered as she shoved a bite of cake into her mouth. The mixture of the moist cake and fudge icing were beginning to ease some of the tension—*barely.*

"Mmm. This is just what the doctor ordered. Chocolate is definitely a cure-all for what ails a body."

Maggie's smile warmed Aimee's heart. This wasn't the same woman who arrived at Paradise Found wearing dread and uncertainty like a cloak. Back then she smiled little and talked less. Once the tattered woman settled in and realized she had nothing to fear and her husband couldn't find her, she became an intricate part of Aimee's little household.

She never realized what a blessing Maggie would be until she began asking to help with the cooking. Her friend could take a little bit of foodstuff and turn it into enough to feed fifteen, with the results, a heavenly concoction.

"As much as I don't want to, I'll go back again tomorrow, even if I have to wait all day for the cantankerous man to show. Or, I could storm his gate." She shuddered at the thought. "No, I'll catch him at the mailboxes. This time, I'll tell him straight out what I want."

Reaching out, Maggie enveloped Aimee in a quick hug. "That's my girl. Now eat your cake. You've got some paintings to frame for Leah's shop. And I need to make the ten pies ordered for the supper crowd at The Forge." She moved to the counter.

"Tomorrow, don't you mince any bones about what you want. Tell him straight out we need his services. And I don't mean stud services either." Maggie stood at the sink, her shoulders shaking with silent humor.

Easy for Maggie to joke about her botched-up job. Her friend didn't know how Branigan scared her spitless—far worse than she was willing to admit. But she'd talk with the man, even if she had to waylay him by jumping into the back of his truck. He wouldn't get away this time without hearing her out and giving her an answer.

Chapter 5

"That man's back in town."

Aimee's heart stuttered to a stop then kicked into overdrive. She didn't have to ask what man Leah was talking about, she knew. There were no secrets between them.

"When?"

"This morning. In fact, you just missed him, no more than five minutes ago."

Leah, a confidant, was her eyes and ears in Ben Wheeler, a safety net of sorts for the women at Paradise. The sale of Aimee's paintings from her art gallery kept Paradise Found afloat and out of the red.

Aimee placed her armload of paintings on the floor next to the art gallery's counter before giving her full attention to her friend.

"Do you know where he went?"

"Right now, he's over at Doc's." Leah motioned across the street at Doc's Hat Shop. "He seems determined. Maybe you better warn Kim she shouldn't go into The Forge today."

"That would be a surefire way for the man to overhear one of the waitresses was missing. He'd wonder who Kim was and why, of all days, she didn't show up for work." Aimee pulled the cloth off the paintings she'd brought to the shop. "But I'll warn her to be careful and be on the lookout."

"That's probably best." Leah picked up the first framed canvas holding it out, giving it a thorough inspection. "But I still worry about you and the girls living way out there by yourself and without a fence around your property. Anyone can just walk right up to your door."

"I know, but at the moment ..." She shrugged.

Leah tilted her head to one side and then the other. "I like what you've done with this one. The reflection of light on the pond is fantastic."

She set the painting aside to pick up the next one. "There's something different about how you're painting nowadays. Lighter, brighter. Not that I didn't like your earlier work. But these ... they have a certain vibrancy about them. I think it's the placement of light."

"Thanks. I'm experimenting with a new technique. The real test will be if they sell."

"They will. So whatever you're doing, I like it. Keep it up." Pursing her lips, she set the painting aside. "I'm still worried."

"Don't be. This man could be smoke in the wind. We'll just have to wait and see."

"You're right. But if he comes in again, I'm going to get his name and see if he has a picture of the woman he's trying to locate."

"Good idea. That way we'll know who he's looking for and if it is anyone at Paradise." She hugged Leah.

"Look, I hate to rush off, but I've got to catch Branigan at the mailboxes."

"Is that why you're so ..." Leah waved her finger at Aimee's clothes.

"You make it sound like I always come in here looking like a slob."

Leah chuckled. "No, but you don't usually look this good either." She wrinkled her brow. "I thought you saw him yesterday."

"I did, but ..." She grimaced. "It's too long a story to go into now. I'll tell you later."

Aimee moved to the door, wanting to stop any further conversation. "I'll give you a call. We'll talk."

Aimee walked out and glanced across the street at Doc's. The sun's glare on the windows made the shop invisible inside. Knowing she didn't have any time to waste if she were going to waylay the illusive Branigan, she hopped inside her truck and fired up the old lady.

She patted the dash affectionately. "Thanks, Gertie. I don't know what I'd do without you."

After backing up, she shifted into first. A quick glance in her rearview mirror revealed a man, medium height and build, light brown hair, walking out of Doc's.

Wishing she had time to stop to get a better look, she headed out of town. Aimee worried the man might be looking for her newest addition, Jill Morris.

She'd learned the hard way, the younger women when coming to Paradise Found sometimes didn't adhere to the rules of no phone calls, texts, or letters home.

Aware the time was close to eleven, Aimee stepped on the gas pedal, hoping Gertie wouldn't take this moment to throw a hissy fit. And hopefully, Sheriff Randall or one of the other officers weren't out patrolling the roads. She wanted to be in place long before Branigan drove up.

Keeping a steady eye on the rearview for flashing lights, she was happy to see the mailboxes ahead and offered up, *sorry God for breaking the law. I hope you understand.*

Glad to see Branigan hadn't arrived yet, Aimee pulled behind some tall bushes that shielded her truck from sight. She figured if Branigan saw her, he'd either drive on by or turn around and hightail it back to his place. That's something she couldn't allow.

Unlike yesterday, Aimee wore her best jeans, a shirt without paint smudges, and a pair of Lucchese boots she'd found at the secondhand store for a song. They were practically new and fit like they were made for her feet.

Her long, unruly hair was pulled back on the sides in a clip, the rest of her hair hung down her back—Maggie's doing. In fact, everything today was all Maggie's doing, with much protest from Aimee.

Her friend's words were still ringing in her ears—*didn't your maw ever teach ya that a gift is more desirable wrapped purty than in an old rumpled sack?*

Aimee climbed out of her truck, leaving her door slightly ajar. She crossed the road to check her mailbox and the others to make certain the postman hadn't arrived. He hadn't.

Branigan's attitude yesterday made her wish she had another choice, but she didn't. He was her one and only choice, like it or not.

She hurried back across the road to hover behind a bush, feeling foolish having to resort to such tactics. Acting like a spy while waiting for a man who wanted nothing to do with her, wasn't her style.

Knowing she would only get one chance at the contrary man, she planned to stay out of sight. If she had to, she would step out in the middle of the road to keep her neighbor from driving away. Hopefully, the cantankerous guy wouldn't run her down.

The sound of a diesel engine had her scurrying to peek through the bush to make certain it was Branigan and not one of her other neighbors.

It was him. He passed, and as usual, parked his truck off to the other side of the road. He was on the verge of stepping down out of his truck when he saw her. He stopped in mid stride, one foot on the ground, the other on the Nerf bar.

She could tell he was thinking about getting back inside his truck and driving off. But she wasn't about to let that happen today.

"Mr. Branigan, may I have a word with you, please." Aimee hurried across the road, ready to stop his retreat. Her heart and mind were racing ninety miles an second.

"I believe you misunderstood my meaning yesterday." Her cheeks burned and it wasn't from the sun. "When I asked you—"

"Listen lady, like I said, I'm not interested. So please, back off and leave me alone." He slammed the truck door, then stomped toward the mailboxes stirring up little dust devils with his boots.

She raced to keep in step with him. "The mailman hasn't come yet."

His mouth rigid, he acted as if she was something dead on the highway. He turned around, heading for his truck.

Aimee touched his arm, praying she could say something, anything to gain the man's attention. She hadn't expected the reaction to her emotions by the mere touch of her fingers. Snatching her hand back, she wondered if he'd felt it too.

If his placid face meant anything, he was unaffected.

"Uh, Mr. Branigan, please. All I ask is that you give me a moment of your time to explain."

He cocked his head to one side, his hot searing gaze pointed at her, or at least that's how it felt. Since he didn't hightail it to his truck, she took it as a good sign.

Swallowing hard, hoping to remove the clog in her throat and the knot of fear twisting her gut, she began, "You were mistaken yesterday as to my meaning."

He stood, arms crossed, distain evident. "I believe I understood you perfectly."

The need to rub her sweaty palms down the sides of her jeans had her shifting her weight nervously.

Trying for bravado, she gave him a short, firm shake of her head. "No, as to what you thought I meant, you were wrong. The services I was asking you to supply —"

He hiked his left brow, leaving her disconcerted.

Focus.

"I-I-It's your survival skills, nothing more. I don't need the other, um, what you were thinking I meant."

"How do you know what I was thinking?"

"Oh, well, as to that, my friend Maggie told me."

"And how does this Maggie person know my thoughts? I don't recall expressing them to her."

"Well you didn't ... express them, that is. But she, Maggie ... we-well, that's not important. What I am —, no, what *we* are willing to offer in exchange —"

Again his brow shot up, at least, this time his lips weren't as rigid.

"Will you stop that please?" Though Branigan hadn't smiled, she had the odd feeling he was finding this amusing.

"Stop what?"

"Stop looking at me as if this is one grand joke. What I have to say is important."

"There you go again, telling me what I'm thinking. Do you and this Maggie person claim to have psychic abilities?"

"Certainly not. Don't be foolish." The insufferable man was making fun of her.

"Would you mind taking off your sunglasses, please?"

"My sunglasses?"

"Yes. I hate talking to people when I can't see their eyes. I'm of the persuasion the eyes are a window to the soul. And I'd like to see yours when I'm talking with you."

"You want to see my soul?"

Her heart jumped into her throat. Aimee didn't know if he was going to take her head off or just leave. Why had she spouted off? She'd gone too far this time.

Seconds, which seemed like hours, ticked by.

Ever so deliberately, he raised his hand, grabbed the rim of his shades, and with a calculated unhurried move, he took his glasses off, lowering them to his side.

One look into Branigan's eyes snatched Aimee's breath from her chest. She'd never seen such gorgeous, unusual eyes. They were deep chocolate brown, embedded with flecks of gold, and surrounded by a ring of green. They pulled at her, that is, until she noticed they were filled with arrogant laughter — directed at her.

Her temper flared. She wanted to kick the irritating man for not taking her seriously.

"Have you seen into my soul, Ms. Hamilton?" He chuckled, if the gravelly sound could be called a chuckle. "Is it as black as some say?"

Chapter 6

Aimee gasped. Her temper evaporated. She was stunned silent by his statement. Her heart ached with compassion for the man, even if he was so annoying.

"Who would dare say your soul was black?"

"I don't think you're here to discuss my soul, Ms. Hamilton. Cut to the chase. What do you want?"

His eyes were cold, snatching the very thought from her mind.

What was it about Branigan that drew her to him and at the same time made her want to punch his lights out?

Aimee cleared her throat and then looked straight at his—chin.

"Mr. Branigan, please hear me out."

He looked at her oddly. "You have exactly two minutes to tell me why you've ambushed me out here before God and everyone passing by." He waved his hand as if directing traffic.

"I need you to teach us self-defense and how to shoot?" She rushed on afraid she might lose her courage or that he might say no. "You were in Special Ops, so I know you have those particular skills."

"And you know this how?" That same brow inched up again.

"Really, Mr. Branigan, you can't expect to keep your military background a secret in a town the size of Ben Wheeler." She smiled confidently, contrary to her churning stomach.

"One could hope," he huffed out. "Let's begin with why."

"Why? Why what?"

"Why do you want to learn to shoot?

"Well as to that ..."

"Get rid of snoopy neighbors?" He let loose a gravelly chuckle. "As you can see, it hasn't helped me much." He looked straight at her.

"No, of course not. I wouldn't shoot a neighbor for snooping."

"Could've fooled me." He folded his arms across his broad chest with an air of boredom. "One minute thirty seconds."

"Would you please stop that?"

He tilted his head. "One minute twenty."

"*Ohhh!*" Her temper boiled as she rushed on. "We want to be self-sufficient, live off the land. You know, be able to hunt deer, wild hog, and other eatable wildlife. Shoot them, gut them, cook them, that sort of thing." She gazed off across the road reining in her emotions, not wanting him to see her desperation. "And we want to learn one-on-one self-defense." She wrinkled her nose. "You know ..." Her voice trailed off.

"No, I don't know."

"Oh, I—"

"When you say *we,* how many are there? And ... just what are you willing to do for me in return?"

She hoped the sparkle in his eyes was an indication he was teasing her over yesterday's disaster.

Well, tease away, Mr. Branigan, as long as you agree to what I want.

"There are six of us, all women." Her voice trailed off again.

"Six ... women?" This time, his brows practically shot off his forehead.

She didn't have any intention of telling him why six. Few people knew, which was how it had to be. And it was none of his business anyway.

Several seconds passed before he narrowed his gaze, cocky-like.

"And, what's in it for me? I believe you mentioned we would both be *mutually satisfied.*" His last two words were drawn out slow and provocatively.

Instead of leaving like she wanted, with what was at stake, she tamped down the urge. "In exchange for your services—"

His chuckle changed the sharp planes of his face, revealing a handsome man.

It took all her fortitude to quiet her racing heart and continue. "We will cook and deliver meals—lunch and dinner—to your house, or you can come pick up the food at my house.

"Maggie is one of the best cooks in the country. You've no doubt tasted her pies and cakes at The Forge or at Moore's restaurant, which speaks well enough for her ability. And"—she had his attention now—"we will also clean your house once every two weeks. And let me tell you, Mr. Branigan, that's a huge bargain for what you'll be doing for us."

He narrowed his gaze. "Why do I get the feeling there's more behind your words than you're willing to say?"

"Mr. Branigan, I don't have some devious scheme up my sleeve. Either you will or you won't. Which is it? I'm not going to stand here all day bantering words with you."

She breathed in deeply, silently praying she could say something, anything that would have him agree.

"On second thought, sleep on it. I'll be here at the mailboxes the same time tomorrow. You can give me your answer then." Aimee paused, giving him a look of indifference so he wouldn't realize how desperately she needed his cooperation.

"Since your land butts up next to mine, I just thought it would be much easier for both of us." She shrugged. "But if you don't want to train us, there are plenty of other men in town who would jump at the chance."

He scratched his chin, studying her.

"Sleep on it." The smile she offered came at great cost. "I'll say good day to you then. Until tomorrow." Aimee turned to leave.

A strong grip took hold of her arm, stopping her from leaving.

"Hold on."

Fear sliced through her, snatching her breath from her chest. Lifting her hand to deflect the blow, she came to her senses seeing Branigan's stunned face and not her ex's.

He released her, stepping back, plainly shocked. "I'm sorry. I didn't mean ..."

Aimee lowered her hand to her side, humiliation forcing her to look away.

"Who hurt you?"

It took all her courage to look him in the face and lie. "No one."

She wondered if he'd be curious enough to probe. If so, what would she tell him? Once again, she moved to leave.

"Hold on. I don't know what just took place here, but if you want my answer, I have a few questions of my own."

"All right. Ask away." Dreading the questions he was bound to ask, Aimee waited.

He smiled ever so slightly.

The dark thoughts faded from her mind. The sun grew brighter. The nervous quiver inside her was replaced by soothing warmth. How could one man aggravate her one second and the next turn her into a hormonal teenager?

"If I agree, when do you want the training to begin?"

That was a question she hadn't expected. "Tomorrow."

He crinkled his brow. "Why the urgency?"

"No urgency. However, I'd like to begin before you change your mind." She forced a cocky smile she didn't feel.

"If I make this bargain with you, I won't be the one to renege." He hooked his thumbs in his back pockets. "Where will the training take place? And who will clean my house? I don't want just anyone poking around in my things."

The elation she had felt seconds ago, dropped in a heap in the pit of her stomach. It was all she could do to keep from telling the man to forget the whole thing. She knew if he agreed, it was going to be a real chore holding on to her temper.

Forcing her shoulders back, she said, "I would like the training to take place at Paradise Found."

He looked at her questioningly.

"That's my place. When I purchased the property, the name seemed to fit." Aimee stopped her explanation, worried he'd delve deeper. "And as to who will clean your house. I'll do it myself. You can rest assured, Mr. Branigan, I have no interest in *poking* through your things."

Branigan studied her to the point of being uncomfortable. Determined not to look away first, she stared until their stalemate became painful and began to do strange things to her insides.

Disgusted with her cowardice and her traitorous feelings, she glanced away. "Look, if this is too much for you, I'll find someone else. Thanks for your time."

She turned to leave, not about to show her disappointment. But one thing was for sure she would have to find someone quick-like.

"I'll do it."

Aimee stopped in the middle of the road, unable to believe her ears. She looked back at him. "Pardon me?"

He smiled an honest-to-goodness smile that nearly floored her. But it disappeared before she had a chance to really enjoy how it changed his looks.

"I'll do it. However, I'd like to inspect your weapons, make sure they're up to my standards. And I want to meet the women I'll be training." He glanced off toward the road. "If they're anything like you, I'll have my hands full." He mumbled the last part.

Aimee couldn't tell if he was joking or serious. However, one look at his bored face she knew he was dead serious.

"You'll find the women you train, unlike me, will probably be frightened of you at first. But they'll get used to you."

She figured she'd better strike while the pistol was hot, or whatever it was that gets hot. "How 'bout coming to the house now and look them over?"

"The women or the guns?" The sparkle in his eyes gave him away.

"The guns," she answered deadpan.

"Since the mailman hasn't come yet, I'll follow you back to *Paradise*."

"You can meet the women, get a taste of Maggie's cooking while you're at it."

"Why do I have the notion that you're getting ready to wage a full-fledged attack against some poor, unsuspecting soul?"

"You can rest assured, anyone I wage a war on will not be a poor, unsuspecting soul. They'll deserve exactly what they get." She turned on her heels and shot over her shoulder. "You can follow me to the house. It'll ensure you won't get lost."

His chuckle floated on the wind, straight to her heart.

"Lady, *you can rest assured*, if anyone gets lost, it won't be me."

Chapter 7

Tom veered his Silverado around one of many major potholes in Aimee's dirt drive. To miss them all would be impossible. He had to pick and choose between the lesser of two evils—the craters or the sinkholes. The lady needed to have some serious roadwork done.

By the looks of her battered old rusty truck, she couldn't afford a decent ride, let alone pay for grading. He figured her house probably wasn't much better.

Aimee was impervious to the pot-marked road. Her truck shimmied and shook as she flew over the holes. How she managed to stay inside the cab or keep the rusty vehicle on the road was a mystery.

Fortunate for him, it had rained earlier that morning, otherwise, he'd be eating her dust. He backed off the gas, putting some distance between her truck since there was the huge matter of her tires spitting rocks and pelting his Chevy. He figured she'd already given him a few chips in his paint job.

Reaching the top of the hill where Aimee's truck had vanished out of sight, he applied his brakes.

The name Paradise Found wasn't far off the mark. The woman had a sweet setup, something he hadn't expected, especially, after the road he'd just traveled.

Nestled in a small valley, backed by a thicket of trees and brush, a large two-story Craftsman style farmhouse sat as a beautiful jewel in the knee high emerald grass, with a garden to one side. A little ways from the house, the sun glistened off a huge pond. He bet there would be some good-size catfish or bass floating in the water waiting to take the bait.

Releasing his foot off the break, his truck ambled on down the hill toward the house.

Aimee motioned for him to park next to hers.

He pulled in and turned off the motor, staring at the picture perfect house. Brightly blooming flowers hung on hooks from the porch header beam. And on the railing, colorful painted pots were filled with flowering plants. Her place had that *welcome home* feel.

Remembering what she said about the eyes being the window to the soul, he reached up and removed his shades. He placed them on the dash, wondering why he felt like obliging her. Something about Aimee made it hard not to want to please her, while at the same time she irritated him beyond belief.

She was tenacious, he'd give her that. He applauded her for her moxie, and at the same time had the overwhelming desire to protect her. To some extent she reminded him of his sister.

Mary Jane was a lot like Aimee — not in looks or size, but in their persistent attitude. They were both like a bulldog, ready to tear into you one minute and the next ... a champion who would fight the world for you and patch up your wounds. Yet, something about Aimee seemed a little off kilter, as if she were hiding something.

It wasn't until he stepped down out of his truck that he noticed the big white barn hidden behind tall trees and bushes. Like the house, the barn looked in excellent shape. Someone had done an outstanding job restoring both buildings, a project he would have enjoyed.

"Sorry about entering through the back door. We seldom use the front."

Tom pulled his gaze away from the barn to the beauty standing in front him. "Back is as good as front."

He sauntered over to where Aimee stood holding the screen door open. The aroma coming from the house tantalized and made his mouth water for what the cook offered.

"Something sure smells good."

"Maggie's doing."

Her brilliant smile caused his heart to constrict.

"This is our mud room, but I won't make you take off your shoes."

"I can if you wish."

"No, that won't be necessary."

Unlike earlier, intent and on a mission, Aimee was nervous and unsure. He brushed it off as a woman's ever-changing mood swings.

Several pairs of shoes, including three pairs of children's tennies in various sizes were lined up on the floor beneath the bench where Aimee sat struggling with her boot.

Did she have kids? Was she married?

He'd never heard anyone mention a husband or any children yet, that didn't mean she didn't. He brushed the pesky thought of Aimee having either out of his mind.

"Here let me help you with that." He motioned at her boots.

"No, that's all right."

Ignoring her, he bent and grabbed the heel of her boot. With small effort, the boot came off in his hand. Her foot was small. The little mudroom grew too small, too cramped, too intimate, and ... she was way too close.

Her brightly, multicolored stockings matched her zany spirit, unconventional and unexpected. He quickly removed the other boot and then stood, breathing in deeply. Big mistake. His lungs were filled with her flowery scent.

Aimee rose from the bench, then stepped back, her cheeks red, her eyes uneasy. "Thank you."

"No problem."

"Shall we?" She motioned at the doorway into the house and gave him a less than confident smile. "The others will be surprised to see you. But don't worry. They'll be accepting of you once I tell them you have agreed to train us."

"I don't wish to intrude."

"You're not. I have an open door policy. Maggie always makes sure we have more than enough food to go around, just in case."

Tom wanted to turn and run, but didn't. He wondered what she meant by open door policy. Did she take in strays or anyone who happened to walk in?

This woman had the skill of a horse whisperer, wheedling her way inside him, turning his will to mush. He still didn't know why he'd agreed. Must have been the desperate look in her eyes when she thought he wouldn't.

Why was she so desperate?

For certain, he would learn the truth before he took on the job.

She led him into the kitchen. "Maggie, we've got company."

The room fell silent. An older woman stood at the stove stirring something in a huge pot. She pulled her brown hair over her right cheek, before turning to look at him.

"Good." A knowing look passed between Aimee and Maggie. And another thing, this Maggie wasn't surprised to see him. *Hmmm. Planned?*

"Everyone, this is Tom Branigan." Aimee motioned to the woman by the stove. "This is Maggie, our excellent cook."

"A pleasure to meet you." Tom tipped his head in greeting. "I hope my coming for lunch isn't an inconvenience."

"Lands sake, no. You're welcome. There's always plenty." Maggie turned back, busying herself with whatever she was cooking.

The other three women stared at him—eyes cautious, fear thick in the room. To say they were skittish was putting it mildly. He figured they would bolt out of the house if he made a move in their direction. Without a word, the three women turned and continued their chores as if he hadn't entered.

Aimee had mentioned six women but counting Maggie and her there were only five. Maybe the last one would show up later.

The owners of the three pairs of tennies, two small boys and a young girl a few years older than the boy, sat at the table watching him. The children were cotton tops, browned by the sun, and at the moment, very curious.

Were these children Aimee's?

"Lands, if I'd known you were bringin' home company, I would have fixed more than stew and cornbread." Maggie took another quick glance at him before opening the oven door.

The aromas mingling in the air made Tom's taste buds clinch with anticipation. His stomach felt like he'd come off a weeklong trek across the desert with nothing to eat but MREs.

"Mr. Branigan has agreed to train us. I-ah-asked him to lunch so he could meet everyone and sample your fine cooking."

There it was again. That slight hesitation, the underlying meaning to what was being said.

A pale woman, with what his mother would have called dishwater blonde hair, crossed in front without looking directly at him, then set another place setting on the table.

"This is Debra Sue. And these are her children."

The mother didn't look at him directly, but she quietly scolded the kids for staring before she moved back to the counter. The children, instead of obeying their mother, watched him with curiosity.

"And the other two helping Maggie are Keisha and Jill, the newest members to our little household."

Keisha, with curly black hair and skin like warm caramel, nodded but kept a wary eye on him. He noticed darkened areas on her arm and one cheek where bruises were fading.

Like Debra Sue, Jill glanced back without acknowledging him, then turned her back to him to help Maggie. She was too thin, making her eyes look huge in her small, child-like face. Her mouse colored hair hung straight down her back and she seemed nervous and out of place. He noticed an ugly, fresh scar that ran the length of her arm from the outside of her wrist disappearing up under her sleeve. Had she been in a car accident?

What was up with these women? Was Aimee running a home for women down on their luck? He hadn't seen a more motley crew since Special Ops.

"You may sit here." Aimee motioned to the head of the table as the others took their places along the sides. She slid in next to him on his right.

Once everyone was seated, a napkin on their lap, they bowed their heads. Fortunate for him, Maggie hadn't dipped up the bowls of the fragrant stew. Otherwise, he would have been digging into his food while the others were saying grace.

He didn't have anything against praying exactly. But after seeing so much death and destruction, he figured God had better things to do than to listen to his prayers. In fact, he couldn't remember the last time he'd prayed over anything, period.

Though he'd wanted to pray a few times, he wasn't certain there was a God. But if there was, he figured his prayers would go no farther than the sound of his voice. Yet, sitting here with these women, it seemed right and natural.

Maggie dipped up bowls of thick, dark gravy with chunks of meat and vegetables. With Tom's first bite, he knew he'd made a good bargain. To have food that tasted this good everyday would be well worth the aggravation he'd go through training these women or having Aimee in his house pilfering through his things.

The room was quiet as everyone ate. He figured there would have been chatter, maybe even laughter if he hadn't been there. For some reason, he'd put a damper on the dinner.

"How long have you been out of the Special Ops?"

He figured Aimee already knew. "Almost two years now."

"How long did you serve?"

Tom wasn't sure why Aimee was probing. If she dug too deep, he'd tell her to back off. It was none of her business.

"Ten years." He shoveled in a mouthful of stew, hoping she'd get the hint and change the subject.

This bargain might not be so great after all.

"Mr. Branigan has agreed to begin training tomorrow. What will you start with first?"

What's the rush on training? "Since we'll soon be in each other's face, it would be best if everyone calls me Tom. Mr. Branigan's a mouthful."

The children laughed. Their mother shooed them but still didn't look his way.

"However, we'll begin with self-defense. I'll give everyone some basic things to work on, demonstrate some of the maneuvers which should scare off anyone who wants to do bodily harm."

"Great. Nowadays, a woman needs to be prepared for every eventuality." Aimee smiled, looking at the women.

Tom didn't need anyone to tell him, most of them were deathly afraid of him. With one look at the silent women, it was obvious. Was it him? Or men in general?

"The first thing you will need to do is get over your fear. Fear can immobilize you, leave you with the inability to think and react quickly." He glanced around the table.

"Don't get me wrong, a little fear is healthy. It keeps you alert. Makes you aware of your surroundings. It also gives you the edge over that person who doesn't know what to do." He set his spoon down and wiped his mouth.

"However, to live through a brutal attack takes skill and confidence and your ability to know what to do and when to do it, along with a healthy dose of respect for your opponent." He narrowed his eyes. "I can teach you, but only you can fight off your attacker."

Though Aimee professed personal protection, he still didn't believe it was the real issue. This training appeared to be the difference between life and death.

Chapter 8

"If you're through eating, we can take a look at the guns." Aimee wanted him out of the room before he scared the women half out of their wits.

"It'll give your food a chance to settle before eating Maggie's excellent dessert. I believe we're having banana pudding." She stood and motioned for him to follow. "This way, please."

"Thank you for lunch, Maggie. That was some of the best stew I've ever eaten. If all of your cooking is as good as the stew and cornbread, I can see I'm in for a real treat." He nodded at the others. "Ladies."

Maggie beamed with Branigan's praise. In fact, Aimee had never seen such a huge smile on Maggie's face before.

When they reached her office, where all her weapons were stored, Aimee reached around the bookcase. Her sawed-off shotgun, resting in the corner, out of sight, was always ready and handy.

She handed the gun to Tom. "It's loaded."

"Nice scatter gun. Mossberg—good brand." He pumped it once, ejecting the shell. He opened the chamber, looked inside inspecting down the barrel. Picking up the shell, he looked it over before reloading it into the chamber again. "The only thing I'd recommend is to use double aught buck shot. It's a more lethal load."

"I'll make a note to get some." Her Ruger SR 45 automatic was next. She removed the clip, jacked the cartridge from the chamber, and then handed him the gun, placing the clip and the bullet on the desk.

Tom didn't hide his astonishment of how she handled the Ruger. "I see you've been around weapons."

"Not before I moved here. But since I can't afford a fence, and being so far from any of my neighbors, you being the closest, I figure a gun should scare off any unwanted visitors."

"Especially, if you jack the shotgun. It's a universal sound that anyone who hears it knows what it means — you're armed and ready." He pulled the slide on her Ruger verifying the gun was empty, and then continued to handle her gun as if it were an extension of his hand.

Unsure if she should pull out her assault rifle, she figured she might as well. He'd find out soon enough she had one. Reaching into the far left corner of the closet, she grabbed her Smith & Wesson .223 M&P AR15. This rifle was more power than she was used to, but she wanted to be competent in handling and firing the thing.

Tom whistled, laying her handgun down next to the shotgun. "Where did I get the idea you knew nothing about firearms?"

"I didn't say that. In fact, not meaning to brag, but I'm a crack shot. I can shoot all them with accuracy. I even have a license to carry. It's the others who don't know anything about guns and I feel inadequate to teach them. Even I know there's more to guns than point and shoot."

She pointed to the assault rifle in his hands. "That one is the newest. I've only had it a couple of months. I'm not as proficient with it as I am with the others."

Tom gave her a strange look before he picked up the Smith & Wesson. As before, he lifted it to his shoulder but only after checking to make sure the rifle was empty. He aimed it at the window, looking down the barrel, before lowering it to his side.

"What exactly do you expect to shoot with this gun?"

His penetrating stare nailed her. She did her best not to avoid his gaze, knowing full well he would recognize she had something to hide if she did.

"I was told at the gun show this rifle would be spot-on target and would fell a deer if I learned to shoot it properly. And that's what I need you to show me how to do. I don't want to maim the animal and then have it run off and die somewhere. I want to bring it down with one shot."

He studied her, then placed the rifle on her desk beside her .45 and the shotgun. She could tell he was working something out in his mind.

"You have some serious weaponry here, lady. At one time I would have said, a bit much for a woman your size to handle. But I've seen recruits as small as you use even more serious weapons than these."

Tom pointed at the shotgun. "That little baby will saw any intruder in half, if cocking one in the chamber doesn't scare them off first. The pistol, aiming at a person's center mass or head, if you're as accurate as you say you are, would blow a man to kingdom come with one shot. But this one?" He picked up the Smith & Wesson again, weighing it in his hands. "This baby, in a good shooter's hands, can take an animal or man down somewhere between 150 to 200 meters. But in an experts hands ... 500 meters or better."

Laying the Smith & Wesson aside he squinted in Aimee's direction. "What are you hunting? And don't feed me the line it's deer or hog, because plainly lady, I don't believe you."

The quiet in the room crackled like electricity on a hot dry day. Tom didn't budge, just stared her down.

Aimee knew if she didn't confide in him in the next few seconds, Tom would walk out the door sealing her fate and that of the other women. However, it was a fifty-fifty chance if she told him their secret he would walk out anyway leaving them high and dry.

She didn't know anyone else who knew more about guns and the art of survival as Tom. That is, if the reports she'd heard about him were correct. She sent up a prayer for wisdom and the right words to sway him.

"Listen, I can tell when someone's not telling me the whole story, and that's something I can't abide." His stance was unwavering. "If you don't trust me enough with the *why*, except to say you want to learn to shoot for food and protect yourself from a would-be attacker, then I'm afraid I'm not your man."

He hadn't moved an inch, just stood there with a hard glare. When she still hesitated, he turned to leave.

"No. Wait. Please." Aimee grabbed his sleeve.

He looked down at his shirtsleeve bunched in her hand.

She released him. "Sorry."

"You have one chance to convince me why I shouldn't walk out that door and not look back."

Her teeth pulled at her bottom lip. She had to tell him the truth. Anything less, he'd see through it and be gone.

"Sit down please. I need to tell you about Paradise Found and why it exists. Maybe then you'll understand why we need your help."

Tom Branigan slipped into her desk chair, stretched his long legs out in front of him, folding his interlocked hands over his trim belly. Once again he zeroed in on her, this time skeptical. "I'm listening."

He had a way of staring at a person that would make anyone else shake in their boots. But not her. She was too petrified to shake.

Aimee moved to the door. With a trembling hand, she shoved it closed before sitting down in her reading chair, perched on the edge, as if ready to take flight or fall on her knees and beg—she didn't know which.

To say she was nervous was putting it mildly. Her food churned in her stomach and felt as if it might come up at any moment. She was about to entrust this man with the lives of her friends and the future of Paradise Found.

Aimee prayed she wasn't making a big mistake. Everything hinged on Tom's ability to keep her secret.

"First, I must have your word that you won't repeat anything I'm about to say."

"If it's not illegal, unlawful, or jailable then you have my word."

She shook her head. "It's none of those, so I'll take that as a yes."

He quirked a brow. "Ms. Hamilton —"

"Aimee, please."

"Aimee, you don't know me from Adam, and yet you'll trust me to keep your secret? A secret that seems to have you scared stiff. Why?"

She glanced down at her clasped hands before looking back at Tom. "I believe you are an honorable man who wouldn't wish harm to the other women or me." She took a breath. "That's exactly what would happen if others were to know the truth about Paradise Found. And ... I have to trust you are a man of your word because you are our last hope."

Chapter 9

Unconsciously, Aimee picked at her thumbnail. Dredging up the past was unpleasant at best and something she would rather stay buried. Yet, she would tell Tom everything, whatever it took, if it meant his compliance.

"It all began when I came to Ben Wheeler a little over two years ago ... well really, it started long before that, but I won't bore you with the details. Suffice it to say, I came here with help from an organization, an underground railroad of sorts, for battered women. Today the organization operates much the same as the runaway slaves' transport did before and during the Civil War."

Though he schooled his features to look unaffected, Aimee witnessed his shock. She felt the old humiliation seep in before she tamped it down and forced it back out.

"Paradise Found is one of many stopping off places where battered women come to heal and move on to the next phase of their new life."

"This organization, they helped you get this place?"

"Not exactly. I–um–inherited some money a few years back which I used to purchase this property and make the improvements. Thankfully, neither building was in too bad of shape. I was able to renovate the farm house and barn into livable space."

His gaze traveled around the room. "From what I've seen of the place, you're to be commended. You've done a nice job."

"Thank you." She remembered the searing pain the money had cost her. However, looking at what she had now, the money, though hard earned, was well spent.

"I did most of the work myself, which took months." She laughed. "You won't believe what I had to do to make this place habitable."

"I'm sure. Did you have help?"

"Very little. Everything you see—siding, walls, roof, paint, I learned how to do on my own either by reading a book, looking on the Internet, or by asking someone who knew how. It took many a sore back and hands, mashed and blistered fingers and thumbs. There were a lot of tears and frustration before it was completed." She glanced around her office, proud of her accomplishments. "I can't tell you how many times I wanted to give up. But it's not in my nature."

"Oh, really? Could have fooled me." He hiked that brow of his. This time a tad of a smile lurked at the corners his mouth.

"I'll ignore that." She smiled remembering how often she wanted to give up but didn't. "The sweat of my labor was well worth the end result."

"I have to hand it to you. You did a remarkable job."

"Yes, well it was for a cause, one I believe in." The heat of embarrassment made her look away and out the window. The view of her pond brought calm and reassurance.

"Once I completed the remodeling and repairs, I opened Paradise Found for women of domestic violence—sort of a halfway house where they come, feel safe, and begin to heal and gain confidence to live without fear or abuse.

"Once they're ready, I send them on to the next link of their journey. They are relocated to a safe area of the country where they receive a new identity, find a job, and begin to live on their own again."

He looked surprised. "You mean Debra Sue, and—"

She nodded. "Yes. All of the women came to me because their husband thought it was their right to use them as a punching bag." She breathed out heavily remembering her own abuse and how she often prayed to die.

"I do what I can to help each of them get their life back, teach them skills to live on their own. And if they have children, coach the kids on their new life and the value of secrecy."

She watched Tom closely. "I saw you looking at the barn."

"I was wishing I had one like it on my property."

"I turned it into living quarters for the women. I can house up to ten women at a time, but would rather take care of four to five so I can give each the individual attention they so desperately need."

Aimee heard Tom's muttered curse.

"After these women have lived, sometimes decades, with a man who has beat them on a regular basis, they don't know how to live without fear, certainly don't have confidence. The beatings become a natural course of their life." She lifted her hands in surrender. "Expected."

"That's where you come in." She hoped he wouldn't back out now that he knew the truth about Paradise. "You can train them what to watch for, how to fend off an attack. Hopefully, it will give them a renewed confidence so they are unwilling to take any more abuse from a man, or for that matter, anyone."

She couldn't keep the bitterness from her voice. "I'd want them to feel confident enough to have a small chance at survival."

He ran his hand through the short stubble of his hair. "You do know a woman is no match for a man."

"Yes. But with the proper training, training you can give, they will have a better chance of survival than before."

"What about their families, won't they help?"

She shook her head. "Some don't have families, but for those who do, the more determined ex-spouse often uses the woman's family to find her and force her back, resulting in escalated violence."

Her loathing was too repugnant to conceal. "My place, and others like this one, is their last hope. When these brutalized women come to me they have cut all ties to families and friends. And there's no going back, no calling, no reference to home. Their previous identity is gone, as if their former life never existed.

"That's one of the hardest things, particularly if the woman has children like Debra Sue."

The painful memory that Aimee might never see her father and stepmother, or even her stepsister again, caused excruciating pain. The stinging prick of tears had her stiffening her spine. She didn't have time for self-pity, especially now. That was the former woman who was afraid of her own shadow, but no more.

Tom leaned forward resting his elbows on his knees. "What precipitated you seeking me out?"

"*Ohhh, my.*" She breathed out. "Suffice it to say, one of the women called home to speak to her mom."

"And?"

"You have to understand, these men are narcissistic in nature. This particular man almost killed his girlfriend. Only by the grace of God did she survive."

He scoffed at her analogy. "In my book, lady, God had nothing to do with it. He was a little too late."

"I won't debate the point with you except to say, I believe God had a hand in her survival and sending her to Paradise Found."

"*Humph.*" The subject was distasteful to him. "And what did the call to her folks do?"

"I believe it's led him here searching for her. Someone has visited Ben Wheeler twice now, asking the whereabouts of a new woman in town who might be his sister. And if it's one of my women, then he's a threat to everyone who lives at Paradise. The man will do just about anything to find his ex, including killing those who stand in his way. Then after he finds her he'll beat her senseless and maybe even kill her."

Aimee shrugged. "You have to understand, men who beat women have a sociopath behavior, lacking conscience where there spouse is concerned that often goes to the extreme—*if I can't have you then no one will*—that sort of thing."

"Is this why you want the lessons, to kill the spouse?" His look was incredulous.

"No. I hope it never comes to that. But, if killing the man enables her to save herself and her children, then yes." The pain of reliving her own abuse bubbled up, choking her. She cleared her throat. "All I want is for the women to have a chance of survival. And I want—"

"So you're staging some kind of standoff? That's what you think will keep you and the others safe and free from these lowlifes?"

She shook her head. "I wish it were that simple."

Tom whistled lightly through his teeth. "Lady, you're asking a lot."

"No. All I'm asking from you is that you teach these women defense so they can at least have a small advantage."

Aimee hoped she wouldn't have to plead. But if it came to that, she would beg on hands and knees if need be. "Mr. Branigan, I'm not asking much. I just need you to help train us, nothing more."

Branigan blew out a breath before his incredulous eyes came to rest on her.

"Lady, when you say you're not asking for much, that's an understatement. I'd say you're asking for a miracle."

Chapter 10

To say he was stunned, put it mildly. The reason he'd moved here in the first place was to find peace, not a war. How in the world had he landed in this hornets' nest? He thought he'd left all the fighting behind.

Aimee was sitting here asking him to enlist in a war of a different kind. Even if he refused, it wouldn't matter. The battle would be taking place practically at his front door.

What had he gotten into? This was far more serious than he bargained for. Even worse than combat duty. At least his men were trained, knew what to expect, and in one-on-one combat could hold their own.

These women didn't stand a ghost of a chance even with what little training he could offer.

She may need help, but he didn't want to be the one to do the helping. Once he started — *no, rephrase that* — if, and that was a *big* if, he took this on, he would go no further than training these six women.

Seeing Aimee's expectant face, he knew she was eager to lock him into helping every pitiful stray shipped her way from ... God only knows where. He shook his head.

Aimee would probably say his moving next door was divine providence. He knew better. It had nothing to do with God and everything to do with total ignorance — ignorance of the fact that his next-door neighbor was a woman with a cause.

And if he knew anything for certain, he knew this spitfire of a woman wouldn't stop until she had him training every wayfaring woman who darkens her door.

At this very moment, that very same woman was looking at him pleadingly to help out with her cause. How in the world did she expect him to step in and train women, who were as frightened of him as they were of their abusive ex. He wasn't a miracle worker.

No way, no how, could he train a pack of women to become aggressive when they wore a badge of fear.

"Mr. Branigan —"

He pulled out of his thoughts. "Tom." When was she going to get it right?

"Tom, surely you can see your moving next to my property, was prov —"

"Stop right there." *How spot on could he be?* He gave a small chuckle with an incredulous shake of his head. "Spare me the nonsense of calling it providence. Nothing about this whole mess has anything to do with fate, providence, or divine power."

He knew what he had to say and do if he were to save his sanity.

"I'll keep my word and train you and these five other women, but that's where it stops. I'm not here to save the world ... or in this case, one woman at a time. I did all my saving overseas. I'm out of the saving business now. All I want is peace and quiet, and to be left alone, without any interference from you or anyone else.

"Do we understand each other?" He gave her a hard stare.

Aimee stiffened. Her countenance changed from pleading to bullheadedness, if he could put a name to the obstinate look in her determined eyes.

He wouldn't, he couldn't soften toward her. A savior to these women, and the trouble that would be coming down the pike if she continued to take women in, wasn't going to be his lot in life to worry about.

What Aimee didn't understand, and he had a good mind to tell her, she would never have peace. She'd have trouble, again and again, until someone killed her for her caring heart.

"I will take what you offer, Mr. Branigan."

She braced her shoulders with obstinacy, reminding him of his old drill sergeant.

"Because frankly, I'm in desperate straits and have no other option. I thank you whole-heartedly for the help you're willing to give. But that won't stop me from praying you see the need to continue helping me."

"Pray all you want, Lady. But don't be surprised if your prayers aren't answered. Mine never were." He'd gone too far. Why didn't he keep his big fat mouth shut?

Aimee studied him then glanced down at her hands. "I don't know what happened to you while you were in the service or if it was after or before, but

I will pray that you find the peace you seek. That's the least I can do for what you are willing to do for us."

She flashed him a beautiful, sad smile, giving him a pang of regret.

"Look, what you're doing for these women is admirable. But like the war, you're fighting a losing battle, one you'll never win. The die is cast. The numbers are stacked against you. There aren't enough hours in a day to save them all. The few you do help are only a drop in the bucket that continues to grow by the minute."

He brushed a hand over his eyes, the topic turning his stomach. "Don't get me wrong, my sympathies are with the women. I believe any man who beats a woman should be taken out and dealt the same punishment but worse, and then hung by the nearest tree.

"However, you are dealing with an element of society that may one day come back to bite you on the backside."

Aimee crossed her arms, giving him a *you poor man, you don't know what you're talking about* stare.

"I'm well aware I can't save them all, but if I can make a small difference in some of these women's lives, then I'll continue to push against the tide." She shook her head. "Unlike you, I believe what I'm doing is important enough to keep fighting, regardless the outcome."

As earlier, Aimee snagged her bottom lip with her teeth. He wondered if she knew she had a telltale sign that she was worried.

"I'm sorry. I didn't mean for this to become a war of words or beliefs between us. I won't say another word about you helping me after the initial training. However ..."

One of the cutest, slyest little smiles he could ever remember seeing appeared as her coffee colored brown eyes sparkled. "If you ever change your mind, just let me know."

The camelback clock on her desk chimed and she stood. "I'm so sorry. I didn't mean to take up so much of your time."

He stood, only a couple of feet separating them. He didn't like how his heart had softened toward her, nor did he like the sweet smell of flowers hanging in the air. The fragrance suited her. "I had nothing better to do."

"Well, good then. I at least made your day a little more interesting."

"I'd say that's putting it mildly." He returned her smile thinking it wouldn't take much to fall for this woman. Becoming close friends would never do. He'd keep a cool head, his distance, and his eyes off of Aimee.

"When do you want me to clean your house? Today, tomorrow?"

Never. "Since the day's mostly gone, why not come by tomorrow."

From where he stood, he was digging a hole that was getting bigger and deeper by the second—one that would swallow him whole if he weren't awfully careful.

"Will eight work? Or are you a late sleeper?"

"Eight's good."

After putting away the guns, Aimee opened the office door and led the way out into the great room.

All the women were gone. Sitting on the table were two bowls of banana pudding with a clump of whipped cream on top.

"I see Maggie left our dessert. It's such a nice day, would you like to take it outside and sit on the front porch?"

No. He wanted to make good his getaway, the sooner the better.

"Sure." He had the willpower of a child with a full bag of candy.

He needed to escape from this enticing woman. Instead, he held the door open allowing her to brush by as she walked outside with their pudding bowls.

Insane for not giving his excuse and making tracks out of here, Tom followed like a lamb to the slaughter. Aimee had a cunning way of insinuating her wants and desires into happening, which wasn't good. Wasn't good at all.

Somehow, staying objective around her was proving more difficult than he imagined. No matter what she said, he wasn't going beyond teaching the six women as he originally agreed. After that ... no more.

"Have a seat."

She motioned to one of the brightly painted Adirondack chairs lining the front porch. He'd completely missed seeing them earlier when he drove up. They had a view of the pond and the western sky. This would be the spot to sit after dinner and enjoy the end of day watching the sun set.

Good grief, what has gotten into him? The way his day was going, any minute now, he'd start waxing eloquently and spouting poetry.

"You have quite a place. Is your pond fishable?" Spooning the first bite of banana pudding into his mouth, his taste buds exploded.

"Wow! You weren't off the mark when you said Maggie was a good cook. This is some serious banana pudding. If the woman cooks this good all the time, I think I'm gonna have to hire her out from under you. As they say, *mmm-mmm good.*"

Aimee's face lit up. Her smile gorgeous.

He spooned in another bite, closed his eyes to keep his gaze off her, savoring the rich, creamy goodness. "Man, something this awesome is too good to be true."

Aimee's uninhibited laughter did a number on him. He watched her with fascination. If he weren't careful she'd make inroads to his heart.

"I give you my permission to try, but I'd be surprised if Maggie says yes." Her words were accompanied by a teasing glint.

She took a bite of pudding, her little pink tongue licking a small drop of the yellowy cream off her bottom lip. "*Mmm,* her pudding is perfection, isn't it?"

The sparkle left. In its place disgust. "Would you believe her husband used to beat her bloody and senseless because he said her cooking tasted like pig slop?"

"Was he the one who did the damage to her face?"

"You noticed?"

He nodded.

"Yes. But I hope you won't say anything to her. The scar makes her self-conscious."

"I wouldn't think of it. However I wouldn't mind meeting her ex in a dark alley someday. He wouldn't be coming back out except on a stretcher."

She nodded. "I understand completely. I felt the same way. Now I just pray he's changed so he won't treat another women like he treated Maggie."

Glancing off toward the pond, she sat in deep thought.

"After Maggie came here, it took me several weeks of gentle care and showing her she had nothing to fear or to be embarrassed about before she would even look me in the eye. It also took another good month before she offered to help me in the kitchen. And to imagine, all that time she was hiding such a wonderful culinary gift."

Aimee held up a full spoon of the creamy mixture. "She believed what her ex had told her for years. Today, the restaurants have standing orders for her pies and sweets. One even tried to bribe her with a very enticing offer just to come cook for them. I can't think of anything that woman can cook that wouldn't put the best chef to shame."

It didn't set well with him the woman, who prepared the wonderful meal, was beaten by the man who should have protected her. Tom's killing instinct rose higher.

"The man should have been horse whipped and then beat to a pulp."

"My sentiments exactly." Aimee filled her mouth with pudding, closing her eyes, smiling.

Watching her was pure pleasure. She was a mixture of sweetness, strength, and unwavering moxie all rolled into one. From one minute to the next she showed him sides of protectiveness, dislike, love, and humor. Aimee was anomaly.

"Maggie's come a long way. She's even taught me a few tricks in the kitchen." She faced him, a twinkle in her eyes.

He studied her, not quite sure what it was about Aimee that made him feel at peace or to want to do her bidding. He found it hard to tear his gaze away.

"What's wrong? Do I have pudding on my face?" She swiped her hand across her mouth.

"No. No pudding." Just one of the loveliest faces he'd ever seen. "How long has Maggie been with you?"

"She was the first woman to arrive at Paradise Found."

Without reticence, she slid her index finger around the edge of the bowl and then deposited the pudding into her mouth. She set her empty bowl on the small table between their chairs. After licking her finger again, she wiped the wet appendage on her pant leg.

Her simple, uninhibited act caused Tom's heart to kick in beating, desiring something best left alone.

"Maggie's been here about a year and a half. You wouldn't have recognized her back then as the woman she is today. Now she tries to boss me around."

Her tinkling laughter surrounded him. He wanted to hear her laugh more, and he wanted to ... *get out of here.*

"She was the one behind the idea to ask for your help. In fact, she made me go back to the mailboxes again today, as she put, *dressed like a proper woman.*

Otherwise, you would have had much the same as yesterday."

Aimee's hand unconsciously moved to the small locket hanging around her neck. She began moving it back and forth on the chain, staring off into space.

"I gave up pleasing a man several years ago. Not that there's anything wrong with it, there isn't." She wrinkled her nose. "It's just not my thing any longer. Now, I have the women. I pour all my energies into them. They need me, and they appreciate what I'm able to offer them. Unlike ..." She looked off toward the pond then back at him.

"Yes, we do have largemouth bass, bluegill, catfish, and last year I stocked some rainbow trout in the lake. Those are really good."

At first he didn't grasp what she was saying, then he remembered he'd asked about the pond when they first came out on the porch. Aimee could drive a man crazy with her penchant for rapid-fire change-the-subject. Did she do it to keep from spilling her gusts?

"I have a couple of ponds on my land, but so far, I've only caught a catfish, fairly good size, but nothing else."

"Would you like to know my secret to a well-stocked pond?"

"Sure."

Again her smile warmed his insides. Yet, by the glimmer in her eyes, he knew she was about to pull his leg.

"I bought 'em."

"Bought them, where?"

"I'll give you the name and number of the man I used. He came out with a truck, dumped a whole load of fish into the pond for a nominal fee and a guarantee. Now we have an abundance of fish for food. All I have to do is catch them. Sometimes that's harder than it sounds though." She rolled her eyes. "I'm not a very patient person."

"Oh really? You could have fooled me." He laughed.

"Don't get smart or I'll take my offer back."

"What offer?"

"To let you fish in my pond until yours is stocked. There's plenty to share."

"Thank you. I may take you up on it." He glanced off at the pond. "Don't be shocked if you see me down there one day sitting on the dock fishing. In the meantime, I would appreciate the name and number of the company who supplied yours." He stood, reached for his bowl.

No matter how much he would love to fish her pond, he wasn't about to become that neighborly. Just one more way for her to get her hooks into him.

"Unless you're going back in for seconds, leave it. I'll take it in. I'm sure you have more important things to do." Aimee stacked one bowl in the other and then stood. She held out her hand. "Thanks for agreeing to take us on. I know it's asking a lot, but it means a lot to me and the others."

As he shook her hand, he noted how it fit in the palm of his, small and comfortable-like, yet not as soft as it should have been. He experienced a jolt that had nothing to do with being a friendly neighbor.

"I'll see you first thing tomorrow, eight o'clock sharp." She released his hand.

He'd been angling to leave from the moment he stepped into her house, but now leaving didn't sit well with him.

"I'll have the gate open. Drive on up to the house. Do you need anything special for cleaning?"

"Nope. Got it all." She studied him like she hadn't seen him before.

"Was there something else?"

"No. Except I was wondering ... why, when you plainly didn't want to, did you agree to train us?"

"If I'd known I was being wrangled into teaching a bunch of frightened runaways, I would have said no." He smiled to lessen the blow of his words. "But let's just say curiosity and your tenacious approach helped sway me." He chuckled. "And ... I figured you'd never leave me in peace unless I said yes."

"You don't know the half." She dimpled up at him. "When there's something I want, especially as important as this, I don't let anything stand in my way."

"I can admire that, as long as you understand ... this is a one-time thing. My training starts and ends with you and the other five." He set his jaw and gave a firm nod of his head. "I'll not train anymore after them."

She smiled as if she'd just been handed a precious gift, one she had begged and pleaded to get.

"After you've slept on it for a while, I think you will come to realize ... you're in it for the long haul." She turned and headed for the front door.

Of all the gall. That woman didn't know when she was defeated. But she'd soon find she'd met her match.

Before she entered the house, she said, "See you in the morning, Tom."

He liked how his name rolled easily off her tongue. She made it sound special, as if they were close friends.

The click of the front door pulled him out of his stupor. Disgusted with his lack of will power where Aimee was concerned, he all but stomped off the porch heading to his truck.

Her cause was a good one. But Aimee would have to find another gullible man to train the next round of women. By then, he will have closed up shop.

Chapter 11

"He's far more handsome than I thought he'd be. But he's a might too scary with his stern looks and serious no-nonsense manner. I'm not certain the other women will take to him." Maggie stood at the sink washing off early spring vegetables Aimee had brought in from the garden. "And if they don't, what'll we do then?"

"I'll have to convince the others he's more bark than bite. This has to work, Maggie, or I don't think these women will make it, especially if the person asking questions is coming for one of them."

Age-wise she was nearer to the youngest of her charges, but Aimee always felt like a mother to the women who entered her home.

"They need to be self-reliant and have confidence. Working with Tom will give them both. When he's through with them, they'll have the backbone they need to feel reasonably safe."

She woke up with Tom on her mind, which wasn't a good thing. And she couldn't figure out how one man could get her dander up so quickly and still stay a constant in her thoughts.

Gathering the supplies she needed for cleaning Tom's house didn't take long. She turned from the sink determined to forget about her elusive neighbor. It didn't help any that she figured Tom was mad at the world. And now, she felt it her mission to help him get over his anger and make peace with God.

Why did she have to be the woman for the task? Why couldn't it be someone else?

She didn't need Tom's brand of trouble, especially while dealing with the women and their needs too. God was asking too much of her.

I'll not give you more than you can bear.

Ok, Lord, I hear you. I'll shut up and do my job.

"I need to get going. Don't want to be late my first day." She chuckled, grabbing the carrier full of cleaning supplies and rags. "I don't want to give him any excuse to back out of this bargain we've made."

"Surely he wouldn't. Not after he gave his word." Maggie looked a little concerned.

"I was just joking. He'll keep his word." She shifted her load to the other hand, latched onto her keys, and headed for the door. "I'll see you around lunch time. Being a bachelor, there's no telling what I'll find or how much work I'll have to do to get his place in shape. Hopefully it's not too bad."

"Maybe I should go with you, this being the first time and all." Maggie picked up the dishtowel and began wiping her hands, a worried scowl in place.

"No, you have too much to do. I'll manage. Plus, I need you here in case we have an unexpected visitor. You know where the shotgun is and what to do."

She had drilled into Maggie the importance of showing strength, and how jacking a load in the chamber should deter most people. And if not ... pull the trigger.

"If I have to go back after lunch to complete the job, so be it. The next time won't be so bad. See you around eleven-thirty."

Aimee walked out the door with less confidence than she'd displayed to Maggie. She placed the supplies in the back of her truck, thinking this was a far cry from what her life used to be. But she wouldn't trade all the days of hard work for all the luxuries she'd had before. This was a better way of living than having wealth and comfort while fearing for your life.

One day soon, she hoped to have enough left over from the sale of her paintings to afford to have her drive graded and eventually a fence.

Today, she'd be taking time away from painting, which would cost her dearly in production, but that couldn't be helped. If she had to burn the midnight oil to keep up with the orders, so be it. That was a small price to pay for Branigan's help.

At the Y, she turned into Tom's entrance. The gate to the Rocking B was open. She noticed there were no holes or ruts to contend with on his smooth blacktopped road. Even her truck hadn't dared to rattle once after crossing the cattle guard.

Almost envious of the man, she remembered the anger and hurt hidden in his gaze. She'd take her potholes any day over the demons he must be fighting.

After several curves, a few ups and downs, and then up a small incline, she caught her first glimpse of the Rocking B. The thing was massive. Huge, or as Debra Sue's Mikey would say *hugungus*.

Aimee figured she'd be here for the next two to three days cleaning. What she should have done before striking the bargain was to have asked first to see his place. That way, she would have struck a better deal. But she wouldn't back out now. Live and learn.

She parked next to Branigan's brand, spanking new truck, turned off her engine, and then sat gaping at the monstrosity in front of her. Though she hadn't seen many log cabins, calling this house a log cabin would be one grand misnomer. Tom's was a huge, beautiful place.

The house had a large wraparound porch with polished logs serving for posts and railings. A log swing sat on the porch along with other log-concocted furniture. Actually, everything was quite well done, lending a certain hominess to the scene.

The floor to ceiling picture windows looked out over a rolling front lawn, which was the size of a football field. A few trees were scattered about, with the lawn ending at the beginning of a thicket of trees.

Though having been used to such opulence in her former life, it seemed a little surreal for something as beautiful as Tom's home to be hidden out here in the backwoods. Was he, like her, hiding from something or someone?

Startled by a woof, pouncing paws on the window frame, and hot doggy breath against her cheek, she barely kept from screaming. She liked dogs, but she hadn't expected one to practically jump in her truck.

"Down, Clyde, heel." Branigan stood at the top of the steps watching her, a grimace in place, as if he'd eaten something rotten.

The dog hopped down and sprinted off toward Tom, tail wagging. He loped up several steps at a time until he sat down next to his master's leg. Tom reached down and gently scratched the dog's head and ears, said something Aimee couldn't hear, then motioned to the side of the house.

Clyde leaped off the porch, heading in the direction of the back woods.

"He won't bite. But you can come out now. He's gone hunting."

"Good morning." Aimee pulled on the handle throwing her shoulder against the door, causing the thing to release. She clambered down. "I wasn't afraid of him. He just startled me, is all."

Leaning over the back panel of her truck for her supplies, she felt a strong arm reach around her and grab the carrier out of her hands. She hadn't even heard his approach, yet here he stood next to her, the smell of aftershave tickling her nose.

A tingle ran through her, not because she was afraid, but because of his close proximity, making her feel-good senses go off the chart.

"Good morning. You won't need the other things. I have my own inside. And cleaning products too." The gravelly tone sounded as if he'd just woken or hadn't spoken before now. His breath on her cheek was soft and warm, and held the smell of toothpaste, unlike the doggy breath of moments ago.

"Be that as it may, until I see what you do have in way of supplies, bring those along." She stepped back from Tom, sorry she'd spoken sharper than she meant to.

"Yes, ma'am."

She heard the laughter in his voice and knew he found humor in her bossiness. Or maybe it was her hasty retreat from him he found so funny.

"You have quite a place. Your house is beautiful. I've never seen one quite like it before. It's huge. Living alone, you must ramble around inside."

"Who said I lived alone?"

"Oh, well I ..." Her face turned hot. "It's none of my business who lives with you. I'm only here to clean—" His rumble of laughter cut her short, embarrassing her more.

"Don't worry. You're not entering a house of ill repute. Clyde is my only resident."

"I wasn't worried. It doesn't matter to me who you invite into your home. This is your house, after all. Clyde or anyone else, it's doesn't matter to me. I ..."

Quit rambling on like a dimwit.

When she reached for her bucket he wouldn't release his hold. She wasn't going to play tug-a-war, so she stepped back.

"If you'll show me the way, I'll get started."

"This way, Princess."

"I've never heard of a princess cleaning toilets before. Surely, you have me mixed up with someone else."

"I'm not so sure."

His under-the-breath chuckle caused her insides to clinch.

Who was this man that could be so distant one minute and teasing the next. She'd rather he stayed cold and aloof, that way her senses wouldn't get all jumbled up. His snarkiness would entitle her to remain surface-friendly, which suited her just fine.

Following him up the steps, she noticed he favored his left leg again. Maybe remnants of a war injury. One thing for sure, she wasn't about to ask.

"I haven't completed the upstairs. It's closed off, so you won't have to clean up there." He opened the front door, allowing her to enter first. "I do a fair job keeping the place clean, but I'm sure you will find it's not up to your standards."

His words stung, making her sound like a prude, which she wasn't. "How do you know what my standards are? You don't know me."

"True. Sorry."

They entered the living area, Tom silent while she took in her surrounding to see what she was up against. The open concept was like hers, only quite a bit larger with doors leading off to other rooms. From where she stood she counted three doors on the bottom floor and five doors on the second level. Thankfully she wouldn't have to clean upstairs or she would be here for two days to bring the place *up to her standards.*

Don't be so touchy.

His house was sparsely furnished, yet she recognized quality in the rich brown distressed leather couch with two matching cattle baron's chairs and end tables. And it didn't take a clairvoyant to know where he spent most of his time when he was home. His morning coffee cup, along with an array of magazines and newspapers were on the end table next to a comfy-looking recliner.

"Would you like to give me the grand tour?"

"Sure. This way."

He led her to a door to the left of the kitchen. "This is the master suite."

The room was on par with the rest of the house — twelve foot ceiling with exterior log walls. His king-size bed, a varnished shiny patina of old barn wood and metal, was rumpled with an impression in the pillow as if he'd just risen. A slight dampness hung in the room, along with the smell of his woodsy cologne, as if he'd recently showered and met her on the steps.

She could well imagine the spectacular sunrises he would witness through the floor-to-ceiling drapeless windows that faced east. Beyond his private porch was a view of a pond and trees.

"Beautiful view."

"Thanks."

Note to self. The man's not one for talking.

Knowing nothing more about Tom except he had served in special ops and had built a monster-size home, she was curious about the man, but not curious enough to ask.

Tom pointed to an open door. "That's the bathroom. The other door is the closet. And that door leads to my private office. You won't need to clean in there. I'll be working while you're cleaning the rest of the house. I don't want to be disturbed."

"You don't want me to dust or vacuum in your office?"

"No."

Don't need to be so touchy. "All right. Lead on." *One less room to clean which can stay dirty for all I care.*

He looked at her peculiar-like, and then turned and walked back out the door they'd entered.

Though more than curious as to what was behind the closed office door, she would respect his privacy and not intrude. But it didn't stop her from wondering.

He showed her the remaining portion of the downstairs — two smaller bedrooms, but not small by any stretch of the imagination, with baths, and another private living area — then left her to clean with the excuse he had work to do.

She wondered what type work he did, but didn't have the nerve to ask. Instead, she grabbed her cleaning supplies, put her ear buds in her ears, turned on the music to begin working. The music always seemed to make the cleaning go faster. It also helped to keep her mind on her work and from listening for Tom.

Beginning with the guest rooms and baths, which took no time at all, she soon moved into the rest of the living space. The house was quiet as if she was the only one here.

She looked out the front windows expecting to see Tom's truck gone. It was still there beside hers. Maybe he was outside. More likely in his private sanctuary.

As she often did, she hummed and sang along with the music as she worked. Surprisingly, she enjoyed cleaning Tom's house. He'd kept the place cleaner than most men, which helped to move through the house quicker than she'd anticipated.

Probably his military background had everything to do with his neatness, unlike one man she had known.

He didn't have a lot of incidental stuff to move and dust. At this rate, she'd be finished by eleven.

She screamed, jerked away from a hand grabbing her shoulder. Her arms swung up ready to defend herself. When she saw Tom's shocked expression — backing away, holding up both hands in front of him — the sting of her humiliation made her want to cry.

Instead, upset over her reaction and his look of pity, she yanked the ear buds from her ears.

"Announce yourself next time." She lowered her raised hand to her throat and felt the erratic beating of her heart, shamed by her display of anger.

"Sorry. I didn't mean to frighten you."

"Well you did."

Her reaction was partially due to the unexpected fright and the old ghost that wouldn't stay buried. She wanted to cry or hit someone, instead she lashed out.

"Don't ever come up behind me without saying something first. You scared me half to death. I nearly jumped out of my skin." She stopped, feeling horrible when she saw Tom's contrite face knowing she should have reigned in her temper and tongue.

"I'm sorry, but I called your name. When you didn't answer, I ..."

His remorse made her feel even worse. She looked away, took several calming breaths before looking up at him.

"I'm sorry. I didn't hear you. It was my fault entirely." She couldn't explain her actions. "Did you need something?"

Unable to look at his pitying gaze any longer, she ran the clean cloth along the counter she'd just wiped.

"I was going to get me something to drink. Would you like a coke or iced tea, or maybe coffee?"

"No, but thanks for asking." She didn't look up, just kept wiping.

"Well, when you do get thirsty, there's plenty to drink in the fridge. Or if you want some fruit, help yourself.

"Aimee?"

She glanced up.

His sheepish grin was endearing. "And I am really sorry I scared you. It wasn't my intent."

"Don't worry about it."

"As a kid, I used to love to scare my sister Mary Ann. She'd scream, then run and tell mom on me. Boy, did I ever get in trouble"

His impulsive chuckle and gleam in his eyes made her wish she'd met Tom years ago when life was simpler.

"You should laugh more. It makes you look younger."

His expression closed, but she continued. "I never had a brother to frighten me. Just a younger sister. The thought to scare her never crossed my mind. We were best friends. With me being older by four years, I was very protective of her." She abruptly turned, not wanting Tom to see her pain.

"Who hurt you?"

"No one."

"Someone did. I see the signs. Your ex?"

He had no right to ask. She almost didn't answer. "Yes."

Tom cursed under his breath. "You were a battered wife?"

"Yes." Suddenly, she felt tired all over. "It was a lifetime ago. Sometimes, the old ghosts come back to haunt like they did just now. But they can't hurt me." Smiling, she moved further away from him, picked up the broom and began sweeping to keep from saying more.

"I'll do your room next. After that, all I have left are the floors. I should be done by eleven, no later than eleven-thirty." She looked back at him.

His brow was knitted together, his gaze narrowed. For a moment Aimee thought he was going to continue to probe, instead, he grabbed a cup, poured it full of coffee, and then took a sip studying her over the rim.

"Everything looks great. If you need anything, knock on my office door."

"Will do."

Her gaze lingered on his back as he left the room. His limp was even more pronounced than earlier, and wondered if he was in pain.

What was he really like?

She knew there was more to the man than met the eye. Private and a loner didn't tip the scales with Tom. Below his rough exterior lurked a caring man. He revealed some of his compassionate side in his smile and in the reminiscing of his childhood, and ... when he wanted to know who hurt her.

Carrying her cleaning supplies into Tom's bedroom made her feel like an interloper. Unlike the rest of the house, this was his private world, a part of him most people never saw. Removing the sheets and covers from his bed, the woodsy scent filled the air and surrounded her, giving her a sense of intimacy.

When she looked for clean sheets, she couldn't find them. And though she didn't want to, she knew she'd have to ask him.

Raising her hand to knock on his office door, she heard a cry of pain and recognized it as Tom's. Without thinking, she opened the door and rushed in.

He was doubled over in his office chair, his legs out in front of him, hand kneading his upper leg, wreathing in pain.

"Tom! How can I help?"

He glared at her through pain-filled eyes. "Get out!"

The angry words were forced through gritted teeth. His hand fisted, he pounded into the meat of his thigh, his moan of pain muted by his clamped, ridged mouth. "I said, get out!"

Unwilling to stand by helplessly, and knowing he wouldn't appreciate her offering to massage his leg, she did the next best thing. She rushed out of the room.

If it was a cramp or torn ligament, she knew moist heat would help to loosen it, then ice to take down the swelling. She grabbed a couple of large towels, ran water over one of them, and then rung out the excess before putting the wet in the microwave to heat. When everything was ready, she grabbed a plastic bag and then ran back to Tom's office with the towels.

He didn't realize she had come back into the room until she knelt on her knees beside him.

"I told you to leave." His words, though still fraught with pain, were less angry.

"You did. But I didn't. I'm here to help."

"I didn't ask for your help."

"My aren't we grouchy. For once I'll let your rudeness slide since you're in pain."

"Some people can take a hint when they're not wanted." He jabbed at his leg again, his face contorted in agony.

"And some people really don't care if they're wanted or not."

She pushed his hand aside and got busy applying the plastic over his jeans to keep his pant leg from getting wet. She placed a layer of dry   and then moist heat, finally placing the dry towel over the wet to keep the heat in.

His face contorted with pain, his fierce glare watched her every move.

"You know it's a shame I can't find a way of harnessing all those heated glares you send my way. I wouldn't have needed to use the microwave to warm the towel." She couldn't keep the sparkle from her eyes. "Now keep quiet and stretch your leg out, point your toes. Try to relax."

"What do you think I'm trying to do? It's rather hard to relax with my leg drawn up tight into a knot, and with some overzealous woman butting in." Though he tried for contempt, he didn't quiet reach the mark.

"The heat should help loosen the muscles and lessen the pain some." She stood back. "How long have these muscle spasms been going on?"

A grunt was his answer.

"I can see from your face, the pain is beginning to ease up some. Once you're a little better, I'll help you move into the living room to your recliner so you can elevate your leg."

While she waited, she looked around his inner sanctum. The room was relatively neat and orderly, but definitely a man's room. No decorator touches here. Well, to be honest, there weren't any decorator touches anywhere in his house.

The office held a big, solid oak desk, a credenza to match, and a wall full of partially filled bookshelves. Tom was sprawled in the one lone leather chair with the ottoman pushed aside, eyes closed for the moment.

Every so often, his computer screen saver flashed pictures of men in uniforms standing, squatting, riding trucks, tanks, hummers, giving a little insight to his former life. A muffled groan drew her attention back to her patient.

"Do you have any pain meds?" She adjusted the towel on his leg.

"In my bathroom cabinet."

Aimee raced out of the room and then brought back the tablets and a glass of water. "I didn't find anything but Advil. Don't you have something stronger?"

Tom gritted his teeth before taking a breath. "No. I don't take drugs. Two of those will do."

While he popped the pills in his mouth and drank the water, she pulled the towels and plastic off his leg.

"What are you doing?" He grabbed her arm, stopping her.

"I'm going to pop the towel back in the microwave and then come back and help you into the living room."

She rushed out of the room with the warm towels. When she came back, Tom was standing holding on to his desk favoring his bad leg, lines of strain crisscrossed his face.

"Here, put your arm around my shoulder." She moved in and put her arm around his waist.

"I can make it on my own."

"I'm sure you can, but I'm not about to let you. You can do it my way and go willingly, or you can fight me, which will only hurt you. Suit yourself, but I'm not leaving."

"You sure are one obstinate woman." He slipped his arm around her shoulder but didn't put his weight on her.

"Lean on me." When he hesitated, she said, "I won't bite."

"I'm not so sure."

His chuckle warmed her. At least he could keep a sense of humor through the pain.

"Come on, lean on me." His dubious expression made her add, "I'm stronger than I look. Too many nights to count, I've dragged —" She latched onto his wrist and pulled him closer, holding on. "Well ... suffice it to say, I've hefted your weight and more many times in the past."

He hobbled next to her. She knew he was doing his best to put as little of his weight on her as possible. Struggling to keep upright and moving, she concentrated on her patient and not the fact that he was draped all over her and too close for her emotional comfort.

Even though Tom was generally surly and cantankerous, it wouldn't take much for her to look past his gruff manner and learn to like the man.

Don't even go there. You don't need complications.

If she were any judge, he didn't need complications either. Yet the more involved with Tom, the more attached she would become. She couldn't help it. It was in her DNA.

By the time they reached the recliner, she was exhausted.

The way he plopped down in the chair, so was he. Beads of sweat covered his forehead and around his mouth. She handed him a dry towel, figuring he'd use it to wipe his face while she retrieved the hot wet one out of the microwave.

Clyde was outside the front door softly whimpering. She wasn't sure if she should let him in or ignore him.

Instead, knowing Tom was her immediate worry, she got the hot towel out of the microwave and quickstepped it to where Tom sat. His head rested on the back of the chair, his eyes closed, the area around his mouth white.

She prayed the Advil would kick in soon and give him relief.

This time when she began placing the plastic and towels on his thigh he didn't push her hands away.

When she was finished wrapping his leg, she stood back and observed the man. It was a treat to watch him without him shooting a hard glare back at her.

Her hand itched to reach out and smooth his tightened brow. She clasped her fingers to make sure she didn't act upon her desire.

Maybe these silly sensations, whenever she was around the man, came because she knew pain and didn't want to see others suffer. Or perhaps her feelings were all mixed up because she hadn't been this close to a man in a very long time.

Whatever the reason, she needed to get past these meaningless feelings, and fast. She didn't have room in her life for a man who was fighting demons of his own. The good Lord knew she had enough difficulty just keeping Paradise Found up and running without adding more troubles to her already full plate. She definitely didn't need to add a man in the mix.

"Would you mind letting Clyde in the house?"

His unexpected words caused her to jump.

Tom released an exasperated breath. "He won't stop whining until someone lets him in. The confounded dog knows when I'm in pain and thinks he has to be here next to me."

"Sure." Had he noticed her staring? She hoped not. Glad for any excuse to leave his side and maybe get him out of her mind, she moved quickly to the door.

The dog slipped inside and past her legs, padding hurriedly to the chair, placing his head on Tom's good leg. Tom's hand moved to Clyde and soothingly ran his fingers over the dog's head.

Aimee marveled at the heartwarming scene of master and best friend.

Tom glanced up and caught her staring. Though the pain had eased some, she could tell he still had some remnants hanging on.

"I'm sorry about that." He motioned toward his office. "But the hot towel appears to have done the trick. Thanks for helping, even if I did just about take your head off." Though his face still held the ravages of pain, his smile showed his thankfulness.

"I'm glad I was here to help." She wasn't sure if she should broach the subject or not, but … "Do you have these spasms often?"

She stood there watching, thinking he wasn't going to answer.

"Not as often as I used to. The doctors believe one day they will eventually stop all together. But until then, I exercise to keep the muscles and tendons loose, and then hope each time I don't overdo it."

He emitted a humorless chuckle. "There's a fine line between just enough exercise and too much. But thanks to your quick action, though severe, the pain seems to be leaving quicker than usual. The stiffness remains, but that'll work out once I rest my leg a bit." He gave a sheepish grin. "Thanks for your help."

"No thanks necessary. Well, if you don't need me any longer, I'll finish your room." She started to leave, then stopped. "Oh, yeah. I don't know where your sheets are for the bed. That's the reason I came into your forbidden sanctuary in the first place."

"Somehow, I didn't figure you'd stay out." He chuckled.

"I did knock ... well, come to think of it, I guess I didn't. I was about to knock, so that counts as a knock in my book. I heard you and opened the door to see what was wrong."

"I know, curiosity." He leaned his head back. "In the bedroom closet."

"What?"

"The sheets? They're in my bedroom closet." He closed his eyes, a smile in place.

"Ok, thanks. If you want me, I'll be in the bedroom." She rushed out of the room, heat filling her face. Her words sounded more like an invitation.

Tom's chuckle lingered all the way to his room.

Chapter 12

Everything was going too smoothly. Aimee, not normally a pessimist, was waiting for that preverbal hammer to drop, all the while hoping and praying it wouldn't.

Over the last several weeks, Tom and she had fallen into a familiar routine that seemed to work well for both of them. Most times he'd eat lunch at her house with everyone else. In the evening, she delivered his meal.

Tom, though tough and expected much, was a good teacher. Their peaceful partnership, if one could call him barking orders and pushing Aimee to the limits during training peaceful, was working without a hitch. The women were beginning to warm towards him, even little shy Jill, her youngest houseguest.

For the sake of the women, Aimee held tight rein on her temper when Tom pushed and prodded her too far. She kept her mouth shut even when what she wanted to do was to give him a good peace of her mind. Wouldn't do any good if she did tell him off, it would just roll off him like water in a shower.

Much to her dismay, he was too easy to like. And those times Tom chose to yell at her, she didn't feel threatened or afraid as she had with her ex. Tom was gentle and caring, in a rough sort of way. And a likeable man even if he tried to act like he wasn't. However, being around him every day was begging for trouble as far as her heart was concerned.

If there was one blessing she could point to in this whole mess, the scare of the man asking questions had passed, at least for the time being. He had left town and as yet, hadn't returned, which hopefully, meant no immediate threat.

Debra Sue, the one who called the meeting, looked around the table at the other women then back at Aimee. "He may be a handsome one, I'll give him that, but he's as mean as they come, especially when he's yelling orders. And there's been a few times, we"—she looked at Jill and Keisha who nodded—"wanted to tear into him for treating you so poorly. There's no call for it."

The way the other women avoided eye contact with Aimee, she knew they were in agreement.

Maggie stood at the counter preparing their lunch, muttering. She glanced back at Aimee, rolling her eyes and shaking her head.

A laugh rolled off Aimee's tongue. "Really, ladies, Tom isn't all that bad. The only reason he picks on me is because he knows I have tough skin and I can take what he dishes out."

"Well, we don't like what he's dishing. When he arrives for lessons, my nerves stand on end and stay that way until well after he's gone. I even yelled at the kids yesterday, something I never do." Debra Sue's shoulders drooped. "We quit."

"Oh, please, don't. Look what he's taught you already. And there's so much more to learn. Give him a little more time. You'll see, Tom's really not so bad." She should be crossing her fingers for telling such a whopper. "You need to think of him as nothing more than a big ol' soft teddy bear." *One that will eat you alive, if you cross him.* She almost laughed at the image.

"He may sound gruff when giving orders but that's his military background. Deep down he's an old softy. For a man like Tom to continue dealing with a bunch of women like us is nothing short of a miracle."

Debra Sue made a scoffing sound. "Call it what you will. But a miracle isn't what I'd call Tom Branigan."

"Well, I didn't mean him exactly." Aimee smiled, doing her best to ease the tension. "Maggie and Kim are continuing. Why not give it another week. If you quit, he may stop training us altogether. And you know, just by the little you've already learned, you've gained confidence, which will give you a small fighting chance. Something you didn't have before."

Aimee motioned at large. "We are all better prepared than we were three weeks ago. Thanks to Tom, if someone were to attack me now, I'd like to believe I could do a fair amount of damage to that person. I feel I have a much better chance of staying alive."

She glanced around the table, feeling bad for capitalizing on their fear, but at this point she'd do just about anything to get them to continue training.

"Don't you remember before Tom came and a man was asking questions around town about us? If he came back today, you'd feel more secure in defending yourself, thanks to Tom. And if you keep training, before you're done he'll make sure you are prepared."

Aimee swept her hair behind her ear. She didn't want to push too hard and frighten them beyond reason. But a small dose of fear might make them see reason.

"I'm not here to make you do anything you don't want to do. We've all had a lifetime of bullies, and I for one don't want another one. But Tom isn't like that.

"All I ask is that you please think about what the training offers. If you do, I believe you'll come to the right decision."

Aimee got up from the table wishing she could shake some sense into the women, but knew they had to make their own decision. She could only guide them so far.

"Maggie, I'll be outside. Call me when lunch is ready."

In the mudroom, she pulled her boots on rather roughly, moved out the door and off the porch needing to let off steam. The women could be so exasperating at times.

She kicked a rock, sending it sailing out into the grass. The childish action didn't help her temper any, but she kicked another one for good measure. Skirting the front porch, she headed straight for the pond.

The women had gone through a whole lot worse with their ex. However, they looked at Tom as an extension of what they had left behind, something Aimee understood and Tom didn't seem to. At least, he wasn't out to kill them, just get them into shape for their future, even if he did yell his commands.

Knowing the only way she would be at peace with their decision, regardless what they decided, Aimee needed to heave all her frustrations onto her Father. She leaned against the railing overlooking the pond.

"God, I come to you asking several favors that I don't deserve. You are the only one who can open their eyes and take away their fear. And while You're at it, Lord, teach me patience and self-control and to be satisfied with the outcome ... whether or not it's what I desire.

"And Father, I hate to ask, but could You have Tom lighten up just a little so he won't continue to frighten the women?

"Oh, and another thing ... please, help me to get over this attraction to him. I don't need any distractions or complications in my life. My plate is full and I don't believe I can handle anymore. However, in these things I pray Your will be done. I need You, Lord. No one else can fill my life like You. Thanks for listening."

Filling her lungs with fresh air, she released a breath and with it some of her pent up frustrations. This talk and little time away from the house had already done her a world of good.

She chose a chair under the dock cover. Her body relaxed as she watched the peaceful ripple of the pond and listened to the sounds of nature. Leaning her head back against the chair, she closed her eyes to dream of a life with no complications, but knew it to be a pipedream.

Hearing Tom's truck, Aimee wished the man wasn't so downright punctual. She remained seated, waiting for Maggie's lunch bell, needing a few more minutes alone.

The soft breeze kissed her cheeks, as the song of a mockingbird soothed her mood. This was living. Not the glitzy lights, the glamorous crowds, the crowded streets and malls, not even the promise to become the first lady held any appeal. No, this was where she was meant to be.

Now if she could just get Tom to be more civil.

Chapter 13

Feeling Tom's presence long before she heard him, Aimee opened her eyes. It didn't make sense how she could be so attuned to a man she barely knew. Three weeks of close contact barely makes a friendship, especially when most of the time Tom ignored her, except to bark orders.

The last time she'd been so in tune with a man it nearly cost her life. Her mistake was in believing. Believing he loved her. Believing it was her fault. Believing he'd stop beating her. He never did.

"I saw you down here. If you don't mind, I'll join you."

Brushing back the hair the breeze had blown across her face, she glanced up at Tom with the odd sensation his being here with her was so natural, so right.

"If I'm intruding, just say so?"

Realizing she was glad he'd found her, she said, "No. Have a seat. I could use the company." She motioned to one of the Adirondack chairs. "I was taking a few minutes for some peace and quiet. With a house full of women, that can be difficult at times."

"Would you like me to leave so you could be alone?"

Why was he being so polite and sensitive to her feelings? She liked him much better when he was his old grouchy self. Grouchy helped her to keep things in perspective.

"No, not at all. Sit down. Maggie should have the lunch on the table soon, but she'll ring the bell when it's ready."

How could a simple smile warm her heart so?

"Does she actually ring a dinner bell?"

"Oh, yes. And you better come a runnin' if you know what's good for you. She waits for no one, not even me." She laughed, then watched him slide slow and easy into the seat beside her.

He leaned back, stretched his long legs out in front of him and got comfortable.

Tom was a good-looking man. Too good looking as far as she was concerned. Her experience with a handsome man had almost caused her death. Erasing that thought she glanced out at the pond. Tom had never shown signs of cruelty even when she'd pushed him beyond his limits.

"I'm glad you came out here. It'll give us a chance to talk."

"What's up?" He looked at her with that intuitive gaze of his.

"There's no good way to say this except to come right out with it." She released her breath, praying he wouldn't take what she had to say the wrong way. "Jill, Keisha, and Debra Sue want to quit." She chewed the inside of her cheek waiting for his reaction.

"Why?"

"In plain English?"

He nodded.

"They're afraid of you."

A sparkle warmed his dark eyes as a grin tugged at the corners of his lips. "Something I said? It surely couldn't be my warm and charming personality."

"There is something to be said about that." She chuckled as she slid to the edge of her chair, her hands clasped, elbows on her knees. "I'm afraid they don't like your looks."

"My looks?" His words came out on a laugh and his brow wrinkled in question. "I've never had anyone complain about my looks. My demeanor maybe, but my looks?"

Why was everything coming out wrong? "Yes. Well ... no."

The sparkle in his eyes had her shaking her head.

"Really, do I look all that bad?"

His teasing had a way of stirring up feelings. "No, you don't. You look ... oh, never mind. You know it's not your looks." She huffed, trying to think how best to tell him. "They don't like how you scowl at them."

"Scowl?" He looked incredulous.

"I've tried to tell them your scowl is worse than your bite, but none of them buy it."

"They're correct, Aimee."

"How so?" *Had he misunderstood?*

"My bite is definitely worse than my scowl. When it comes to training, I'm a bear. I won't worry about their *little* sensibilities or feelings. If you're looking for an easy teacher, then I'm not your man." He shrugged.

"A sniveling, weak-kneed woman can't expect to survive a personal attack. She won't last a minute if she has an emotional meltdown when confronted by danger. She needs to be capable of gouging the man's eye out without hesitation.

"I won't temper my harsh voice or excuse them because they don't feel good or it's their time of the month, because frankly, *darlin'*, their attacker won't care either."

"There's no need to be crude." She tried to keep the irritation out of her voice but failed miserably, knowing he was right.

"Listen, Aimee, I'm just speaking the truth."

She nodded, squeezing her cupped hands. "I know. What do you suggest I do?"

"About the women?"

She nodded.

"Nothing."

"Nothing? But …"

"If those women are afraid of me, what do you think will happen when they come up against a real threat?" He shook his head. "They've got to develop a backbone and be ready to fight at a moment's notice and not just because you've pushed them into it. They have to want to on their own."

"I'm just not sure they can."

"I can't give them the will, neither can you. And I can only train them. Strength is something that can be developed, but there also has to be a want in their gut to survive." He poked his rock hard stomach. "Without it, they're putty in their attacker's hands."

It felt like her heart was being squeezed. She wanted the women to succeed but ... at what cost?

"How's your leg doing? Have any more problems lately?" She didn't think he would answer. He looked at her oddly, then glanced out at the pond. "All right. We can change the subject, but it won't change the fact they either have a will or they don't. And my leg is better."

She wrinkled her nose and glanced at him sideways. "Why do I get the feeling you wouldn't tell me if the pain were nearly doubling you over?"

"I wouldn't."

"Ah, I get the picture now. You aren't much different than the women I take in."

He made a scuffing sound without looking at her.

"With you, pain isn't an option. With them, fear is a constant. So if we operate in the guise that neither exists, that makes us stronger?"

Tom gave her a narrowed-eyed stare.

"Well, tell me Mr. Special Ops Man, what happens when your pain throws you to the floor like it practically did a few weeks back? Or, when Debra Sue faces an angry demon in the form of her ex — you? In both cases, it incapacitates, both are uncontrollable."

"But mine is physical." He picked up a small stray rock and lobbed it up and down in his hands several times. "Though I don't like to admit I have a disability, I continue to work to overcome my handicap."

He lobbed the rock up in the air again, but this time he caught it before throwing the stone as far as he could out over the pond.

The rings in the pond grew huge until they disappeared completely.

"These women are allowing their fear to dictate how they live. In order to get past that fear, they will need to face it head on, whether by facing me or by facing their ex."

Her penetrating stare never wavered from his face. "Have you ever experienced a fear so strong that it made your heart stop? Or knew with one blow of a hand he could kill you or inflict so much pain you wished you were dead? And then by some miracle or curse you lived through the beatings, but the injuries took weeks to heal before it started all over again."

Aimee breathed in deeply then released her breath along with some of her pent-up frustrations, sorry she'd revealed so much. She stood and moved to the deck railing and leaned her elbows on the edge.

"Those memories can never be erased. In the back corner of your mind, you'll always wonder if this is the day he'll find you? And maybe this time he'll kill you."

Turning her gaze on him, she asked, "Tell me Tom, how does one handle that fear?"

Tom's expression hardened and then instantly turned lethal. She knew his anger wasn't directed at her, but at some unknown monster in his mind. He moved from the chair to stand next to her.

"Is that what happened to you, Aimee?"

She shuddered, turning her gaze before he could witness in her eyes the ghastly horrors of her ex-husband's deeds, too appalling for words.

"I'm sorry he hurt you. But not all men are like *him*." He rested his hand on her shoulder. "No woman should ever have to experience that kind of pain from someone who should have loved and protected them."

The hum of locust and the soft ripple of the pond filled the silence as they sat locked in their own private world. His strength was the comfort she needed. Why couldn't she have met someone like Tom first?

His hand dropped away and she felt the loss. By his odd expression, he didn't know what to say or where to go from there. He shoved his hands in his pockets.

"You know my awful secret now." She offered a humorless laugh.

"Yes, and if the man was standing here today, I'd give him a hefty dose of his own medicine. I'd break every bone in his body, but leave him alive. And when he had mended, I would do it all over again, just so he could experience a small portion of the pain you had to endure."

She touched his arm to gain his attention. The fury in his eyes would have terrified most but she knew his rage wasn't directed at her.

"Tom, though he may deserve that and worse, it's not the answer. But maybe now you have a little insight to what the other women have endured, which is as bad or even worse than what I suffered. Their fear, though debilitating, it doesn't define them. And prayerfully, one day, like me, they will grow beyond their fear. But I believe they will get there sooner if you help them."

"That's what I'm trying to do." Tom rammed his hand through his spiky hair, and then moved to lean his back against the railing.

"I know you are, but it would go so much smoother if you show them a little compassion, a bit of your congenial side."

He chuckled, shaking his head. "Congenial? What's that?"

"You can be quite pleasant once a person gets to know you. And you have a compassionate heart, which you try your best to conceal. I've seen it when you weren't looking, like now." She dimpled up at him. "Let them warm up to you. Get to know you like I have."

He chuckled again. "And you think you know me?"

"Yes. I know that you hate to acknowledge your pain. You'd rather be in Afghanistan, or wherever, fighting alongside your men. You're hiding from the world, just like we are, unable to face the harsh reality of why you are here instead of there." She motioned behind her at the world at large.

"You know nothing about me. And don't presume you do."

The fierceness in his voice would have shaken her faith in him before today, but she knew it was all bluster. Yet something had soured him on life.

She squinted up at him and smiled in spite of his glare. "Did you ever think you might be here because of us? Maybe you were sent here to help these women." She wondered if she'd gone too far this time. He looked surly and ready to tear into her.

"Not hardly. I'm not a coaxer or a prodder."

"That may be true, but I think, if you dig deep inside, you'll find that guy who once laughed and you might begin to enjoy life again. I've seen sparks of him, even though you've tried your best to hide him from me. You're one of the good guys, and don't let that devil on your shoulder tell you differently."

She motioned toward the house. "Shall we go on up? Any minute now, Maggie will be ringing the dinner bell, and I for one don't want to miss lunch."

Tom walked quietly beside her. She had touched a nerve. But like the battered women who came through her doors, he needed to hear the truth, learn how to forgive and move on. And whether he liked it or not, she was determined to show him how.

Chapter 14

No matter how much Aimee tried to engage the women or Tom over lunch, everyone sat solemn, giving minimal answers. Maggie gave her several looks as if to say, *fix it,* to which she shrugged. She didn't know how to *fix it,* but it certainly didn't bode well for this afternoon's training.

"Tom, why don't you tell us a little about yourself?"

He looked at Aimee as if she was speaking gibberish.

"I'm not sure what you'd like to hear." His spoon clinked against his bowl. He sat back staring a hole through Aimee.

"Oh, anything. Your childhood, your service in Special Ops, whatever."

If it were possible, he looked like he would rather pulverize Aimee into dust.

"*Humph.* Well. Let's see. Nothing major growing up, besides the normal scrapes and bruises. No DWIs. No drug problems. No killings. That came later."

There were a few intakes of breath from the women. Aimee figured he was on a roll and getting even with her for prying.

"At eighteen I enlisted into the service to serve my country and to get my college degree. I found I had a real knack for Special Ops." He nailed her with his hard glare. "Did my share of killing, don't know the exact count. Got blown up by an IED, which killed all my men. Then after a long stint in hospitals and rehab centers, I landed here. That about sums it up." He gave everyone a forced grin that didn't agree with his eyes.

To Aimee, he shrugged as if to say, *that went well, didn't it?*

The women were looking him over for injuries, positively distressed over the, as he put it, blown up part. *Well,* maybe the killing part, too.

Aimee cleared her throat and said, "Maggie, the soup and sandwich were wonderful. Tom might like another bowl."

Maggie moved to get up.

He waved her off.

"No more for me. Too much food can make a man soft."

He wiped his mouth with his napkin and then slapped it down on the table. "You're one good cook though. I mentioned to Aimee that once this training gig is over, I was going to try to hire you out from under her."

Maggie laughed. "I'm not sure you could afford me. But I might work out something with you to pick up your meals for a price."

"I'd be interested in that deal." He shoved his chair back and gave everyone a huge smile except for Aimee. He didn't look her way. "Ladies, thank you for the pleasure of your company."

His smile was contagious, all of the women were beaming, even Debra Sue.

Aimee figured he could be a real charmer when he wanted to, and right now he seemed to want to.

"I'll see you ladies out in front of the house in twenty minutes." He stood. "Aimee, I would like to discuss a matter with you outside."

She wasn't sure why his words struck fear, and she sure as shootin' didn't want to go outside with the man. Something in his voice or how he avoided looking at her, told her this wasn't going to be a casual stroll or a pleasant discussion. More like pistols at twenty paces.

Picking up her dishes, and then reaching for his, their hands collided, causing her to withdraw quickly, feeling a little panicky.

He followed her to the sink, set his dishes and glass down, then nodded at the door. She led the way outside then stopped on the porch.

"Walk with me." The words were not a request, they were an order.

No doubt, seeing the stubborn set of her jaw, he gave a tight-lipped smile. "Please."

Putting her hands behind her back, she headed down toward the barn. He fell in step with her, the crunch of gravel breaking the silence.

When he touched her arm, she glanced up at him.

"This is far enough. I didn't want the others to overhear."

"Oh, so this *is* going to be a scolding after all. I thought you just wanted the pleasure of my company." Her smile froze on her face.

"Not entirely a scolding. I want to make something perfectly clear."

"And that is?"

"My history is my business and no one else's. Understood?"

"Yes, but I—"

"In the future, my personal life is off limits. So don't ask questions."

"I'm sorry. I just thought if the women knew a little about you they might be less afraid. I'll not bring it up again–um–unless … well … sometimes talking helps."

Tom stared at her in disbelief. "I might say the same to you. What's your story? Poof, you just landed here and thought it might be fun housing a bunch of wounded women?"

He had no right! She felt like telling Mr. Smarty Pants it was none of his business. He was the one who needed help … maybe she did too. At least she was working through her issues.

"I thought so." His gaze never wavered. "Share Tom, share, but don't ask me to. Is that how it works?"

"I'm sorry." Aimee looked back at the house. All of the women were standing on the porch watching. She smiled and waved not wanting them to be alarmed or think that Tom and she were at odds.

She motioned back at the house. "Shall we? It looks like you have an eager bunch of students waiting to begin training."

"Not so fast." He latched onto her elbow.

Aimee felt the shock of his touch go straight up her arm to her heart, but this time, not because his grasp was unexpected … because she was falling for the big ox. She didn't need or want a man in her life, especially this cantankerous old goat.

"Let's get a few things straight. Don't go asking questions about my background or history. If and when I feel like sharing, I will. It's not for you to go digging around trying to fix me."

She could tell he was getting up a full head of steam, yet she wasn't afraid of him.

"I don't want any complications in my life. And you Aimee Hamilton are a bucket load of complications. Scratch that, you're a truck load of trouble." He pocketed his hands, whether to keep from strangling her, she couldn't be sure.

"Furthermore, I'll teach you and the others. But don't presume to dictate to me how I am to run the class or handle the women." He gave a no-nonsense shake of his head. "I won't have you undermining my authority or my job. Do I make myself clear?"

She felt like saluting and clicking her heels, but figured he wouldn't find humor in her actions. "Perfectly."

Still stinging from *she was a complication and trouble,* she said, "Mr. Branigan—"

"Tom."

"Tom, you should know a few things about me. I'm quite docile unless I get riled, which is rare."

He laughed. "Docile? I would call you anything but..."

"Be that as it may, know this, if you hurt one those women," — she nodded back at the porch where their audience was straining to hear what was being said — "you'll learn what real trouble is, and it won't be complicated."

How this arrogant man, wearing a smile bigger than a carved pumpkin, could rile her temper more times than she'd like to remember was a mystery.

Aimee turned to leave.

The infuriating man had the nerve to chuckle.

She shot over her shoulder. "Unless you want to stand here laughing all day, the women are waiting. Are you coming?"

For such a large man, he sure could move silent and quick-like. He was by her side without any effort and ... still chuckling. The sound rapped around her like a warm blanket. His cologne lifted on the wind, making deeper inroads to her heart.

If she wasn't careful, Tom Branigan was going to wiggle his way into her life and that would be disastrous.

"Why is it I get the odd idea before this bargain of ours is over we're going to butt heads continually?" He chuckled.

"If there's any head-butting going on, it'll be you. I never butt heads."

His laughter carried to the women on the porch. Aimee saw their tension ease as they smiled and talked amongst themselves. She knew nothing could have worked more in his favor than for them to see the man's lighter side, if there was one.

"And I bet you don't like having the last word either, do you?"

She increased her speed, which was nothing for him. "Certainly not."

"Hmm, why do I get the feeling I've been conned by a real pro?"

She tried not to smile while affecting an accent thicker than swamp mud. "Why, Tom Branigan, whatever do you mean?"

His laughter filled the air and melted her resistance down around her feet.

This man was the answer to her prayers where the training was concerned, but he was going to be the demise of her well-planned life, if she wasn't awful careful.

Chapter 15

Exhausted from the rigorous training Tom dished out today, Aimee took the dirt road to the mailboxes slower than normal. Fifty pushups, after hand-to-hand combat with the man, made her feel like a rag doll after washday—all wrung out and left out to dry. One of these days, he'd push her too far and she'd give him a good piece of her mind.

Would never happen, not in a million years.

She laughed, thinking she'd have very little of her mind left if she did. And she wanted him to stick around and train not just these women but also the women who would be coming to Paradise Found in the future.

At least, since their talk, Tom hadn't been scaring the women with his fierce looks and harsh commands. Instead, he picked on her.

Aimee could take it, so long as the women didn't rebel.

She pulled and parked across from the mailboxes, but didn't budge. Instead, she leaned her head back against the window, closed her eyes. For a moment, she enjoyed the peace and quiet without all the demands. She could take this short span of time where the world ceased to exist. There were no commitments, no problems to solve, no worries, no threats, just Tom. If only ...

Aimee sat upright. This wasn't a time for *if onlys. If onlys* were for people who didn't have responsibilities, and right now she had plenty.

There were canvases back at the house to paint, the women to care for, and there was Jill, still moping around for her lowlife of a boyfriend. Why couldn't the girl get it into her head, men like Jimmy never change. *Why?*

She pulled on the door handle, disgusted with her train of thought, giving the door a good bang with her shoulder. Hopping down out of the truck, she was about to head for the mailboxes when a beige car turned off the highway and stopped across from where she stood.

Not recognizing the man or the car, her heart sped up. She gave a quick glance around and knew this man and she were the only ones out here. Even if she yelled for help, there was no one within shouting distance to hear.

The driver's window rolled down. A man in his late thirties, early forties wearing shades much like Tom's, smiled and nodded. And though he didn't look threatening, she didn't like the fact that she didn't recognize him. Why had he stopped out here anyway?

"Hi, I think I'm lost. I was wondering if maybe you could help me?"

The man, like Tom, had the same military bearing, buzzed hair, stern features, but he seemed friendly enough. Though a likely request, she couldn't tell if he spoke the truth.

"I'm looking for the town of Ben Wheeler. Would you be able to tell me if I'm on the right road and how much farther it might be?"

She shielded her eyes with her hand, trying to get a better look at the man without moving closer. Something about him made her uneasy. However, any stranger would have done the same.

"If you continue the way you were headed, west on FM 279 for a couple more miles" — she pointed at the two-lane highway he'd just turned from — "you can't miss it."

"Do you live in the area?"

Her radar antenna went zinging skyward. "Yes."

"I'm looking to relocate. Someone told me Ben Wheeler was a small, friendly town. Do you know where there might be property or a house for sale?"

"Afraid not. You might ask in town." Her heart was racing. A stranger asking questions didn't bode well, but one asking for property or a house didn't ring true. She turned to her truck, fingers wrapping around the handle. "Have a nice day."

She yanked on the door, but the stubborn thing wouldn't open. With a silent prayer, she gave another yank and almost flew backwards when it released as easy as sliced pie. She climbed in and started the motor, hoping the man would get the hint and leave so she wouldn't have to.

For several uncomfortable minutes, he continued to study her, and then finally rolled up his window.

He made a U-turn, then turned out onto the highway in the direction of town.

Aimee, feeling like a ton had lifted from her shoulders, released a pent up breath. Her hands were shaking and her whole body was buzzing like a beehive.

Coincidence? She couldn't be certain. But she wasn't going to take any chances. She would alert Maggie and Kim. Times like these made her wish she had a locking gate and a fence around her property. It might not stop an intruder, but it sure would slow them down some.

She turned off the engine. Resting her head against her locked hands on the steering wheel, letting out a *thank you, God,* while she allowed her heart rate to slow to normal.

Why hadn't she thought to carry her handgun?

~ ~ ~

What a stroke of luck.

If he were a betting man, Frank Thornton would bet his whole commission the woman back at the mailboxes in the old beat up truck was none other than Jennifer Stanley.

Her hair, long, curly, and a beautiful auburn color instead of short, blonde, and straight, would be easy to change. Her clothes looked old and worn, not from Neiman's or a pricey boutique. But there again, expensive clothing would stick out like a flashing billboard out here in the country. They'd only serve to make her a target for anyone who might come looking for her. And the fact when he asked for directions she was too skittish by far, was an additional indicator.

Yep. That woman had to be Jennifer.

Now to locate where she's been hiding all this time. Somewhere close by no doubt. Probably down that dirt road. She was heading toward the mailboxes when he drove up and spooked her.

Frank knew better than to ask around town or drive down her road. She'd get wind of someone looking for her and hightail it for parts unknown, and then his hunt would begin all over again. He'd play it out as usual while he searched the general vicinity to locate where she lived. Only this time he'd be a buyer checking for property, not searching for a lost relative.

Once folks got used to seeing him in town, driving around the countryside looking for land, they'd loosen up and start talking. It might take a few days. But then, the woman might even resurface. But if not, he'd eventually find her.

Frank pulled up and parked outside of Leah's Fine Art Gallery. In the front window on display was a large painting of Texas bluebonnets with mist hanging in the air and the early morning sun barely peeking above the horizon. The whole scene was beautiful, and something Jennifer Stanley would have painted, if her painting on display at UT art center were any indication.

He couldn't believe it. He'd hit the jackpot.

The bell above the door announced his arrival into the art gallery. A rather tall, nice looking woman with long highlighted dark hair came from the back room dressed in stylish bohemian.

"Hi, may I help you?"

"I saw the painting in the front window and thought of my friend who's looking for a bluebonnet scene to go over her mantle. Could I take a closer look?"

"Certainly." The woman was pleased with his selection. "I just got this one in yesterday. It won't be here long." She turned the easel around so the painting faced the interior of the shop. "It's called "First Light," and priced at thirty-four hundred. Worth every penny."

"I'm sure it is." Frank moved closer, inspecting the painting. "Aimee Hamilton. I don't believe I've heard of this artist. Is she local?"

"Everything in my shop comes from East Texas artisans."

"And they come with a certificate of authenticity?"

"Certainly."

She moved to the counter, strangely, a little indignant over his questions.

Frank stepped back, looking around the shop. "Do you carry other work by this artist?"

"Yes, you will find Aimee's work scattered about the gallery. Have a look around. And if I can answer any other questions, please let me know." The woman made herself busy with paperwork, but continued to keep an eye on him.

Frank took his time looking around the shop and found a great number of Aimee's paintings hanging on the walls among a few other artists. Leah knew more than she was willing to divulge about the artist, at least to him.

He lifted a small painting from the wall with a similar tone and feel of the one in the window, handing it to Leah. "I'll buy this one for myself. That way my friend, if she likes what she sees, I'll bring her back in to take a look at "First Light.""

Leah smiled. "Good choice. But tell your friend not to wait too long. I won't be surprised if "First Light" isn't sold by this weekend."

"She lives in Athens. Maybe I can get her to meet me here this weekend." He pulled out cash to pay for the painting. "Would you happen to know of any property for sale around here? I'd prefer some acreage with a fixer-upper, but would take land if a house isn't available."

Again he was met with suspicion. He hoped he hadn't tipped his hand too soon.

Leah pulled out brown paper and began wrapping his purchase.

"Sorry, but I haven't heard of any. The closest realtor is in Canton, west of here. They should have all the listings for the surrounding area and towns."

"Thanks. I'll drive to Canton then Athens." Frank glanced out the window. "Do you recommend The Forge for lunch?"

She slid the painting on the counter toward him, still reticent to say much. "Yes, their food is good."

Picking up his package, he smiled. "You've been most helpful. When you see the artist again, tell her I'm a great admirer of her work. Have a good day, and thanks again."

After placing the painting in the backseat of his vehicle, Frank jaywalked across the highway to The Forge. He figured no time like the present for the small town to become accustomed to seeing his face. Hopefully, it wouldn't take too long for him to become part of the local color. With a little flattery, some down-home charm, their tongues should loosen up eventually.

Once he had the proof and location, he'd give Rick his report to collect his hefty fee.

Frank loved it when things came together so smoothly and with little effort. If only all of his jobs went this smoothly, he'd have it made.

Chapter 16

Tom wished he'd never met Aimee Hamilton or agreed to her harebrained idea of training. That woman could make a sane man crazy.

The only reasonable answer to his lapse in judgment of steering clear of her ... he'd been taken in by a pair of toffee eyes, auburn hair, and one fiery disposition all rolled into one fine package. And the one and only pitiful excuse ... he'd been on his own far too long.

A pathetic defense, but the only one he could come up with on short notice. Otherwise, he'd have to agree, he was out of his ever-lovin' mind training these women.

He couldn't comprehend how he'd allowed Aimee to roll right over him like a steamroller and flattened him into a pastry. At one time, he would have been impervious to such a woman. However, the past two years must have made him soft. Living out here in virtual isolation probably helped him become susceptible to her charms.

Charms? She didn't know the first thing about charms. Oh, she knew how to push his buttons and finagle her way to get him to do her bidding, even rile his temper, but charms? The only charms that woman had were the kind she wore on a bracelet.

Come to think of it, it was kind of fun and certainly easy enough to push her buttons to get a rise out of her, especially when her temper matched her fiery hair.

He released a pent up breath and closed his eyes. No matter how hard he tried to forget about Aimee, he found it impossible.

He'd already settled into a routine—training the women, eating his noon meal at Paradise Found, and his evening supper delivered by Aimee.

From the first, when Aimee delivered his meals, she stayed no longer than to set his dinner out on the table, make sure he had a glass of sweet tea, and then left. Then one night he asked her to keep him company while he ate. And now she stayed to eat dessert with him.

Like today, he shouldn't have done it, but he yelled at Debra Sue and Aimee interfered, that's when he let her have it. He could still see the unyielding fire in her eyes that said ... *no man will ever get the better of me, even if it kills me.*

Inwardly, he applauded her stubborn resolve when he told her to drop and give him fifty for questioning his orders. She gave him a look hot enough to sizzle his hide, then dropped to the ground and started her pushups.

At first, the other women stood around giving him daggered looks, which soon turned into a cheering session for Aimee on her last ten. When she finished, she didn't stay on the ground exhausted like he thought she would. Instead, she jumped up and asked rather flippantly, *would you like me to do more, or will that do, sir?*

Tom's chuckle dissolved into a moan as he eased his tired body down into his easy chair. He flipped the lever up relieving the pressure of his aching leg. He must be getting soft. Two years ago, her kind of smart mouth would have received a reprimand, another fifty push-ups, ending with a five mile run. He shook his head. *Pitiful.*

Country life must have weakened him or was it Aimee who had gotten to him? Whichever, he'd have to work to solve the problem.

An annoying buzz pulled him out of his stupor. A glance at the clock on the wall showed six o'clock. His men would have called him a baby for taking a nap in the afternoon.

His body felt stiff and sluggish. His legs and arms wouldn't cooperate. Neither would the unrelenting buzz from the front gate. He should have left the blasted thing open.

At the moment, he'd like nothing better than to ignore the stupid intercom. However, he figured it wouldn't stop Aimee. She'd probably crash his gate to see why he hadn't answered so she could deliver his dinner.

The move from his chair to the intercom was slow and painful. Eventually he made the short distance to push the button.

"For Pete's sake, would you let up on the buzzer?"

"My, aren't we testy. If you'll open the gate, I'll … Oh, thanks. I'll be right up with your dinner. Maybe you'll growl less after you've eaten."

Aimee's pert little quip made him smile. As a substitute for niceties, he growled. "If you didn't have a lead finger, I'd be less cranky."

She didn't answer him. Instead, her peal of laughter and the sound of her truck's grinding gears pulling away from the gate came through the intercom, filling the silence. A yearning welled up inside him, making him wish he had someone to fill the quiet of his lonely life. Someone like Aimee.

Disgusted with his train of thought, he limped to the kitchen, filled a glass with water, and then popped two aspirins into his mouth.

The woman spelled trouble, the kind of trouble he didn't need, especially now. And furthermore … what woman in her right mind would want a broken-down man like him, with nothing to offer but a house.

Her squeaky truck alerted him she was outside. He listened for the pop of her truck door. Her singing got louder as she stomped up the stairs.

"Hello, Clyde. I can't scratch your ears right now. Wait until I put this food down then I'll give you a proper welcome."

Before she could kick the metal door guard, which she was prone to do, Tom swung the door open.

She avoided looking at him.

Lately, he'd been able to read her as well as he used to read his men. Aware of her mood, he figured she was ticked-off about something. Maybe the fifty pushups earlier. He'd have to tread softly or she was apt to leave and take his supper with her.

He smiled, knowing she'd do no such thing.

"Here, let me have that." He reached for the box.

She sidestepped him. "I'll carry it to the counter. You're in no condition to carry anything with that leg of yours acting up."

"My leg isn't acting up." About that time his injury made a liar out of him. He nearly buckled under the pain. Clamping his mouth shut over a groan, he hated that Aimee could read him just as easily.

"There isn't any shame in pain. The good Lord made us so that we would realize our limitations. And right now, you need to get off that leg of yours."

Clyde nudged his hand. He playfully roughed the dog up, then scratched him good behind both ears. "Sorry, ol' boy. I forgot you were outside. Go eat."

Clyde gave a soft *woof* before padding into the kitchen to the little recessed nook that held the dog's food and water bowls.

"You want me to set up a tray so you can eat in your recliner and get your leg up?"

Though full of sass, Aimee hadn't looked at him once in the eyes. Something was going on. What? He didn't know. But he'd get to the bottom of it, even if it were the extra pushups from this afternoon.

"No. I'll eat at the table." He continued to watch her fuss around the kitchen.

Familiar with his house now, she never had to ask where anything was, which was a good thing ... or maybe it wasn't. At times, his house felt more like hers than his with the personal touches here and there that she'd added.

Just the other day, she talked him into purchasing a few pieces of furniture she'd found at some estate sale. She had an eye for decorating. The things went well with the other furnishings in his house.

"Suit yourself. But don't complain if you can't walk tomorrow all because of your pride."

Irked that she would think he had pride, or that she would mention his injury again, he stomped to the kitchen sink to wash his hands.

Pride? The woman didn't know what she was talking about.

Sitting down, his gaze lingered on her as she filled his plate and brought it to the table. He didn't move. Instead, his gut wrenched as images filled his head of Aimee being used as a punching bag by a man who professed love. One day he hoped he'd run into the man. Her ex would never touch another woman again.

"You better eat before it gets cold."

"Have a glass of iced tea while I eat. Unless you're in a hurry to get back."

"I should get on back." She glanced at the door as if to escape.

"What's the rush?" He liked her company and didn't want her to leave, not yet anyway. It was too lonely here by himself, especially at night. "I'd like to discuss the training."

Aimee snorted. "Nothing to discuss. I already know what you think on that subject, but I'll get a glass. Go ahead and start."

Though starving, he waited until she had her iced tea and sat down. He picked up his fork to take a bite.

She cleared her throat and looked at him daringly.

He bowed his head, said a quick silent prayer, and then dug in like a starving man. After shoveling in a bite, he glanced at her and saw the sparkle in her eyes.

"What? Do I have gravy dripping off my chin?" He wiped his mouth with his napkin.

She shook her head smiling.

"My shirt?" Glancing down he didn't see any stains.

"No. I just don't remember ever seeing a man enjoy his food as much as you do."

"You've never had to eat in a mess hall, or be in the field eating MREs. That's as close as you can get to dog food."

Clyde whined.

"Sorry Clyde, but Aimee doesn't know what it's like to eat a cold MRE while out on a mission. If she did, she'd appreciate Maggie's food like I do." He glanced back at Aimee.

Her smile faded too quickly.

"You want to tell me about it?"

"About what?" Aimee wouldn't hold his gaze. Instead she ran her finger along the pattern of the wood grain in the table, then brushed an imaginary speck onto the floor.

"About what's bothering you?"

"I don't think the women are progressing fast enough."

"Aimee, I told you—"

She held up her hand. "You aren't to blame. You're a wonderful teacher. It's them. They just don't have the spirit to fight, at least not yet. Not like me. Maggie and Kim are ready to take anyone on, but the other three, I'm not so sure. And after today"—she rolled her eyes and shook her head—"with your show of testosterone in making me give you fifty, the three of them just about swore off working with you again."

Three little crinkle lines showed up between her brows as she stared at him. "What were you trying to prove? You're the boss. I'm the weakling. Well, you made your point loud and clear probably at the loss of their training. I know I coerced you into teaching us when you didn't want to, but I thought ..." She started to rise.

He grabbed hold of her hand. The warmth of her skin made him desire more than mere friendship. What was wrong with him? Next he'd be down on one knee—*no way*.

She glanced at him and he released her.

"Sit down. Let me explain." When she hesitated, he added, "Please."

He pushed his plate away. The food was good but he'd lost his appetite, especially with Aimee looking at him like he was an executioner.

She sat down, her warm, sad gaze making him nervous. He had no earthly idea what he was going to say or why he asked her to stay. He just knew he didn't want her to leave, not yet anyway. Then she broke the connection by looking down.

His first instincts were correct. Something more than the women was bothering her.

"Are you going to explain what's really bothering you?"

When she didn't answer him, he said, "As to the fifty pushups, I'm sorry." He gave her a sheepish grin. "When you told me to back off of Debra Sue, I needed to show them I was running this training, not you. There can only be one boss."

"I wasn't bossing you."

He raised his brows and gave her a look of, *oh yeah?*

"Well maybe a little, but—"

"You were acting like a mother hen, which in your case is a good thing except when you interfere with the training."

"I just thought you were being a little too harsh."

As he studied her, she averted her gaze again. "What is really going on, Aimee? There's something more you're not telling me."

Overwhelmed by the desire to shield her from whatever was bothering her, he felt inadequate. He couldn't protect her any more than he was able to protect his men.

Her shoulders slumped forward. "You've done enough already. It's nothing I can't handle."

"You want to tell me about it. You'll find I'm fairly good at solving problems."

She shook her head. "No this is something I'll handle on my own. But thanks anyway." Aimee's smile wasn't convincing.

Don't get involved. She may need it, but she doesn't want your help.

He knew better. Whatever had her spooked, he wasn't about to allow her to take it on her own, not when he was here and could help. Thinking he had a pretty good idea what was bothering her, he asked, "Is this about the man asking around town about property?"

He knew he was on target by the way her body stiffened and she jerked to attention.

"What have you heard?" Her gaze searched his face.

"Nothing much. I was in Leah's this afternoon. She mentioned some man was in town asking questions."

She nodded, worry etched in her face. "I'm pretty sure he's the same man who stopped me at the mailboxes earlier today."

Tom wanted to tear into the guy and would have if he knew where to find him. "Did he touch you? If he did, I'll—"

"No, he just asked for directions to Ben Wheeler. But there was something about him that didn't fit. He was too observant, too ... oh, I don't know ... like you. Made me think military. He wore sunglasses and his hair was cut like yours."

"Nothing wrong with my cut." He ran his hand over his spiky hair, smiling.

"I didn't say there was anything wrong. It suits you, as it suited him. And though he wore dark shades, I could feel him staring at me, really looking me over, like he might have recognized me. Or as if he were looking for someone but didn't want to come right out and ask." Aimee gave a dismissive wave of her hand. "But this isn't your fight. I can handle him."

"I think you've made it my fight when you asked me to train you and the others. And, if at all possible, I'm not about to let anything happen to you."

Chapter 17

"Any word from Jill this morning?" Aimee walked into the kitchen and grabbed a cup from the cabinet.

"No. She hasn't come back yet. Probably took off with that skunk of a boyfriend." Maggie's voice held contempt as she dumped a load of carrots from a basket into the sink and then vigorously attacked the carrots, scrubbing.

"I saved you a cinnamon roll and some bacon. It's over there." She pointed with her scrub brush.

"Thanks, but right now, I don't believe I could eat anything. I'm worried." Aimee poured water from the steaming teapot, then prepared a cup of tea before sitting down at the table.

"How late were you up?"

"Well past midnight. But then I didn't sleep sound thinking that Jill might be in trouble." Aimee rubbed the back of her neck, worry eating at her gut over the girl. "Last week I really thought I had her convinced she could make the break."

"That girl doesn't have a lick of sense when it comes to that lowlife." Maggie slammed a carrot down loudly on the counter then turned to look at Aimee. "She doesn't know when she's well off."

"You know as well as I do, these women aren't thinking straight. They have to give up everything to start a new life. Some make it. Others don't. Maybe Jill wasn't ready yet." Aimee took a sip of her tea, staring into space, as her mind conjured up all sorts of horrible happening to Jill. None of them good.

"Did she talk with any of the other women before leaving?"

Maggie shook her head. "No. Debra Sue said she didn't mention anything to them. But Jill was acting kind of skittish yesterday morning. Kay said she talked about how much she missed Jimmy and how he really didn't mean to hurt her." She gave a disgusted snort. "All the same gibberish women like us are trained to believe."

Hearing a car drive up outside, Maggie turned to the window. "It's the sheriff. This can't be good." She wiped her hands on the towel hanging from her waist.

Aimee didn't want to move fearing the worst, but she stood. "I'll go see what he wants."

She headed for the mudroom, each step harder than the next. When she opened the door she noticed the sheriff was already on her porch.

"Aimee." Sheriff Randall removed his hat and nodded. The grave look on his face didn't bode well.

"Good morning, Sheriff, what can I do for you?"

"Can we step inside to talk?"

She opened the screen door wider and then motioned for him to enter. "Where are my manners? Certainly, come on in and have a cup of coffee. I believe Maggie may even have a cinnamon roll left with your name on it."

His chuckle came out stiff and tight. "No thanks, but I'll take you up on that coffee."

He followed Aimee from the mudroom, stopped just inside the kitchen door. His fingers shifting the wide brim of his hat anxiously around in his hands as he avoided her gaze.

Aimee was a far better judge of character since running away and starting her home. She had seen enough nervous gestures in people to know Sheriff Randall's news wouldn't be good.

"Please be seated, Sheriff." She motioned at the table.

"Maggie will you get a cup of coffee for the sheriff, please." She turned to the officer. "Sugar? Cream?"

"Black, please."

"Is this a social visit or a formal one?"

"I'm afraid formal." He sat down and placed his hat on the table, pulled a small note pad from his shirt pocket before thumbing through the pages. He stopped to look over his notes then glanced up at her.

"Early this morning, we received a report of a woman's body on one of the back roads not far from here."

Maggie's hand jerked as she was setting Sheriff Randall's coffee cup down on the table, causing it to spill. "Sorry about that." Her hand trembling, she used the towel hanging at her waist to clean up the coffee.

"No problem." He took a sip then set the cup back down. "Like I was saying, when we arrived, we found a young woman, in her early twenties. No ID.

Badly beaten. However, the reason I'm here, knowing what Paradise Found is all about, I wondered if she might be one of yours?"

Aimee's hand rested on her throat. Her heart felt like it might explode. She didn't want to believe this woman could be Jill.

"The girl had long straight brown hair, huge eyes, and weighed about one hundred ten pounds. She wore jeans with a purple T-shirt that read *Live Life To Its Fullest With No Regrets.*"

Maggie sucked in breath. "No." The tormented cry was cut off by her trembling fingers over her mouth. She turned her back to the room, her shoulders shaking with silent grief.

Unable to speak, Aimee closed her eyes and choked back the cry burning her throat, Jill's death ripping her apart. Was this how a parent felt when they lost a child?

She swiped at the tears, pulling it together to answer Sheriff Randall.

Swallowing first to dislodge the stinging lump, Aimee got out, "I hope I'm wrong. But, I believe the person you're describing is Jill Morris. She left here yesterday afternoon without a word and hasn't returned."

"I'm sorry. I kinda expected as much." He pressed his lips together as he made a notation in his notebook.

How could this happen? Jill was supposed to be safe here at Paradise.

Jill, with huge haunting brown eyes. Timid yet eager to please. Thoughtful but shy. A daughter, a friend, and someone who didn't deserve to be killed and dumped alongside the road like unwanted trash. *Gone.*

"I'm sorry for your loss. However, I'll need you or one of the others to go with me to Tyler to identify the body."

So unemotional, almost rote. Was this how officers dealt with death, detached and just another job?

Aimee nodded. "I'll go."

Looking closer, she noticed lines of fatigue around Sheriff Randall's mouth and the corners of his eyes. Distaste rode his face as if he'd eaten something that hadn't set well with him. He wasn't coping with Jill's death as easily as she first thought. With someone so young, life before her, who could?

"Do you know who might want to hurt"—he looked down at his notes—"Jill?"

"I only know she was running from her abusive ex-boyfriend. His name is Jimmy." Aimee shook her head. "I'm afraid I don't know his last name. However, the Houston women's shelter should be able to give you his full information."

"How about the next of kin? Do you have their number?"

"No, I'm sorry. When the women come here, I'm told little to nothing about them. All I know is they are here to escape an abusive relationship. However, the women's shelter should have that information."

Aimee stood. "Finish your coffee while I get the information you need and my things together to go with you."

She walked from the room, tears streaming down her cheeks, steeped in misery over her failure.

Run ... You Can't Hide   *Janice Olson*

~ ~ ~

The ID confirmed, Aimee came home to a solemn and quiet household.

The women, each in their own way, mourned the loss of Jill. Even the children were unusually quiet. Aimee asked Tom to suspend training for a couple of days to allow the women a chance to recover.

She met Jill's parents in Tyler to give them their daughter's things. Though they didn't blame Aimee, the weight of responsibility rested heavy on her shoulders.

"How did it go?" Maggie walked onto the dock and then sat down beside Aimee.

"As well as could be expected. Jill was their youngest, their baby." Her voice broke.

Maggie slipped her arm about Aimee's shoulder and gently squeezed.

"Maybe I shouldn't be doing this?" Aimee moved her fingers nervously in her lap.

"Doing what?"

"The women. Helping them. I can't keep them safe. Maybe I'm the wrong person for the job."

Turning Aimee to face her, Maggie shook her gently to gain her attention.

"Listen to me. You're just feeling bad because this is a first. Don't you go a blaming yourself for Jill's poor judgment. You have a calling. I should know. Look at me, scars and all." Her voice cracked on a wry chuckle. "This is not your fault. They have a free will. They make choices, whether good or bad. This is just a setback, that's all."

~ 154 ~

"Thanks, Maggie. I hope you're right. But I'll tell you right now, I'm not sure I could take another one of these setbacks."

Chapter 18

Bingo! Pay dirt.

Frank smiled. The old truck he'd seen at the mailboxes the other day drove up and parked in front of Leah's. The same young woman got out, pulled some paintings from the truck bed and then carried them inside the shop. The little lady was none other than Aimee Hamilton, and if his guess was correct, a/k/a Jennifer Stanley.

Not too bad a strategy he'd put in play. All it took was a little time to get acquainted with the locals, and thankfully, the Ben Wheeler residents were a friendly lot.

Once he posed no threat, most of them were amenable and willing to talk. He ate at the two local restaurants, talked with the people in town, searched out the property suggested, and even gave them a full report later as to his findings. And it worked.

The one exception ... Leah Franklin, the owner of the art gallery. Though he'd seen her in passing on several occasions, once in the restaurant, and another time in her shop while looking over the paintings again, she remained guarded, suspicious. She had pegged him as up to no good.

Today had to be one of those *perfect storm* moments. Now if only Roni Peters would arrive, they could meet the artist, look at her paintings, and at the same time he could get a better look at the woman up close to make a positive ID.

Afraid he would miss the opportunity to verify his hunch, he decided not to wait any longer on Roni. He crossed the street and stepped up on the boardwalk when a horn honked.

Roni waved at him as her Suburban pulled in to park.

"I'm sorry I'm a few minutes late, but I had to wait for Drake. He and little Marcus are spending the day out on the range herding the long horns." Roni gave Frank a hug. "Is this the place you were telling me about?" She glanced at the front window.

"Yeah." Frank pointed. "And that's the painting."

"It looks like what I had in mind. Let's go in and have a closer look."

"That's what I figured. Shall we?" The bell jingled when Frank opened the door holding it for Roni to pass through.

Leah and the woman from the truck turned to look.

Frank moved closer. "Hi, Leah, this is my friend I was telling you about. She'd like to take a closer look at the painting in the front window." Trying not to be obvious, he studied the young woman with Leah out of his peripheral.

"Certainly." Leah looked none too happy to see them.

"Jennifer?" Roni cocked her head to one side plainly puzzled. "Is that you? It is." She rushed up and grabbed the woman in a full bear hug.

When Roni pulled back, the auburn haired beauty gave her a questioning look. "I'm sorry, you must be mistaken."

Roni smiled. "Don't give me that. What's going on? What are you doing here? Where have you been? I've been worried sick."

Frank had seen plenty of fear in his time to recognize the signs. The momentary terror the woman exhibited seconds before shifted to acceptance.

Jennifer Stanley wasn't out for revenge or to harm her politician ex-husband. She was hiding out for protection. He had to reassure her he wasn't here to harm her or turn her over to Stanley, not now, at least.

"Hi Roni, how are you?" She sent a cautious glance in Frank's direction.

"I'm fine. But more to the matter, how are you doing? The last I heard, the news had you as missing and presumed dead. What's going on?"

Aimee took a deep breath. By the time she released it her transformation was complete. She stood erect, shoulders squared, her demeanor one of an indomitable foe.

"I'll explain everything, but first introduce me to your friend." Her narrowed gaze directed at Frank was anything but friendly. She was assessing him as he had assessed her seconds ago.

"Oh, I'm so sorry, I forgot about you, Frank." Roni pulled him up next to her. "Jennifer Stanley, this is Frank Thornton, a very good friend of mine. And if you ever need a good PI, he's the best."

"I'll keep that in mind." Her words sounded caustic, without a hint of a fear or surprise. "We finally meet."

She inclined her head, already pegging him as her nemesis.

"However, I go by Aimee now, Aimee Hamilton, which I believe you already know."

She held her hand out to him.

Frank was amazed Jennifer or Aimee, whatever she's called, could offer him the pleasantries of polite society. If he'd been in her shoes, he would have kicked his backside out the door and then hightailed back to wherever she was hiding.

Clasping Aimee's hand in both of his, he realized she was a very savvy woman, one that shouldn't be underestimated.

"Trust me, it's a pleasure to meet you. And your secret is safe with me. It'll not go beyond these walls."

"What secret?" Roni glanced at both of them, plainly puzzled.

Aimee turned to the proprietor. "Leah, may we use your apartment for a few minutes."

The woman looked ready to take the broom and run him out of town. "Are you sure?"

"Yes. At least we now know. The threat is aimed at me."

Chapter 19

Aimee's sense of security vanished the moment she recognized Roni and Frank. She should have known then he was up to no good.

Where did she slip up?

And Roni? Where did she fit into the picture?

"Have a seat." Aimee motioned to the sofa. She aimed her question at Frank. "Why are you here?"

"I was hired to find you."

"By Rick?" She already knew, but she needed his confirmation.

"Yes."

"Frank, what's going on?" Roni looked confused. "Why would you make me a part of this? If you'd asked, I would have told you about Rick and his partiality for abuse."

She turned to Aimee. "I'm sorry. I had no idea Frank was working for Rick."

"Don't worry. It's not your fault." Aimee waved her off, sending her next question to Frank. "What I want to know is what you plan on doing with the information?"

"First off, when I invited Roni to meet me here to see your paintings, particularly the one in the window, I didn't expect to find you at the gallery. And as far as the information goes, Rick will never know I found you." He ran a hand over his spiky hair much like Tom often did.

"I took the job because I felt your family deserved answers as to your whereabouts, or closure if you were actually dead as reported."

Aimee wasn't sure if she should believe Frank. He could be like Rick—deceptive.

He turned to Roni. "I saw Aimee some days ago by accident on my way here to Ben Wheeler. I was fairly sure who she was then, but when I saw her paintings in the shop here, I was ninety-nine percent certain I'd found Jennifer Stanley."

"What did my paintings have to do with anything?"

"A hunch about your art led me here, which paid off."

"My art?" Aimee couldn't imagine how he could track her by her art, especially when she hadn't painted in years or used her real name.

"Yes. You may not realize this, but you have a unique and very unusual style of painting Texas scenes. Especially, the way you paint light to direct the viewer's eyes through the picture. Subtle, yet distinctive in nature. A tale of sorts." Frank shrugged.

"I saw one of your paintings at your alma mater, UT, while doing research to locate you. I had a hunch that someone who could paint as good as you, if you were in need of cash flow, art might be an avenue you'd pursue since you hadn't before."

"I did need the money." She wished she had found another way to make a living.

"I figured as much. Why else would you take a chance at discovery?" Frank folded his hands in his lap. "My search led me to a few art galleries around the state. When I found a gallery with a similar painting style, yet, with more depth, more maturity than your UT painting, I figured I was on the right track. That is, until I saw they were painted by Aimee Hamilton, on consignment from Leah's Art Gallery in Ben Wheeler, Texas. However, on a long shot, I came here."

He turned to Roni. "You became involved because I knew you were looking for a Texas scene with bluebonnets to hang over your living room mantle. I wasn't aware you knew Aimee. But knowing her paintings are some of the finest bluebonnets I've seen, I figured you would like her work. Her showing up today at the same time as you was unexpected, but fortuitous."

"For you maybe." Aimee's words were more scathing than intended. Raising from the chair, she moved to the window, her back to Roni and Frank.

Heart heavy, thoughts chaotic, she watched a small dust devil whirl down the street heading for a planter in front of Doc's. The delicate purple flowers were ripped from the dirt, tipping the planter, spilling the black soil on the sidewalk. And then, just as quickly as it appeared, the dust devil vanished, leaving wilted flowers and trash scattered across the street.

A shiver raced over Aimee's skin. Was she to be uprooted, and the delicate women in her charge strewn to the wind? *God, forbid.*

She crossed her arms facing Frank. "So where do we go from here? How much time do I have before you report to Rick, or have you already told him?"

"No. And I don't plan on reporting you. The only report he will receive from me is that I'm no longer on the case." Frank ran a hand over his chin. "I'm normally a good judge of character, but Rick is one slick politician."

Aimee's derisive chuckle was her response to Frank's hindsight.

"I should have listened to my gut. Something about Rick's tale didn't ring true. When I saw you the other day and then again today, I felt my first instincts were correct. You couldn't be as bad as he painted you." Frank rested his booted ankle on his knee.

"I can imagine Rick's story was very believable." Aimee knew how persuasive her ex could be with his honey-coated words. She'd been proof of it over and over again until he almost killed her.

"If you'll trust me, I think I have a plan that will work and make it so you won't have to worry about your ex ever troubling you again."

Aimee frowned. "I think I know Rick Stanley a whole lot better than you. He won't stop looking for me until I'm dead."

"Oh, Jennifer, I'm so sorry. No one knew where you were or what had happened to you. I wished I'd known." Roni's concern was heart-felt. "Why didn't you come to me or at least call? I would have helped."

"I was too ashamed to involve others, and there was nothing you could have done. At the time, you had your hands full proving Drake's innocence for his father's murder."

Aimee cringed at what she had to endure at Rick's hands. Most were too horrible to put into words. They were locked away in a dark corner of her mind and would probably never be uttered to another living soul.

"Well, Frank will see to it that you aren't bothered by him again." Roni turned to him. "Won't you Frank."

Aimee smiled at her friend's passionate confidence, knowing it wasn't that easy.

"I'm not so sure it's that simple." Frank lowered his leg, leaning forward, his elbow on his knees, his hands cupped together. "If I've taken Rick's measure correctly, he won't stop until he's found you."

"You're correct, he won't."

"After meeting you, I believe Rick is planning your death." Frank cleared his throat. "And ... there's something else you need to know."

She didn't like Frank's hesitation or the look in his eyes.

"Rick Stanley is engaged to your sister, Melissa. He claims Melissa made him promise to find you before she would marry him."

"No." She wrapped her arms around her middle, closing her eyes, seeing her innocent sister under Rick's power. It felt as if a vice had tightened around her heart. "Not Melissa. He'll kill her. She isn't strong enough. He has to be stopped."

Since nothing else had succeeded in getting her to come back, Rick knew she would come, if for no other reason than to save Melissa. She turned back around determined Rick's cruelty wouldn't touch her sister.

"I have to call Melissa, warn her about Rick."

Frank narrowed his gaze. "I would caution you not to act hasty. Rick would like nothing better than to know your whereabouts. It could be why he pursued Melissa, thinking she or your father might know where you were. If I'm correct, he means to draw you out of hiding by using her."

"That's exactly what he's done. Melissa isn't his type. And believe me, Rick has a type. Melissa isn't blonde, sexy, or a Barbie to hang on his arm as a trophy. She's sweet, kind, and trusting. Some might call her gullible, but in a good way."

Aimee shook her head. "I should have left the first time he struck me, then maybe none of this would have ever happened."

Frank shook his head. "I'm not so sure. It's been my experience, men like Rick consider their wife or girlfriend their personal property. They don't play nice. They don't let go."

"Well, no matter. I can't stand by idly and do nothing. Melissa isn't strong. He'll kill her if he abuses her like he did me. I've got to warn her."

Aimee ignored Roni's shocked intake of breath. She'd never told any of her friends how bad it had been living with Rick, and never would.

"I think we can devise a plan where both you and your sister will be safe."

Though Frank looked confident, she knew nothing about the man. And furthermore, Frank didn't know

Rick like she did. And what if his gesture was a ploy to allow Rick time to get here.

"I've survived this long on my own. I don't need your help."

Roni moved to stand by her, putting her arm around Aimee's waist. "Jen, listen to him. Frank's good at what he does. Let him help you. He helped me prove Drake's innocence. Or call Madison or Phillip, they'll even vouch for Frank. He's one of the good guys. He can't be bought by Rick."

Roni's avowal swayed her decision some. "You have one chance to convince me why I should trust you, otherwise, I'll do it my way."

Frank cocked his brow as a grin slowly played across his lips.

A good-looking charmer to be sure, but could she trust him?

"If you would have come to me first, I could have buried your trail so deep no one would have found you."

Aimee's brow wrinkled in question.

"I relocate women like you, those who live in abusive situations. I've done it for the last five years. I hate spousal abuse, always have. If I could, I'd kill off every man who has ever tried to harm a woman." His look was vicious and then he smiled. "But that would land me in jail and then I couldn't help anyone else. Instead, I get even in my own way. One woman at a time."

For the first time since Frank had walked into the gallery, Aimee felt she could trust him. Maybe because Roni vouched for him. Maybe because he helped women like her. If her trust were misplaced, not only would she have to endure Rick's wrath, Melissa would suffer too.

And if Frank's plan didn't work, she was prepared to die defending what belonged to her, starting with her sister. She wasn't about to let another women she knew suffer abuse or die like Jill.

"You have one opportunity to show me what you can do to stop Rick from coming after my sis or me. But if you fail, then I'll go it alone."

Chapter 20

The short time he had known Aimee, she'd never once been late for lunch or not shown up for training. Yet here he sat with a table full of women that, even for them, were unusually quiet with no Aimee to fill in the silence.

Something wasn't right.

When he mentioned Aimee's absence, Maggie didn't think it strange. He didn't believe her.

Though the food was excellent, it wasn't sitting well on his stomach. Tom couldn't wait to excuse himself and head for the door.

On the porch, he leaned against the railing. He couldn't help but notice Aimee's truck was still missing. She'd made mention of seeing a stranger at the mailboxes. When was that? ... Three, four days ago? A week, two? He couldn't remember.

Aimee never brought up her past except once briefly and then she hadn't told him much. But he gathered, like the other women, she was here hiding from her ex. The man she'd seen at the mailboxes could be here for her for all he knew. Maybe he'd already grabbed Aimee and taken her back to whom? To where?

He fumed, getting angrier by the second. He didn't have a clue if Aimee was her real name or not. Or where she lived before coming to Ben Wheeler. Not even a mention of her family, or if she still had one.

She'd be no match for a man, no woman would. And he doubted she took her gun when she went to town, or wherever she went this morning.

At the moment, he wanted to punch something, but knew there'd be no satisfaction in that either. The only pleasure he would have was when Aimee returned home safe.

The screen door squeaked, then shut quietly behind him. Maggie moved up next to him to lean on the railing. Her gaze followed the path of the long drive up the hill.

"I didn't want to alarm the others" — she nodded back at the house, speaking softly — "but this isn't like Aimee. It's not like her at all. She always calls when she's going to be held up in town."

Tom's body tensed. Worry gnawed at his gut. But to keep from upsetting Maggie, he smiled down at the little lady who had cooked her way into his heart.

"Maybe she got to talking and forgot the time. Do you know where she went?"

"Leah's. She took some paintings to the shop first thing this morning around ten." Maggie shook her head. "But that ain't Aimee's way. She always calls to tell me she's running late, but she didn't this time. I'm tellin' ya, something's wrong. I'm worried."

She glanced up at Tom, resting her hand on his arm. "I don't want her to wind up like ..."

Tom knew she referred to Jill but couldn't say her name.

Without thinking, Tom slipped his arm around Maggie's shoulder and gave her a hug.

"She won't. She's all right." He didn't believe his own words but he hoped he could convince Maggie. "When she returns, you'll see you had nothing to be concerned about."

"I hope so."

Tom released her and then stepped off the porch. "Tell the others I had some business I had to take care of. I'll see them first thing tomorrow."

"Where you headin'?"

"To town. I'll see if I can spot her truck and find out why she didn't come home." When he reached his truck, he shot over his shoulder, "If she gets here, give me a call. You have my cell number."

Though his truck had double duty shocks to offer a smooth ride, the speed he traveled and the potholes in Aimee's drive caused him to bounce relentlessly in his seat. He could slow down, but he had the need for speed and a burning desire to find Aimee.

If anyone hurt her, neither God nor man could keep him from killing the guy.

Jill's face flashed before his eyes. His gut twisted as he forced his truck to go faster than he should have on the dirt road. Feeling his back wheels begin to fishtail, he let up on the gas. He'd do Aimee no good if he flipped his truck.

At the point of turning out of Aimee's drive and onto the main dirt road, Tom saw a rooster tail of dust heading his way. He stomped on his brake, skidding to a stop. It could be one of their neighbors, but at the rate of speed the red cloud was coming toward him, he figured it was Aimee.

As the vehicle got closer, he recognized Aimee's old battered Chevy. He smiled. A ton of weight was lifted from his chest. Then ... his anger kicked in.

She slowed her truck and stopped next to him. A beautiful smile rode her lips.

After the dust settled, he rolled down the window and looked her over, or at least the portion he could see. There were no tear-stained puffy eyes, no marks on her face or arms, and she looked healthier than a new born calf.

Quicker than lightning strikes earth, he was hit with a realization. He'd fallen hard for this woman that didn't seem to give a care that she'd scared ten years off his life.

He shoved the gear into neutral, pulled on the brake, allowing his anger full reign.

"Where in the world have you been? Didn't you think it might have been nice to let Maggie or someone know you wouldn't be home for lunch or practice? Or were you having too much fun to care?"

Her beautiful smile dissolved into two rigid, hard lines. Anger and hurt replaced her excitement at seeing him.

Why hadn't he had the good sense to keep his big mouth shut? Lately, all he seemed capable of doing was to push her buttons, when all he wanted to do was to show her how much he cared.

"It's none of your business, but if you must know, an old friend came to town and I forgot about the time."

She looked straight through him. "I thank you for all you've done with the women, Tom, but you're not my keeper. Have a nice afternoon."

Aimee released her clutch and tromped on the gas, leaving Tom to eat her dust.

His window wouldn't roll up fast enough to keep the fine red stuff from coming inside his cab. He coughed as a thin red layer settled on him and on the dash.

In his rearview mirror, Aimee's truck vanished from sight. He figured he'd have the devil to pay when she delivered his supper tonight, if she came at all.

And who was this friend? Was the friend male or female? If a man, were they mere friends or maybe serious? How would he find out?

Leah. She'd know. But would she tell him?

Instead of turning into his drive or going back and apologizing to Aimee, he headed straight for town. When or if she came tonight, he'd say he was sorry. But first, he was going to find out who the person was she called friend.

He wasn't jealous exactly, more like curious. He scoffed at his own lie.

The only other time he'd felt jealousy, but nothing this strong, was over Linda. Then he'd had good cause when he found her in the arms of another man. But that was history well forgotten. Aimee was always honest and straightforward. Nothing like Linda

The only reason he was checking up on her, he wanted to make sure it wasn't someone who would harm her. If it was a man, he'd find out who, then look him up to make sure he wasn't a threat ... to her, of course.

Who was he fooling? If she was seeing another man, he'd work him over and tell the guy to hit the road and don't look back.

Tom began whistling then stopped. He loved her. There was no other explanation.

No wonder he got so all-fired mad over Aimee's explanation. Imagining her with another man made him want to punch the guy's lights out.

Now what was he going to do?

Nothing, that's what.

He wasn't about to make a move on her. She deserved a whole man, not one with a bum leg, nightmares too horrible to imagine, not to mention his anger with God for not saving his men.

No, he wouldn't saddle Aimee with all of his baggage, regardless of how much he loved her.

Tom approached town, his mood getting sourer by the minute. Maybe he'd eat at The Forge tonight, or run over to Edom and eat at The Shed. It would serve Aimee right for scaring him half to death. And ... he wouldn't have to deal with his feelings.

He pulled up in front of Leah's gallery, cut his engine, and then sat staring at the painting in the window. Had to be one of Aimee's.

"Well, are you coming or going?" Leah stood in the open doorway of her shop, her hand shielding her eyes, smiling.

His decision made, he got out of the truck. "I'm coming. How are you doing?"

"I've been better, but I'll do." She moved from the doorway allowing him to go inside. "What brings you in, as if I didn't already know?"

Tom liked Leah. She was straightforward and to the point. No stepping around the issue. "If you'll be breaking a confidence, don't answer. But if not, was Aimee here today?"

"I think you already know the answer." She motioned to a stack of framed art leaning against the counter. "She dropped off those paintings this morning."

"Did she meet anyone while she was here?"

Leah looked at him sideways, squinting. *"Tisk, tisk."* She raised her brow. "And you're asking why?"

"Oh, never mind." He looked around the shop. "I'd like to buy a painting. I'm partial to the one in the front window. But didn't you have a different one there yesterday?"

"Yes, but I sold it just a little bit ago." Leah moved to the window and turned the easel around to face Tom. "However, this is one she brought in this morning and it's my personal favorite."

Tom recognized the scene immediately.

It was Aimee's pond with the rolling hills and the forest in the distance, and the sun dipping below the horizon. The colors were soft, gentle, and easy on the eyes, pulling him in for a closer look.

Standing on the dock, a man and woman faced the sunset. He had his arm around the woman's waist, and her head rested on his shoulder. If he hadn't looked closer, he would have missed the dog resting at their feet.

A deep longing gripped him. To cover his emotions, he cleared his throat and asked, "How much?"

Leah chuckled, giving him a knowing look. "This one will cost you. It's thirty-nine hundred, but well worth the price."

Without thinking twice, he pulled out his credit card and handed it to Leah.

He wouldn't allow himself to pursue Aimee. However, he could buy her art as a reminder of her and the sweeter side of life, something he would never experience.

"Good choice. I'll wrap it for you." Leah carried the painting to the counter. "To answer your question … yes she had a friend drop by. Any more than that, you'll have to ask Aimee."

Fat chance of that happening, especially after this afternoon. He wasn't about to open that can of sardines and have Aimee raise a big stink.

"Is he a good man?" Why was he punishing himself? It was none of his business. If anyone deserved happiness, it was Aimee.

She looked at him oddly, handing him the painting. "If you're asking if I like the man, I do. At first I wasn't sure, but once I heard how he was going to help Aimee, he won me over."

Tom's heart sank.

She walked him to the door. "Hey, big guy. When are you going to tell Aimee how you feel about her?"

Tom stopped in his tracks and glanced in Leah's direction. "Never. And I'd be much obliged, if you didn't either."

"Be bullheaded then. But I won't say a word. Have a good afternoon." Leah's chuckle followed him to his truck.

His mood black, his disposition sour, he figured he'd best go home and cool down. No use treating Aimee to his nasty temper.

Aimee deserved a good guy and a chance at happiness. It just couldn't be him. But, as long as he was around, no one would ever lay a finger on Aimee again or they'd forfeit their life.

Chapter 21

Aimee sat starring up at Tom's front door thumping her thumb on the steering wheel. The open gate meant he was expecting her but she wasn't too sure she wanted to face the bear in his den. Maybe he'd be in a better mood than this afternoon. If not, a quick in and out is what she'd do.

The man had no right to be so angry and on the attack with his questions. Her business was none of his except where training was concerned. Anything else was ... well it was off limits, or at least it should be.

Sitting here won't get his dinner delivered. Get on with it.

Aimee turned the handle and gave a good shove with her shoulder. Fortunately, the door opened. She climbed down, reached in and got the food carrier, and then trudged up the front steps to his door. Inhaling deeply, she raised her hand to knock.

"I was wondering if you would get out of the truck or if you were going to make me come get it."

Aimee screeched as she turned to glare at the insufferable man.

Tom jumped to his feet and rushed over to where she stood. "Sorry about that."

Her trembling hand rested on the rapid thumping of her heart. "I didn't see you sitting there. You scared me half out of my skin."

The effort to rein in her temper didn't work. Her emotions were jumping all over the place, bouncing somewhere between excited to see him and ready to strangle the man.

"Here let me have that." Tom grabbed the carrier. "Come sit down and have a glass of tea while I eat." His smile was that of an unrepentant little boy daring you to laugh at his pranks.

She wanted to punch him for being so irresistible.

"I was sitting in the swing waiting for you. I thought you saw me when you drove up. I really am sorry."

"Sure. I just bet you are."

"No really, I am."

"Well, I didn't see you. Why else would I scream? Next time, say something instead of sitting there like some axe murderer waiting to pounce. I—"

The sparkle in his dark eyes stopped her flow of words. His fresh scent, as if he'd just stepped from the shower and splashed the woodsy cologne on, rooted her in place.

He placed his hand at the small of her back, steering her toward one of the tables already set for dinner. Pulling out a chair, he removed his hand from her back and then motioned for her to be seated. "Please."

Even after sitting down, she could still feel the warmth of his hand resting on her waist.

While Tom unloaded the carrier, she noticed he'd gone to the trouble to add a glass for her, and a small dessert plate. *Ahh, so he was still expecting their nightly ritual.*

She would stay, but only because she felt sorry for him and didn't want him to eat alone. Who was she kidding? She wanted to stay.

Their evenings together had given her a chance to gain some insight to the man who was becoming ... what? A close friend, a confidant—she wouldn't go that far, but they were getting to know one another and she liked him.

He had fierce loyalty and strong values and a no nonsense approach. She liked him for the way he treated the women. And ... he wasn't bad on the eyes either.

Aimee sipped her tea, watching Tom over the rim of her glass as he filled his plate. When he was finished, he sat down, bowed his head and blessed the food.

He gave her another boyish smile. A little less certain this time. And then as if he were a starving man, he began chowing down.

The awkward silence from their unfavorable greeting, along with his earlier grilling of why she hadn't shown up for lunch, had Aimee on edge. She looked around for something to say, wanting to keep it neutral.

"It's a lovely evening. You couldn't have picked a better night to eat out here on the porch." *Good, keep going.* "The breeze is quite nice, really great for dinner al fresco. And your view from here is spectacular. You really have a nice piece of land with the woods and pond at the base of the hill. And your house—"

Tom's chuckle stopped her and had her glancing at him.

"What's so funny?"

"You."

"Me? Something I said?"

"No." His grin said otherwise.

"Unlike you, I was trying to make polite conversation."

"A little one sided, don't you think."

"Well, you were eating." She rubbed the frost off her glass with her thumb. "I can sit here quietly, if you'd rather." She tipped her nose into the air.

"No, please don't." That sparkle was back in his eyes. "I find it adorable that you rattle on when you're nervous."

"I don't ..." She started to get mad, then laughed. "You're right. I do tend to ramble when I'm unsure or worried."

"You want to talk about it?"

Aimee shook her head not wanting to broach the subject of this afternoon for fear he'd want to hear more than she was willing to share.

Tom shoveled another bite into his mouth and then leaned back in his chair studying her as he chewed.

How the man could make chewing and swallowing so appealing was a mystery to her, but she could watch him for hours. If she'd tried to pull off something like he was now, she'd look like a cow chewing its cud, or have food dribbling down her chin.

As if he had read her thoughts, Tom reached for his napkin. He wiped his mouth, leaning his head to one side studying her.

Looking away, she fidgeted with her glass.

He stood, held out his hand. "Come sit in the swing with me."

She wanted to say no. It was on the tip of her tongue to say no. But her heart and mouth wouldn't cooperate.

With little effort, her palm slipped into his hand and somehow she rose to her feet without stumbling. Time was suspended as they stood holding hands, facing one another.

The fragrance of his cologne was so him, weaving around her, drawing her in. His closeness woke sensations she believed lost forever and evoked a certain intimacy.

He leaned toward her.

Her heart pounded wildly.

Without releasing her hand, he reached for her glass of tea, handed it to her, then grabbed his glass.

Disappointment crowded in around her. She kicked herself for being such a ninny, when she should be thankful it was the glass he'd latched onto and not her lips.

How stupid can you be? Tom isn't interested in you.

She didn't want him to be. *Liar.*

His hand holding hers continued to play havoc with her emotions. If he'd kissed her, what would she have done? Slapped him or hung onto him and never let him go.

She felt like a silly schoolgirl on her first date—nervous, excited, energized, and a little let down—and this wasn't even a date. More like friends passing the evening together.

Get a grip.

Without speaking, he led her to the porch swing, allowing her to settle in before he sat next to her. With the toe of his boot, he gave a small shove, causing the swing to gently sway back and forth, the movement and his closeness weaving her further into a cloud of fantasy.

She leaned her head back against the polished wood and closed her eyes.

The evening was too perfect. Tom sitting close felt right, even if they were just friends. The warmth of his side radiated through her, lulling her into a sense of security and wellbeing. If only this moment could last and trouble wasn't out there somewhere waiting for her.

The feel of Tom's thumb rubbing the back of her hand jerked Aimee out of her stupor. She sat up and extracted her hand but immediately regretted her action.

Flustered, without looking at him, she said, "I really should go. I have a painting to finish."

When she began to rise, he gently grabbed her arm to hold her in place. "Stay, please. Keep me company just a little longer, please."

Her first reaction was to scramble out of the swing as fast as she could and get her tush back home. But when she glanced at him, she was no match for the loneliness she recognized in his gaze.

"I'll stay if you'll talk to me, and not make me feel like I have to babble on and on like an idiot."

He chuckled, arousing those feelings again.

"I love to hear you babble. It keeps the dark thoughts at bay."

"What dark thoughts?" At first she thought she'd gone too far.

He breathed in heavily, while gazing at their intertwined hands. "Wow. That's quite a question. How to answer it?"

"Like you, I'm a good listener."

When he didn't speak, she wondered if she should continue to prod.

"You don't have to tell me unless you want to. But sometimes it helps to speak aloud the demons that bother us. It's kind of a way of releasing them. Therapeutic."

Should she continue?

"When I first came to Ben Wheeler, I lived with Leah. She's the one who taught me the demons of my past can't harm me unless I allow them to by living in fear."

"What brought about your move, and why did you start Paradise Found?"

That was a question she would have rather not answered. However, if she wanted him to open up to her, he had a right to ask the same.

"It's not something I like to speak about, except to others like me to encourage them to fight."

"You don't have to tell if you don't want to."

The compassion in his eyes was her undoing.

"I want to tell you. But if you don't mind, I'll give you the short version." Aimee took a deep breath, doing her best to settle her heart.

"I was a victim of spousal abuse just like the ladies that come to my home. When I'd had enough and reached the point of not wanting to be the recipient of my husband's anger or his punching bag, God sent me Marty from the Houston Women's Shelter.

"I won't lie and say the decision was easy, it wasn't. It took a near death experience before I would listen to Marty and leave Rick." She leaned her head back against the wood, exhaustion taking over as it usually did when she told her story. Today seemed to be a day of reliving the past, and though it couldn't hurt her any longer, it still had a way of needling her mind.

"Your ex isn't a man. He's a jerk if he got his jollies by beating a defenseless woman. In the service, we had a name for someone like him, but I won't sully your ears." He squeezed her hand. "If he ever comes around you again, I hope I'm here to show him what weak and defenseless looks like. Believe me, when I'm through he'll never hit another woman."

Aimee chuckled. "You may soon get your chance."

Tom searched her face looking for answers. "Was he here today? Is he threatening you?"

The fierce look in his eyes made her realize he would be a force to reckon with.

"I'm sure glad you're on my side." She chuckled. "But no, he's not here. However, I got word he hired someone to look for me. And thanks, but I don't think you beating him to a pulp will be necessary, regardless how much pleasure I'd have in seeing it done."

She shook her head chewing on her bottom lip. "No, I don't mean that. A while back, I would have enjoyed seeing Rick beaten bloody and senseless. I wanted him to feel the same hurt and pain he caused me, but not now. God says, *revenge is mine*, so I've left Rick in His hands."

Aimee looked down at Tom's strong hand holding hers. With him, fear would never be a factor. She knew his hands would only bring comfort and love.

"Rick's mind is warped—whether something from childhood, family"—she shrugged—"whatever, doesn't matter. All I feel for him now is pity. And believe it or not, I pray for him." She took a calming breath needing to purge her soul of the dark thoughts Rick had brought about.

"Anyway, if he comes around, you've already shown me how to fight him, and for that I'm thankful. And if that doesn't work, my gun will." The smile she displayed was anything but heartfelt. She didn't want to kill Rick, but neither would she allow him to beat her again. "He won't beat me again if I have anything to say about it."

Tom covered their hands with his other one. "I'm here for you. You know that don't you?"

"I know. But Frank's going to send Rick looking down a rabbit trail far away from here so he won't find me."

"Frank?" Tom stiffened next to her but didn't release his hold.

She felt the coolness in his attitude. Should she tell him who Frank was? For some reason she didn't want to.

"Is he the friend you met in town today?"

"Yes." Not a lie exactly. If Frank could be trusted he would be a good friend to have.

"Is this Frank special to you?"

Though she wanted to tease him and say yes, she wasn't going to torment him a second longer.

"Frank is a friend, and he's the PI my ex-husband hired to locate me."

"And you trust the guy?" He looked incredulous.

"I have to, if I'm going to sleep at night. I would have thought Rick, my ex, would have given up by now. But it seems his hatred knows no bounds, at least where I'm concerned." She glanced up in time to see a flash of Tom's anger.

He studied a spot off in the distance as if it were the most important thing at that minute, then he turned to her.

"Look, you may not like what I'm about to say, but I want to build a fence with an automatic gate and lock system around your property, or at least the part that is open to the road and accessible by foot. Something like I have here. For you, it wouldn't hurt to go down and around the house and barn either."

"I can't afford that. Maybe one day." She would like the fence and gate, even have her road graded. But as it was, she was barely keeping everything afloat, something she wasn't about to tell Tom.

He scrunched his brow in thought. "Look, I've got money. I'll give it to you. Even hire the men. The company who installed my fence will give me a good deal. I feel sure they can have the fence up and done within a week or two. What do you say?"

"No. Plain and simple."

"Why? Because of pride? I would think the women's safety was paramount. Look what happened to Jill."

His words pricked the tender spot in her heart. "It's not my pride. I can't because I don't' have any way of paying you back and probably never will."

"Did you hear me say I expected you to pay me back? I said I'd give you the fence."

"No, but—"

"I don't need the money. It'll be my gift, if not for you, then for the women. Because one day, one of their ex's will come calling. At least this way, you would have a fighting chance with a gate and fence in place."

Aimee wanted to accept his gift. Instead she shook her head without looking at him.

"Did anyone ever tell you that you're one stubborn woman?"

A gurgle of laughter slipped through her lips. "I believe that's been mentioned a time or two before."

"I don't doubt it." He stood. "Well, I don't know about you, but I'm ready for my dessert. What did you bring us?"

When she started to follow him, he waved her off. "Sit there. Don't move. I'll bring dessert to you." He dug inside the bag, pulled out a container, then lifted the lid revealing a huge portion of Maggie's Dump Cake. "I don't know what this is, but it looks good enough to eat."

"Maggie's Dump Cake is always good."

Tom picked up two forks, carried the container with the cake over to where she sat. He handed her a fork, then scooted in beside her on the swing again.

"Dig in."

She looked at him skeptical.

Tom dug his fork in and began eating the cake straight from the container.

"Come on. Don't be bashful. If you don't hurry, I'm gonna clean the bowl."

He held the cake in front of her. She slid a nice size bite onto her fork, then into her mouth. "*Mmm.*"

Though she'd spent many an evening sharing dessert with Tom, tonight was a first. The intimacy of sitting next to him and eating Dump Cake from the same bowl had her insides as quivery as a new born calf standing for the first time. Yet, she couldn't let him know how much his nearness was weaving its way around her, drawing her closer to the man.

Without thought, she dipped her fingers into the container, and then held it out in front of him. "Here."

He looked at her oddly, and then when he was about to lick it from her fingers, she smeared the whole gooey mess all over his mouth and then started laughing.

He recovered quickly. "Now you've asked for it. The war's on." He grabbed a handful of cake.

"No." Aimee tried to dodge. "Please, I'm sorry."

"Sure you are."

She was pinned in the swing as he leaned over her, rubbing the gooey mess over her mouth and chin. Jumping up, she ran to the other side of the table. He followed and slathered more goo down her arm.

"You're not playing fair. You have the bowl and longer arms."

"Who said I play fair. I never lose regardless what it takes to win." He caught her off guard again, swiping her cheek this time, and then licking his fingers. "On second thought ... truce. This cake is too good to waste on a food fight."

He dipped his fingers into the cake and pulled out a huge bite, which he slid into his mouth, closing his lips around his fingers before extracting them for more.

Safe from retaliation, she came out from behind the table, grabbed a napkin and began wiping her face. She glanced inside the bowl then looked up in surprise as the gooey substance was slathered down her cheek to her neck.

"No fair." She slapped his arm. "You called truce."

His devilish smile melted her heart. "But I did warn you. I said I would do whatever it takes to win."

She'd never seen this lighthearted, playful mood of him before. Normally, he was all business or shut off from others. Tonight he was young, alive, and handsome, and he'd completely captured her heart.

Chapter 22

Tom clunked his partially empty cup down on the patio table. Lukewarm coffee sloshed over the rim onto his fingers. Shoving his chair back roughly.

Aimee was driving him crazy.

From the first day they'd met he knew she'd be trouble, and last night was proof.

He'd acted like a schoolboy with no control, obsessed with the beautiful girl. Yet he couldn't be blamed. She'd started it, and he couldn't resist her playfulness.

Like a child looking at the candy in front of the glass window, he couldn't seem to get enough of her. The result was disastrous. He'd wanted to be her friend, help her with her problems, but after last night, they were far beyond being friends — at least he was anyway.

Aimee invaded his personal space, intruded into his dreams, and now she seemed to be constant in his thoughts. His house bore the mark of her more than him with her personal little touches everywhere.

Wasn't anything sacred?

He leaned against the railing looking off into the line of trees. Even now, Aimee was keeping him from enjoying his daily ritual of sitting on his bedroom deck drinking coffee while watching the sunrise. How she managed to break through his line of defense and storm his heart, something he'd worked hard to protect, was a mystery.

Self-discipline had never been a problem for him. His men had called him ironman because nothing affected him. Which was true until he lost his men and now ... Aimee.

He had little to no control over her gradually wheedling her way and inserting herself into his life.

Her impish laughter, her sparkling eyes, her crazy, fun-loving spirit all worked against him, drawing him.

The image of Aimee's face and arms slathered in chocolate and her trying her best to retaliate while he held her at arms-distance, brought about a smile. Last night, what he really wanted to do was haul her into his arms and kiss her senseless. Luckily, he'd come to his wits in time.

Last night was a mistake. He shouldn't have let it get out of hand.

Attuned to his surrounding, his gaze searched for the source of rustling dry leaves and found Clyde romping back and forth, teasing a rabbit. Tom leaned against the railing as his dog darted off into the woods in hot pursuit of the cottontail.

Again his thoughts turned to last night with Aimee. It had been years since he'd felt so alive and lighthearted and he owed it all to her. If he wasn't so messed up inside, he'd pursue Aimee like Clyde did the critters around his house. Unlike Clyde, he wouldn't play catch and release. He'd play for keeps.

Disgruntled with where his thoughts had taken him, he grabbed his cup and went inside.

Aimee and he together were too foolish to imagine. She deserved more. She deserved someone who was whole. Someone who didn't have nightmares or dark thoughts, and whose self-worth was a whole lot higher than his.

If he ordered her fence, his problem would be solved and he'd see less of her.

Without another thought, he picked up his phone and dialed the man who had fenced in his property. It took no time at all to work out a deal and set the wheels in motion.

The material would be delivered sometime today, and a crew would be out either late this afternoon or early in the morning to begin installing a fence and an automatic gate on Aimee's property. The chunk of change it cost him was well worth the investment, if it meant her safety.

Once Aimee saw the fencing dropped off on her land, he figured she'd hightail it over to his place and give him what for. He smiled at the feisty image in his mind.

Tom tapped in a couple of picture hangers into his office wall across from his desk. After hanging Aimee's painting, he stood back and admired the scene.

Humph. Having Aimee as a friend was becoming expensive. First the painting, and now the fence, but he didn't begrudge either. The cost was minimal compared to his peace of mind.

He smiled. The way he was doling out the cash he'd have to do some hefty trading to recoup his expenditures. But the fence was worth every cent he'd invested.

If it weren't for his expertise on the stock exchange, he wouldn't have been able to help Aimee. As it was, he could and he was glad he could.

Like today and every day, his routine was much the same.

Wake up, trade on the NASDAQ for several hours, take a break and drink his coffee on the deck, then trade some more. Over time, along with a few mishaps, his trading had turned into a profitable business, growing his investments. As it was, if he didn't want to, he'd never have to work another day in his life. But work kept him sane.

Today, except for the few pesky thoughts of Aimee interrupting his work, which seemed to be happening more and more frequently, he had already recouped his outlay of cash for the fence.

He whistled a tune, then stopped, shaking his head. The woman had made him daft. He was going around whistling and smiling, which wasn't like him.

After several more hours of trading, Tom grabbed his keys, a couple bottles of water, then headed for his truck. His gate had stopped working yesterday and he knew it wouldn't get fixed on its own.

Parking in the middle of his drive, he pulled out his tools, and attacked the problem. Several of his neighbors from down the way drove by, honked and waved. One stopped to talk for a few minutes.

He knew some of his neighbors, even had spoken to a few of them, but mainly he knew them by sight and the vehicle they drove. That's why he picked country living. Country folk were always friendly, but also left you alone.

Hearing a vehicle approach, he looked up. The man glanced his way but without waving, drove on by. Both, the car and the man weren't familiar to him. Tom continued to watch until the car drove past Aimee's road and out of sight. Within a matter of minutes, the same vehicle drove back and stopped in front of Aimee's drive then hooked a left into her property.

He couldn't be up to any good.

Tom slung the tools in the back of his truck, hopped in, and took off after the man. Impervious to the bumpy ride, he was bent on stopping the guy before he got to Aimee's house.

He smiled when he saw the car a little ways ahead. The driver was taking Aimee's drive slow and easy because of the potholes. At least something could be said in favor of her road.

Tom whizzed around the man on the grass just before the other vehicle got to the house. He pulled a sliding stop with his truck across the road causing the man to panic stop and preventing him from going any farther. Dust and rocks flew around both vehicles while the other man stared at Tom in disbelief.

Before the dust had settled, Tom was out of his truck and opening the car door of the other vehicle.

"Who are you and what are you doing here?"

The screen door banged, and someone came running toward them. Tom didn't take his eyes off the man.

"What's going on?"

Without turning to Aimee, he said, "I saw this man enter your property and thought I'd find out what business he had coming on your land."

The man, at first studied Tom, then looked over to where Aimee was standing, then flashed a cocky smile.

"Quite a watchdog you have there, Aimee. Would you like to tell him I'm one of the good guys and introduce us before he takes my head off?" The last was said on a chuckle.

Not caring who the guy might be, Tom was ready to reach into the car and drag him out by the nap of the neck. The only thing that restrained him from acting on his impulse ... Aimee's gentle touch on his arm.

"Tom Branigan, meet Frank Thornton, the PI I told you about last night."

When the PI climbed out of the car, Tom noticed several things about the guy. Thornton was about the same height and weight as he was, and his gaze didn't miss a thing. Right this minute, he didn't like the way Thornton was eyeing Aimee—as if she was his Christmas package and he'd like to take her home and unwrap his present.

Another thing ... that crack about him being Aimee's watchdog rankled. And as far as Thornton being friend or foe, the jury was still out. He'd watch him. Make sure the man was here to help, because anything less, and the man would be seeing stars.

Knowing he had no claim on Aimee, Tom simmered down, stuck out his hand, and was met with a strong grip, one Tom reinforced.

"Glad to meet you." Thornton chuckled under his breath, nodding. "Aimee, I like your guy."

"He's not my guy." She turned a bright shade of pink. "Tom's my neighbor and a good friend."

"I can see that." Thornton looked back at the house.

All the women were standing on the porch ready to jump into action. Maggie, shotgun in hand, had lowered the gun to her side seeing there was no immediate threat.

Tom was pleased to see some of his training had taken hold.

"Is there some place where we can talk?" He looked again at the women and then at Tom. "Somewhere private?"

Tom wasn't about to leave Aimee's side. He was going to tag along to hear what Thornton had to say, even if it meant pushing his way in and upsetting Aimee.

She motioned to the dock. "We can talk there. It's quiet and away from everyone." Turning toward the house, she waved. "Everything is OK. I'll be right back."

She started off then stopped. "Tom, if you have the time, I would like you to come and listen to what Frank has to say? I believe this will ultimately affect you also."

"I'd be glad to." The pleasure of her request left as quickly as it came when Thornton stepped up to walk beside Aimee, a little closer than called for.

Tom moved up next to her on the other side and heard a deep, under-the-breath chuckle again coming from Thornton.

Come to think of it, a little of Thornton goes a long way. He might not wait to punch the guy's lights out after all, especially if he keeps flirting with Aimee.

Chapter 23

The charged atmosphere between Tom and Frank was enough to ignite the city of Ben Wheeler, or, at the very least, her little compound. The men were like two bulls, heads down, pawing the dirt, ready to charge at the drop of the red flag. Aimee's only hope ... get out of the way if they decided to hook horns.

If she had known asking Tom to come along would fuel the competitive fervor, she wouldn't have asked. It must be a male thing.

A possessive Tom was puzzling. She'd never seen this side of him before. Usually, he acted as if he couldn't be bothered.

At the dock, she positioned her chair carefully. She faced Tom *and* Frank, motioning for them to be seated.

"What's up?" She rested her elbows on the arms of the chair, fearing the worst from Frank's visit so soon.

"I assume Tom knows your history?"

"Enough to make him party to this conversation."

Frank nodded. "I called Rick and give him notice that I wouldn't be working for him any longer. He had several choice words to say about my decision and what he'd like to do to my anatomy, which I told him would be physically impossible." Frank gave an indifferent shrug.

"However, during his attack, he let slip that he knew where you were and wouldn't need me anyway." He stared at Aimee not happy with what he'd delivered. "I don't think he was bluffing."

A chill crept up Aimee's neck causing her hair to stand on end as she gripped the ends of the armrests. Faster than she could get out of the way, her world was crumbling down around her feet.

"If that's so, then I can't stay here and endanger the others." She directed the statement to Tom.

He leaned forward. "You and the others can camp out at my house until it's safe to return. He wouldn't know where you were."

She shook her head. "Thanks, but I couldn't."

"If not with me, you could move to Tyler. My sister would put you up until the scumbag gives up hope of finding you."

"It's not that simple. I can't hide. I have mouths to feed, bills to pay, and he'd find me anyway."

"The offer stands if you change your mind." Tom scooted back in his chair plainly frustrated.

"Or, we" —Frank directed his remark to Tom— "could make Aimee's house a fortress."

"What do you have in mind?"

Though Tom was willing to entertain Frank's idea, she wasn't so sure she could.

"Between the two of us, we can devise a plan to catch the man or men he hires to do his dirty work. I could be wrong. I don't figure he'll come. He'll send someone else."

"I'm not so sure." Both men looked at her. "With Rick, it's a matter of principal. He won't send some minion to do the job he'd rather do. He'll want the satisfaction of taking care of the problem—me—himself." What she failed to mention, her ex enjoyed inflicting pain to the point of her praying for death.

"So much the better. If you agree"—he glanced at Tom—"we can protect her and the others 24-7. I'll send off for a couple of my guys. We can set up a camp near the road—"

"Hold on a minute. You're moving too fast. I can't involve you or Tom in my fight."

"Aimee, if you won't come to my house, then Frank's idea is the only sensible solution."

She knew Tom was right, but she didn't like embroiling others in her fight. What if one of them got hurt?

"I'll listen to your plan, but I won't make any promises. At the moment, I feel like I'm being run over by a steamroller. I know Rick and what he's capable of doing a whole lot better than either of you do."

"I'm sure you do," Frank grunted, his distaste clear.

Tom looked ready to kill.

A disconcerting silence settled around them.

No one, not Frank or Tom could know what an awful hell she'd lived in, or the many, many times

Rick had beaten her then apologized only to do it again another day.

"The final word would have to come from you." Frank waited for her reply.

Shoving the horrors from her mind, she said, "Thank you."

"If you're in agreement, my men, Tom, and I will set up camp tomorrow afternoon close to the entrance. We'll be able to catch anyone trying to come onto your property." Frank raised his brows and laughed. "Hopefully, we'll catch them a little quicker than Tom caught me today."

She could tell Tom found no humor in Frank's wisecrack.

Frank turned serious. "How many people live with you?"

"Six women, three children."

Tom reached out and squeezed her fingers, still holding on, his thumb rubbed the back of her hand. "Aimee." Tom waited until he had her full attention. "If you won't move everyone into my house, the next best thing is what Frank's proposing. It offers the best possible safety for you and the others."

"If we set guards near the entrance and along the front, he'd have to come through us to get to you. If that happens, you and the others will know he's on his way and know what you need to do to be prepared for him. Frank's plan is the only sensible way."

"What if he takes out you or Frank, or one of the other men? I couldn't live with myself. I can't let you do this for me."

"Aimee, please listen to reason." Tom's concern snagged at her heart. "This man has to be stopped. And you know by experience the authorities are of little help in matters of domestic violence. They can only arrest him if he's caught in the act. Him getting that close to you is unacceptable."

He squeezed her hand. "This is the only smart way to handle the situation. With Frank's and my skills and that of his men, I believe we can stop this sadist before he hurts you or anyone else again."

Their plan was viable, but it meant playing with other people's lives, something she vowed never to do. "And if an innocent bystander is hurt, what then?"

"My men are well trained for this type of situation."

Frank glanced around her property and then up the hill. "You have a pretty spread."

"Thank you."

"But you need a good fence around this place. It would make it a lot harder for someone to get onto your property."

"A fence will be up by the end of the week." Tom's response was spontaneous.

Aimee's gasped. "What?"

Tom avoided looking at her.

"Good." Frank nodded. "I think—"

Motioning Frank to silence, she tried to remain calm. "What do you mean I'll have a fence by the end of the week?"

"If you remember, we discussed putting up a fence last night before dessert."

His grin was sexier than all get out, but it didn't cool her temper. She knew Tom referred to her total lapse in judgment of last night's dessert fight. Heat ran the full gamut from her head to her feet.

"And I remember specifically telling you I couldn't afford a fence."

"Yes, and as I explained, the cost was immaterial compared to your safety. It's too late anyway. All the fencing material should be here within the hour. The men will begin work later this afternoon or in the morning. So it's a done deal."

"Well, you can just undo the deal. I won't have you paying for my fence."

"I can't call it off. No refunds."

Tom's smug smile irked her. By the stubborn set of his jaw, Aimee knew Tom wasn't going to back down. Well neither would she.

"Then I will pay back every last cent with interest." Her heart sunk. She had priced a fence last year and it was over forty thousand dollars. Where would she get that kind of money? It would take her a lifetime of painting day and night to pay the pigheaded man back, if she lasted that long.

Sending a defiant look in Tom's direction, she said, "We'll talk later."

He cocked his head to one side. "That's fine with me. But if my hearing is as good as I know it is, that diesel sound coming from over the hill is the material being delivered."

Tom hadn't bested her. *Well, he had.*

At the moment, she'd like nothing better than to wipe that silly grin right off his face and give him a good old fashion tongue-lashing. However, with

Frank silently watching and chuckling over what he probably thought was a show of testosterone versus hormonal imbalance, she figured she'd show some restraint.

"Since we've settled that, can we move on with plans? Shall I send for my men?" Frank posed the question to Aimee.

She wanted to refuse but at the moment she didn't have a better plan or a good enough excuse why he shouldn't, except ...

"Not so fast. What's your fee?"

"My fee?" Frank looked at Aimee as if she was speaking German.

"Yes. What's the fee for around-the-clock protection?" She would be working for years to pay back Tom and now with the added charge of Frank she'd never see the light of day again.

"Since I have others that depend on me and I'm not made of money, and now there seems to be the *huge* matter of a fence ..." She sent a scathing look at Tom that didn't faze him. "I know a PI and a couple of men twenty-four seven won't come cheap."

"Let's just say your ex is paying for this."

"How so?"

"Our original agreement, whether or not I decided to take the job, was a nonnegotiable and non-refundable preliminary fee upfront, which was hefty. So in good conscience, I couldn't spend his money unless it went for a good cause. In my opinion, protecting you and the others is a good enough cause."

Shaking her head, she said, "I can't—"

"Like Tom here, I won't take no for an answer. I'll be back tomorrow with my men."

"Since you are doing me a huge favor, and the closest motels are in Canton, then I insist that you and your men stay with me. There's plenty of room in my barn."

When Frank wrinkled his nose, she laughed. "My barn was converted into a mini-hotel with central heating and AC. I have ten separate living quarters with baths, and a main gathering room in the center."

"Pretty handy."

"I think you'll find the accommodations comfortable. And of course, you'll eat your meals with us. Ask Tom. He'll vouch for Maggie's cooking. She's the best."

"It sounds like we've struck a good bargain. I look forward to some good home cooking for a change." Frank stood.

Aimee and Tom followed suit.

"I'll head on back to Dallas and set up everything. We'll be here around noon or earlier." He reached into his pocket. "Tom, here's my card. If you'll give me your number, I'll touch base with you sometime later tonight or in the morning."

While Tom and Frank exchanged information, Aimee turned to look out over the water. It would only be a matter of time before Rick found them and her peaceful existence would shatter.

God, I'm scared. Not for me but the others. I don't know what trouble the day will bring, but you do. I can't run again. Please watch over and protect everyone. I place everything into your capable hands. Amen.

"Aimee." She felt Tom's hand on her shoulder. "Frank's leaving."

She turned. They were both looking at her oddly.

"I'm sorry. I was just preparing my mind for what's to come." She stuck out her hand. "Thanks for your help, Frank, and for all you and your men will be doing for us."

If she'd had any doubts in Frank, his compassionate smile erased them.

"I wouldn't be human if I didn't offer my assistance." Frank wrinkled his nose. "Your ex may know where you are, but he'll have to come through us first."

"There's something you should know about Rick. He's shrewd and doesn't give up easily. He'll kill anyone to get to me, and that's not just a silly woman talking."

"Let him come."

Tom's menacing look chilled her.

"He better think twice before he touches one hair on your head. If he does, he'll not live long enough to regret it." Tom looked meaner than a junkyard dog ready to rip Rick's throat out.

Chapter 24

How dare the man put up a fence without her say-so. If Tom hadn't left when Frank did, Aimee would have lit into him right then and there.

And another thing that chapped her backside raw, the coward didn't have the nerve to show up for lunch. He probably figured there'd be a showdown at noon. And he would have been right.

The smell of Tom's dinner drifted up from the container causing her non-existent hunger pangs at supper to kick. If that bullheaded man wasn't home, she'd wait until he got there, if it meant waiting all night. They were going to have the *fence talk* whether he liked it or not.

Seeing the pile of fencing supplies up by the road made her temper flare. She continued to simmer at a steady boil as she turned onto Tom's road.

His gate stood open, which meant he was either expecting her or he was still having trouble with the automatic opener. The closer she got to the house, the less she felt like having words with him. He didn't deserve her anger. After all, he purchased the fence to protect her and the others. Except for the money he had spent, which was huge, what fault could she find in him wanting to help?

Her anger vanished and a tingle of excitement flared when she saw Tom leaning against the porch post, his arms and legs crossed, waiting for her. The man, too appealing by half, caused any leftover remnants of anger to fly out her open window. Her breath hitched in her chest like a baby with hiccups when he straightened to walk down the steps toward her truck.

She remembered to breathe, barely.

How did she let this happen?

Overnight, their relationship had gone from friends, at least on her part—if one could call verbal sparring and daily disagreements friendship—to this sense she would be lost if he walked out of her life.

As rain was to the earth, she knew Tom was essential to her wellbeing, and it scared her beyond reason.

The warm smile and glint in his eyes brought home the staggering realization that Tom had gotten past her radar, torn down the walls she'd erected, and gone straight for her heart. How had she let this happen?

Aimee shook her head to dislodge the incriminating thoughts while giving herself a good, sound scolding. She should have seen it coming and safeguarded her feelings long before now. But no, she had fallen for the guy … *hard*.

When he pulled on the truck handle, the faithless door opened as easily as a new one. No screeching, groaning, or loud popping sound. *Traitor.*

Apparently, her truck was as susceptible as she was to Tom's charms.

Doing her best to think of him as a friend, didn't work. Yet there would be no way on God's green earth she would act upon her feelings. What man in his right mind would care to be saddled with all the baggage she carried? And then there were the women.

"Wow. You look gorgeous, and smell good too. I hope it was for my benefit."

Tom helped her out of the truck. Like a marksman, his compliment flew straight to her heart. The jitters began to build in the pit of her stomach and work their way through the rest of her body.

Though she'd taken more time on her appearance than normal, she didn't want him to think she had. "I hate to disappoint you, but I believe your eyesight must be failing. And you're smelling? Well, that must be going to. What you smell is Maggie's cooking."

"No, ma'am. That's where you're wrong. My eyesight is perfectly fine. And I like what I see. And my sense of smell is just fine too?" He leaned in and sniffed of her hair. "Your hair smells like flowers."

Self-conscientiously she said, "Thank you." She ran her sweaty palm down the side of her jeans. His close proximity had her excited and confused.

"Since you missed lunch, Maggie figured you might be hungrier than usual. She packed extra."

Once again she was chattering and feeling nervous. Tom looked so good she couldn't bring herself to give him one good scold—at least not yet, maybe later. Just seeing him had waylaid her plans.

She reached inside for the food carrier. Tom beat her to it. He moved in closer, the handle already in his hand. He waited for her to move aside and then he shut the door. Placing his hand at the small of her back, he led her up the stairs. The warmth of his touch seeped through her, managing to stir up her chaotic feelings even more.

When they reached the table, the same table where they'd had the dessert fight last night, her heart jackhammered inside her chest until she could hardly breathe. The panicky feeling compelled her to turn around and hightail it back to her comfort zone where everything was normal and on an even keel, but she couldn't. Yet, she didn't need any of these uncontrollable impulses taking her for a ride.

Tom began unloading the basket.

Complicated she didn't need, and Tom fit in that category. And the last thing in the world she wanted was Tom getting her off focus, especially with Rick on his way.

Backing away, she hoped he wouldn't notice she was acting skittish, or that his nearness was causing her to act like a woman gone mad.

"I think you nailed it."

Startled, thinking she had spoken aloud, she asked, "What?"

"Maggie went overboard. I can't eat this much." His golden-brown eyes sparkled with hope. "Have you eaten?

Tell him yes. Tell him you can't stay. Get back to your truck and go home.

His face showed he expected her to make an excuse to leave.

"To tell the truth, I am a little hungry. I didn't feel much like eating earlier." What was wrong with her mouth? Why had she agreed?

"Good. Then you can eat with me."

"Thanks, I'll get another plate while you pull out the rest of the food." Aimee gave him an uncertain grin, then left.

She kicked herself for accepting his invitation.

Inside, pulling together her place setting, she heard Tom's cellphone ring. She moved toward his office, and heard it again behind the closed door. Not sure if she should enter his private domain or tell him about it, she figured it might be important. To save him some steps, she'd take the phone to him.

Feeling like an interloper, she opened his office door and saw his cellphone on the desk. Though it had stopped ringing, she grabbed it, slipped it into her pocket and was about to leave when she noticed her painting on the wall.

Humbled that Tom would think so highly of her art to buy it, she took a moment to gaze at the pond and the couple on the deck who were painted in as afterthought but certainly enhanced the picture.

Looking at it now, she knew why she'd felt compelled to add the man and woman. Though painted in the abstract, the figures were Tom and she. Their shapes, coloring, even their posture were the same. She could see it now. Even the dog she'd added was Clyde.

Had he noticed the resemblance?

"What are you doing in here?"

His gruff question had Aimee turning red for being caught where he had explicitly told her not to go. Tom's displeasure flustered and confused her.

She fumbled for his phone drawing it out of her pocket. "I-I ... your phone was ringing." She handed it to him. "I thought it might be important, so I came in here to get it and bring it to you."

He pushed the button to look at the readout. "Thanks, but it's not important. It can wait. The food is getting cold." He waited for her to pass.

The firm snap of the door being shut left her a little embarrassed and rattled.

The frequent tension-filled dinners with Rick, often ending in abuse, came rushing back, caused panic to bubble to the surface. No longer hungry, she hesitated then grabbed her plate noticing her hand shook.

On the table were two placemats, two glasses filled with iced tea, and a cloth over the food. Tom pulled out her chair, pocketed his phone, and then sat down facing her.

Rick was easy to read, but she couldn't read Tom. She always knew when to stay out of Rick's reach, which didn't work most of the time. Though she didn't fear Tom, he hid his feelings and thoughts too well.

She nearly jumped out of her skin when he grabbed her hand. Her heart lurched to a stop and she shrank back, anticipating the blow from the back of his hand.

In that split second, he knew what she had thought.

Shame washed over her when she saw Tom's shock turn to hurt, then anger. *"That jerk!"* His barely audible mumble was ground through his clinched teeth.

Leaning back, he lifted his hands to show he meant no harm.

"Aimee, I would never lay a finger on you in anger." Tom was a mixture of cross and contrite.

"I know you wouldn't. I'm sorry." She felt horrible.

"However, right at this minute, if he were here, I would beat your ex to a pulp."

Her shame caused tears to sting her eyes, pooling at the edge of her lashes, and distorting her vision.

Not once had Tom shown her anything but kindness. Not when she argued with him. Not when she'd pushed him too far. Not even when she'd irritated him to no end, which she seemed to do on a regular basis.

"Tom, I know you're nothing like Rick." She glanced down at the table, nervously fiddling with her utensils. "My only excuse is you caught me off guard." Giving him a weak smile, she asked, "Will you bless the food, please?"

Her eyes closed, several seconds ticked by as she willed her tears away and waited for Tom to pray.

Tom's deep voice resonated, soothing her soul as he said a lovely blessing over the food. He even asked God for protection from the coming threat.

"Thank you. That was a lovely prayer. Again, I'm sorry." She lifted her hand then dropped it to the table. No words could take away the humiliation of her actions. Should she explain? Or would he be sickened by her confession?

"It's a built in mechanism that I've yet to conquer. But I am getting better. Years of abuse is hard to erase. Especially when the cruelty came from someone I believed loved me yet showed me his fist."

Tom's sharp intake of breath had Aimee wanting to stop but for some reason she couldn't. The floodgates had opened and there was no stopping the flow of words.

She traced the intricate woven design of the blue fabric placemat with her nail.

"Just like this fabric, God had interwoven people into my life, like you, enabling me to trust and forgive." She smiled, feeling the ironic sadness. "Then when I think I've conquered the demons, one raises its old ugly head, like now.

"True, my reflexes when touched unexpectedly leave a lot to be desired. But one day soon, God will heal that aspect too."

"I would never knowingly hurt you."

"I know you wouldn't. I trust you with my life."

"Good." He squeezed her hand. "Since we have that settled, shall we eat?" He released her. Picking up a fork, he stabbed a piece of fried chicken. "I'm starved."

"By all means, I would hate to stand between a man and his food."

His chuckle warmed the cold places of her heart.

"You're one smart woman." He attacked the meat with a vengeance.

They ate in companionable silence, the food tasting better by sharing it with Tom. She didn't know how she would work out the unexplainable sensation of love she felt toward him, yet, with God's help, she would.

Tom was a good man and a good neighbor. For now she would enjoy his company and build upon their friendship. Soon she'd be over this infatuation. Maybe even count him as a good, close friend — *just not too close.*

"I missed lunch today because Frank wanted to do some planning. So I obliged him and took him to The Forge instead. I figured it would be less unsettling for the women." He looked at her sideways. "I would have rather eaten with you though."

Aimee ignored the last. "I hope no one overheard you. If they did, they doubtless thought you were getting ready to nab a group of terrorists in Ben Wheeler."

"We have one in town?" He scrunched his brows together, giving her a teasing look.

"No, but you know what I mean."

He wiped his mouth, his face grave. "This is far more serious than terrorists. This guy is coming after you, Aimee. If he does, I'll kill him."

Worry gnawed at her. She placed her hand on his arm. "No. Don't say that. He's not worth it. At one time I would have said, yes, go for it, but no longer. All I pray is that he goes to jail for a very long time. I don't want him hurting another woman like he hurt me."

"I won't make you any promises. But I will try my best to subdue him and turn him over to the authorities."

"That's all I ask."

He cleared his throat. "My other reason for missing lunch, I thought it best to give you some time to cool down."

"You're a wise man." She cocked her one brow, admiring Tom's honest approach.

"I try to be most of the time. Sometimes it works, sometimes it doesn't." He cracked a smile.

"Ordering the fence, when I expressly told you not to, was definitely a *doesn't*."

"I know, but if I say I'm sorry will you forgive." He held up his hand. "On second thought, I'd be lying." He gave her an impish grin. "I figured a fence would never be built if I waited for you to agree."

"You figured right. However, since it's a *done deal* as you put it, I'll live with it. But I plan on paying you back."

"I don't want or need your money."

She gave him a stern look.

"However, if you're bound to have it your own way—"

"I am." She crossed her arms.

"We can work out something later, once they're through building the fence and this mess with your ex is outta the way."

"You can bet on it." She moved her plate over then stood. "I think I am ready for some of Maggie's banana pudding. How 'bout you?"

"Are you sure you will eat yours and not smear it all over me like last night?"

The glint in his eyes caused her heart to accelerate. He was way too appealing. "I'll do my best to refrain."

"Good. Maggie's pudding is too good to waste."

Aimee served up a heaping bowl of pudding for Tom and a smaller amount for her. He stood, grabbed his pudding and then clutched her free hand. "Grab your bowl." When she did, he pulled her over to the swing. "This is more relaxing."

A tingle of excitement flared to life. Her self-declaration to keep Tom at a distance and as a friend, howbeit, a very close friend, was shot to pieces when he sat down next to her.

The warmth of his side seeped into hers, crumbling her resolve, turning her into one weak-kneed, lily-livered individual without an ounce of willpower.

She took a bite of pudding to get her mind off Tom, but it didn't work. For some reason she couldn't keep from feeling a deep-seated need to be close to him, sense his strength, his calm attitude.

She latched on to the first thing that came to mind. "I noticed you bought my painting."

He didn't say anything, just sat quietly eating his pudding, which either meant the pudding was too good to talk or the subject was off limits. Maybe he was still mad that she'd invaded his private inner sanctum. Or maybe the painting was just another piece of art to him—pretty but nothing special. The last thought stung.

He cleaned his bowl, scraping up every last drop of pudding, before setting it on the side table next to the swing. Seeing her bowl was empty, he took it and placed it next to his. Then as natural as if this was what they always did, he slipped his arm along the back of the swing over her shoulder. He pulled her into him, cradling her head in the crook of his neck.

A shove of his foot sent the swing slowly moving.

Instead of feeling odd or forced, everything felt so right. The gentle rock of the swing, the south breeze brushing softly against her skin, the sun barely touching the horizon, all of it wrapped around her, giving her a sense of security. She didn't want the night to end.

Her earlier intentions crumbled beneath Tom's tender touch.

She marveled at how in tune she was with Tom, how he affected her in ways Rick never could. Just the simple pleasure of resting in his arm, saying nothing, was something she had never experienced before. Deep inside she felt the shudder of his breath. The rapid beat of his heart felt natural and as though it was hers. Surely there was no harm in enjoying this intimacy for a little while.

"Yesterday, I went into town to ask Leah about your friends."

She stiffened and started to pull away, but he gently held her in place.

His chuckle rumbled deep inside her as his head rested on top of hers, causing her flash of anger to dissolve.

"I was worried about you."

"I can take care of myself."

"I know you can. But I had to make sure for myself that your friends weren't here to hurt you." Tom fell silent.

By all rights, she should be mad at him poking his nose into her business. Yet, she was unable to muster up one ounce of anger. Instead, she burrowed deeper into his side, if that were possible.

"And?"

He laughed. "Leah wouldn't tell me one blasted thing, except she liked your friends. So I had to take her meager words, as you were in no danger from them."

"I wasn't in danger."

"I know that now, but I didn't yesterday."

His easy manner seeped into her bones causing her to relax and enjoy the security of his arms.

"When I saw the painting, I recognized the pond and dock. I knew I had to buy it."

"What did she charge you?" She started to look up at him. He held her put.

"Enough." He chuckled.

"For all you've done for us, I would have gladly given it to you."

"I didn't want you to know I bought it."

His words sunk in as silence hung heavy around them.

"The couple …"

Aimee held her breath hoping he hadn't guessed what she'd only discovered earlier.

"I hoped … no, to be truthful, I imagined the couple standing on the dock was us. That's why I bought it. Well, that and it's a great painting. You're a talented artist. Your paintings show emotion and hope."

"Thanks." Unlike Rick who belittled her art, Tom's praise gave her confidence.

"I hung it where I could look at it while working. It's a reminder of something I want but will never have."

Chapter 25

Tom felt Aimee stiffen next to him.

He'd gone and done it—opened his big mouth. He could have sat here all evening long with her resting in his arm without saying a thing. Why hadn't he?

"How can you say something like that?"

He allowed her to pull away from him this time. She glared up at him as if he'd lost his marbles.

"Easy. I don't have much to offer a woman, but if I did, I would come closer to offering it all to you than anyone." He breathed in. The pain in his chest hurting worse than anything he'd ever experienced from the IED, knowing he'd have to let her go. "You deserve a whole man, one who can make you happy, not me."

Aimee's eyes snapped with anger. "Tom Branigan, shame on you. You have more to offer a woman than most men walking this earth. You're good, kind, decent, even if you do try to hide the fact. And furthermore, any woman would feel fortunate to call you her man, including me."

Stopping the swing, he leaned forward, placing his elbows on his knees. "You wouldn't be so quick to say those things if you knew half of what I've done, all of the deaths that lay claim to my name." He refused to look at her, not wanting her to see the raw pain hovering at the surface.

The ghosts of ten years of killing continued to plague him to this day. The vivid pictures were never far from his thoughts. The carnage of men, women, and even children, though done in the line of duty to preserve the life of his men and the people they were there to defend, had carved their image into his mind. Even his inability to die with his men left him nursing a heavy weight of guilt and shame.

"Look at me."

He didn't move. He couldn't expel the hideous images.

"Tom Branigan, you better look at me." She jabbed his ribs with her elbow.

Her aggressive approach caused a smile and gained his attention, pulling him out of the dark pit that threatened his sanity at times.

"When we first met, you said your heart was black."

"You don't know how black." Looking at this innocent slip of a woman who was pure, decent, and good, made him want to hide the atrocities so deep that she would never glimpse the evil lurking in his soul.

"I'm not going to sit here and argue the point, but I'll say this ... if you were the despicable man you believe yourself to be, I wouldn't be sitting here next to you. Whether you want to recognize it or not, you're one of the kindest, most generous people I've ever met. And though you do your best to hide it, you have a caring heart."

Feeling like an imposter, he wanted to tell her she was way off the mark. He wasn't any of those things. He wasn't that guy and never could be. And though he knew his feelings for her were hovering on the brink of love, a man like him didn't deserve a woman like Aimee.

"You're patient, though I seem to rile your temper some."

"Some?" He chuckled remembering all the times he'd worked hard to see how far he could push her before her fiery anger would explode.

"You will do just about anything for anyone. Just like my fence. Though I told you not to, what did you go and do? You bought me one anyway, which I'll be dead before the fence is ever paid off. But don't you worry though—"

"I don't want your money."

She sliced her hand through the air cutting him off.

"You don't have any say-so in the matter, Tom Branigan. But that's a discussion for another time. Don't interrupt me."

"Yes, ma'am." He loved to see her all fired up on a mission. She didn't know that he would give everything he owned, down to his last cent, to keep her safe. The fence was a piddley sum in comparison to her life.

"And furthermore, the women at Paradise Found? Although it took them quite a while to warm to you and at times you still scare them some, they absolutely adore you. Even Maggie is besotted with you. She believes you can walk on water. But I know better than that." She snorted, shaking her head.

"Why do I not find that surprising." Love shot through him piercing his heart while hope sprung to life.

"And look what you did for me since you learned Rick is on his way here to try and finish me off." She wrinkled her nose.

"Over my dead body." He growled. He'd like nothing better than to wrap his hands around the neck of that putrid piece of dog meat.

"Don't say that. I don't want you to die."

"Thanks for the vote of confidence in my abilities. But I don't plan on dying any time soon," he grumbled.

"Good. I'm glad that's settled." She gave him a teasing grin. "Nevertheless, what man in his right mind would put his life on the line for me? And, besides, I couldn't love a man whose heart was black. So don't you dare say that again, do you hear me?"

He couldn't have heard her correctly. "What did you say?"

She huffed out a breath shaking her head, plainly put out with him.

"Weren't you listening to anything I was saying?" She rolled her eyes. "I said your heart isn't black. And if you say that again in my presence, I'm liable to blacken your eye to match the color you believe your heart to be."

"No not that part. The other part where you said you couldn't—"

"That's irrelevant." Aimee waved him off while wrinkling her nose. She turned to glance down toward the bank of trees to the south of his property.

"Oh, but it's not irrelevant to me."

Her gaze was glued to the scenery while her hands nervously gathered the hem of her shirt.

"Aimee, look at me."

Her body went rigid with her refusal.

"Now who's being stubborn?"

"I'm not stubborn." Her chin jetted out.

"Oh, but you are." He gently turned her to face him. "You're one tenacious, spitfire of a woman, who has a stubborn streak a mile long. Which isn't all bad." He smiled.

"In fact, those are just a few of your many qualities I've found hard to resist. But what I love most about you is your indomitable spirit. Regardless what you come up against, you just keep on truckin'."

"Keep on trucking, huh? *Hmm.* Like a Peter Built or Mac truck?" She dimpled up at him, a sparkle in her eyes.

"Does it matter?"

"Well some folks say a Mack is dependable. Others say ..." She huffed. "You're right though. I have people who depend on me, as I do them. I can't just roll up into a ball when things aren't going fine with my world. That's why, as you say, I keep on *trucking.* " She folded her arms.

"I'm here now. I'll not let anything happen to you or the others."

He wanted to laugh at the mulish set of her jaw, but didn't.

"We can't depend on you or Frank forever. If you don't catch Rick this time, he'll be back, or some other husband or boyfriend will find us. It's the nature of the game these sickos play." She inhaled and expelled a deep breath. "We will always have another threat, another man lurking around the corner."

"Why do you do it when it's such a losing battle?" He understood loyalty. It was something he had with his men. But they had gone through years of training and fighting together as a unit, unlike Aimee. She barely got to know the women before they were gone or ended up like Jill.

"Do what?"

"Paradise Found. The women. "

"Do you believe in the law of reciprocity?" She cupped her hands in her lap.

"I know what it means. I'm not so sure I believe in it though."

One of the sweetest, most beautiful smiles he'd ever seen began to spread across Aimee's face.

"Oh, but you will. You have given over and over again to us. God won't let that go unnoticed or unrewarded."

"*Humph.*" He would have loved to fill her ears about what he thought of God and His law of reciprocity. He knew better. His men were proof. Why would God take notice now when He didn't care enough to save his men? And what about Jill? What happened there?

"Marty, a counselor from the Houston women's shelter, helped me to see my way out of my abusive relationship. The last time Rick tried to kill me, someone found me alongside the highway. I landed in the hospital with contusions, broken ribs and was unrecognizable from the injuries Rick inflicted. Marty helped me see that I didn't have to live that way. Something she said finally clicked in my brain."

"And what was that?" Wanting nothing better than to slam his fist into the face of a man he didn't know but hated, he held his temper in check and his thoughts to himself.

"Marty said I was priceless, worth more than a king's ransom of diamonds and rubies. And because I was priceless, I deserved the best this world had to offer, and it wasn't Rick."

"She's right. You are priceless and you do deserve the very best." He knew it wasn't him.

"I know that now, but then, it was hard to admit to the world that I was a failure and my marriage was a sham. Especially since Rick always said the beatings were my fault, that I had made him do those things to me." She braced herself while tears collected in her eyes.

The burning desire to find the man had him clinching his jaw. If he ever found her ex, he'd keep him alive long enough to learn what real pain meant and then he'd kill him very slowly, inch by inch. Even then it would be more mercy than he deserved.

"Anyway," Aimee swallowed, "Marty turned me around. Consequently, I help these women. And then there's you."

"I don't see your point."

"You, Mr. Tom Branigan, were sent to teach us skills and to know the difference between cowering-debilitating fear, and the healthy fear that enables us to stay alive." She titled her head, giving him a curious look. "For you, a retired Special Ops, to move next door to me, what are the odds?"

He sat mute. What could he say?

"It's like ... what grace you measure out returns to you multiplied." She dimpled up at him. "And if I remember correctly, the Bible has a lot to say about giving and grace."

"That may be true, but where was God when your husband nearly killed you? Where was he when Jill was beat to death? Where was God when my men were blown to bits? And where was God when He allowed me to live instead of dying with my friends?"

Catching a rugged breath, he stood and moved away from her, knowing he'd said too much. He leaned his elbows on the railing looking out at the dusk hovering in the trees. The anger he held deep inside roiled and churned like the ocean pounding the sand, dredging up all the ugliness buried deep beneath its surface.

He felt Aimee before she slid her arm through his, joining him at the railing.

"I can't answer the whys, but what I can say ... you and I were saved for a reason. For all intents and purposes, we both should be dead, but we aren't. God spared us. We're here together. And I for one, am glad God didn't allow you to perish with your men. He brought you to me when he knew I was ready and I would need you most."

"You're a good man, Tom. Stop beating yourself up for being alive." She released his arm and then leaned over and kissed his cheek. "Good night, Tom." Aimee slipped away and down the stairs, heading to her truck.

"Aimee."

He started after her, but when she didn't stop, he didn't follow. He braced his hand along the top of one of the posts, watching her, not able to turn away.

Did she mean she liked him or was she just glad they'd met so he could train the women? Perplexed as to her meaning or why she rushed off in such an all-fired hurry, he figured he'd ask her that question tomorrow.

She jerked on the cantankerous door several times before it opened, nearly knocking her to the ground.

He laughed when she practically vaulted into the driver's seat as if hounds were nipping at her heels. The grinding sound of the ignition until it started had him wishing she had a better truck. One day that truck would have her stranded along the highway.

The thought had him growling and nearly coming off the porch to hand her the keys to his Silverado. He could buy her a truck, but then she might kill him. Smiling at the thought, he waved her off.

Buying her a dependable vehicle would have to wait 'til she calmed down over the fence ... then he'd buy her a pickup.

Chapter 26

The noise of truck engines and men's voices seeped into Aimee's groggy brain. She pulled the pillow over her head then jerked it off.

"My fence." She groaned. "Or, since I haven't spent a dime on the thing, I should say *Tom's fence.*"

The front of her property was a good city block or more away from her house. However, the noise traveled through the windows and walls as if they were right out her front door.

Unless the men putting up her fence were fast workers, she could count on a good number of mornings waking at the crack of dawn to the sound of equipment noise.

"So much for peace and quiet." She stretched, rolled out of bed, and then remembered last night ... Tom's questions, and her too-close-for-comfort declaration.

Her cheeks burned. Thankfully, she'd caught herself before she blurted out how she truly felt about him. Then to kiss his cheek and react like a silly schoolgirl by running away ... what had come over her?

Pure, plain, and simple ... she was scared. Regardless how she worked hard to conquer the fear and her emotions, it was like fighting a battle she had no chance of winning.

With Rick, she'd made a mistake that nearly killed her. Could she trust her feelings this time? Or better yet, could she trust Tom?

She shoved the ridiculous thought out of her head. With Tom, it was a no brainer. He was a good man and she loved him, even if she didn't want to. And she could trust him with her life.

"Enough of this. I've got work to do and a fence to inspect."

Dressed and anxious to meet the fence crew, Aimee left a note for Maggie, saying she'd be back in time for breakfast, then rushed out the door. She stopped up by the entrance where several pickup trucks were parked and men were milling around.

When she got out of her truck, a rather stocky, older man walked over to her.

"May I help you?"

"Hi, I'm Aimee Hamilton, and I believe you're putting up my fence."

"Charlie Atterman." He tipped his battered cowboy hat. "Please to meet you, ma'am. And yes, we are."

"I was wondering how long you think it will take to build the fence?"

"A couple of weeks." He scratched the stubble on his chin. "But if I'm able to hire a couple extra men, maybe sooner. We'll see."

"That long, huh?" Now that she had one going up, she was hoping for sooner.

"Yep." He nodded, making his tan weathered jaws shake. Signaling with his fingers, motioning along the front of her property. "We're working on this here section first. We'll be going all the way across the front with wrought iron and an electric gate over the road. Barrin' no complications, we'll have the wrought iron part done by Monday, Tuesday the latest."

"Monday or Tuesday?" *Couldn't the man give a definitive answer to a question without waffling?* She smiled

"Yep. This being Friday, I don't pay time and half for Saturday work unless the customer says so and is willin' to pay the extra cost."

"No. Monday or Tuesday will be fine." She owed enough on this fence as it was.

"We're putting up barbed wire down the west side, and Mr. Branigan gave permission to tie into his fence on the east there." He pointed at Tom's property. "There's posts to set, brush to cut and haul, and a few saplings will have to be removed before we're done. But I don't anticipate the whole thing taking much longer than a week and a half or two."

"Well, if you need anything or if you have any questions, just come to the house and knock on the back door. Someone's always there."

"Thanks, but we shouldn't have a need to be botherin' ya'."

"Well, if something does comes up, you know where to find me. Have a good day."

"Will do, and same to you." Mr. Atterman tipped his hat again. He moved over to four guys who'd been loading metal posts into a pickup while at the same time checking Aimee out.

Figuring it was a male thing she ignored them.

To the far side of her front property line, a man looked through a surveyor's device. He signaled another man at the opposite direction, who waved and then pounded a stake into the ground. When he was through he tied off a string line that ran the whole length to the one surveying. The surveyor in turn pulled the string up taunt, tying it off.

She walked over to one of the stacks of wrought iron fencing, annoyed that Tom would pick out something so costly to use for the front of her property. Unlike him, whose property front ran back about sixty feet then fanned out into a huge V, hers ran the full width of her property, a little over 600 feet.

Instead of buying wrought iron for the front, and by the looks of it a very expensive wrought iron, Tom could have purchased barbed wire at a fraction of the cost. Four or five strands of barbed wired would have worked just as well as the eight foot tall iron fencing. The gate she understood, but it too could have been a little less fancy to save on money.

One thing for sure, the fence would set off her property and be difficult to climb, deterring most men. But ... *how in the world would she ever repay Tom?*

What's done is done, and no use stewing over burnt turnips. Come to think of it she didn't even like turnips. She smiled, releasing her frustration as she walked back to her truck.

She climbed in behind the wheel and noticed one of the men continued to watch her, but when he saw her looking, he turned and walked off. Dismissing him and the fence that might or might not be done in two weeks, she turned on the engine, knowing Maggie probably had breakfast on the table.

When she drove up to the house, Maggie and Kim were on the porch shielding their eyes while looking up the hill.

"Well, are they doing anything up there besides making a bunch of noise?"

Aimee smiled at Maggie's pragmatic call.

"Yes, the front fence will probably be done by Tuesday." She cocked her brow, her attitude effusive. "And a *real* pretty entrance it will be too, thanks to Tom Branigan."

Maggie laughed. "Well, come on in. You're breakfast is getting cold."

"I thought you were going to put in barbed wire." Kim held the door open, plainly confused.

"I was when I could afford a fence. But Mr. Branigan had his own idea of what was best for me."

A couple of the women quietly laughed as she headed for the sink to wash up.

After the blessing, Debra Sue glanced up. "So, we will have a fence sometime this coming week?"

"No, more likely in two weeks. The foreman can't quite make up his mind." She grinned. "When asked, he gave me two different times, like the front may be done Monday or Tuesday. The remainder of the fence will be done in a week or two." Aimee laughed, shaking her head. "Regardless, once they get the front in place, it'll give us a little more security than we had before. Once it's done, no one will be able to drive on my land, or come in unannounced."

The sound of a truck driving up had Aimee looking out the kitchen window then moving to the back door to greet Tom. Heat flooded her cheeks. Yet, she wasn't going to hide from him just because she'd run like some silly teen last night.

"You're just in time for breakfast." Tom looked good. Too good for her peace of mind.

"Thanks, I've already eaten. But I will have a cup of coffee, if Maggie has an extra cup."

"She always does." Aimee held open the door. "Come on in."

"Mmm, smells good." He took hold of the door, allowing her to enter first.

Good, he's acting normal. Now if I can do the same.

"Maggie baked muffins, and if my nose serves me right, bacon too. There's plenty if you want some."

"On second thought, I believe I will have a muffin with my coffee."

The women had already moved around, making room for Tom at the end of the table next to Aimee. Butter, a muffin, and a cup of coffee were already waiting on him.

Nothing stayed a secret for long with all these sweet Nosy Parkers living with her. They knew she was still a little upset about the fence, and they also sensed something was up between her and Tom, if their curious glances were any indication. Thankfully, they didn't know what. And that *what* she wasn't about to supply.

She sat down trying to act ordinary. Well, as ordinary as one could act whose pulse was frantically racing and whose senses were shooting off the chart.

Tom's fresh scent had her attuned and nervous as a child about to receive a shot. And the fact that he was studying her with his keen, observant gaze didn't help any either.

Aimee picked at her muffin and sipped at her tea as the women, one after another, asked Tom something about the fence. Her mind elsewhere, she barely kept up with the conversation.

"If you're through decimating that poor muffin, would you join me out on the front porch?"

Tom's question pulled her wandering mind to attention. Aimee looked up from her plate filled with crumbled muffin, her nerves too unsettled to eat.

"Shall we? I have a few things I'd like to discuss."

Befuddled, yet gaining the jest of what Tom was asking, Aimee got up from the table, dumped her muffin in the trash, filled her cup with fresh tea, and then walked out of the house. She didn't wait to see if he followed, but she sensed him behind her.

Afraid of what he wanted to discuss, she bypassed the porch and headed for the dock. No use giving her Nosy Parkers more food for talk by overhearing their conversation.

"Whoa, slow down." He grabbed her arm, sloshing her tea over the edge. "You going to a fire?"

She shifted the cup to the other hand, slinging off the warm tea before wiping them on her jeans. "No, just figured ..." *Figured what? Why I left so quickly last night.*

Walking beside her, he matched her steps. "I talked with Atterman, the fence foreman. He said you were up earlier looking over the fence."

"I was."

"He also said you looked none too pleased."

"I wasn't."

"Would you like to tell me why? Did you want something different? If so, I can have them change it to whatever you'd like."

He was actually concerned that she hadn't liked his choice.

She shook her head. "Nothing to discuss. As you said the other day, *it's a done deal.* Talking will solve nothing." They had reached the dock and she motioned for him to be seated. "The fence will be beautiful and … costly."

"Aimee, please, I know you're upset with me for buying the stupid thing without your permission. But you needed one and I had the resources to make it happen. Can we at least put it aside for now? We need to discuss what'll take place this afternoon when Frank's men get here."

"I'm listening." She shuddered, hoping Frank's standoff wouldn't turn out to be a shootout leaving the best men standing.

"Between Frank, his men, and me, we will be taking shifts guarding your property. To ensure that the men get proper rest, they will bunk at my house. That way, the children and the women won't have to change their routine or be quiet while the men are sleeping."

"That'll work. But I insist the men take their meals here, including you." She had to repay them in some way for their service.

"Sure. I have no problem with that. But won't that put more work on Maggie? And what about the cost of the food? I'd like to help with that."

She shook her head. "We can manage. Maggie and I have already discussed the matter. She's always been good at stretching food by adding a little more to the pot. And she wouldn't have it any other way." She shrugged. "We've got enough food, that is, if the standoff doesn't go on any longer than a couple of weeks.

"All right, but here's the thing. Your property won't be secure in front until next week." He frowned. "However, I believe you and the women will be safe with us guarding the front. No one's going to drive down the road in front of your property without a reason for being there."

"I'm not worried. I know everyone will do their best to keep us safe. But Kim and I will still go about our day as normal. She has her job in town this weekend, and I have trips to Leah's and a couple other shops."

"Until we know for sure what Rick is up to, Frank thinks it best, one of us goes with you."

"Really, is that necessary?" She didn't want a babysitter.

Tom's thunderous look told her she'd just crossed an invisible line he'd drawn.

"Yes, if you want to stay safe. It's you we're worried about. Your ex could have someone watching and grab you while you're out. Think of your escort as an extra pair of hands toting and fetching. It'll make it easier for you."

"*Wow*, thanks. Just what I needed. Another pair of hands."

He hiked his brow at her sarcastic tone then smiled.

"Now that we have that settled, would you like to tell me what's going on?"

Her heart stopped. She didn't want this conversation.

"Or are we going to ignore the fact that you ran off last night without telling me why?" His gaze never left hers. "Did I offend you?"

"No, nothing like that." How could she tell him her emotions were all jumbled up where he was concerned?

"Aimee, come quick! Little Mikey's gone missing."

Chapter 27

"When did you last see him?" Aimee, out of breath, tried to keep calm so she wouldn't alarm Debra Sue further. She knew it wasn't like Mikey to run off or even leave the yard without saying something to his mama or one of the other women.

"A little after Tom and you walked out to the pond. But I just thought he was out back playing."

Tom looked around the yard then up the drive. "I'll drive up to the front and see if he's there. With all the noise and talk about the fence, he probably got curious."

"Search the yard and out back again. He might have gone into the woods and didn't hear you call." Aimee was trying to think where he might have gone. "And one of you check the barn again to make sure he isn't hiding, thinking this is a game." Aimee tuned to Tom. "Wait up, I'm going with you."

They tore off in Tom's truck toward the front gate, gravel pinging the undercarriage. The cab held the smell of new leather and Tom's aftershave. Aimee scanned both sides of the road for any signs of the boy. She figured Mikey would love riding back in Tom's pickup with the cool air blasting from the vents.

"If he's not up by the workers, do you think the men will help us look for him?"

"Don't worry, they'll help. But he's probably up there asking all sorts of questions. Little boys are like that."

"You're probably right." Her heart sank knowing there were plenty of places around her property for a little one to get lost or hurt. "Debra Sue and the kids have gone through so much, I don't know what she'll do if we can't find Mikey."

Fear for Mikey's safety tore down her confidence as unthinkable scenarios played out in her mind.

"He's only six, but a very adventurous six-year-old. The woods would be a likely choice for him to explore if he's not up by the road."

"Nothing's going to happen to Mikey. We'll find him." Tom slammed on the brakes, his truck coming to a skidding stop.

The dust hadn't settled before they were jumping out of the truck. They rushed over to the small group of men taking a water break.

"Have you seen a little blond-headed boy, about this tall?" She held out her hand about the height of her waist. "He's only six. He's wandered off from the house."

Mr. Atterman parted from the other men. "The only ones I've seen are you and Mr. Branigan."

The men with him agreed.

"Are you certain?"

"Yes, ma'am." He glanced down the county road where a pickup truck was coming toward them. "Let me ask these other men."

Mr. Atterman waved them down.

One man was in the cab and two were in the back. The driver leaned his arms on the door.

"Henry, have you seen a little boy wanderin' around?"

The man shook his head. "Can't say that I have. Did you ask Steve or Mike?"

Atterman signaled to the man with the surveyor equipment to come over, then glanced in the opposite direction. "Where's Mike?"

"Don't know." Henry shook his head. "Haven't seen him, but then I wasn't paying him any mind either."

Steve drove up and stopped a few feet away. "What's up?"

"Have you seen a little boy running around here?"

"Yeah. He seemed to be a friendly tyke. He took right up with Mike. Mike was here at the gate working when he came up. I was still at the far side making adjustments. He motioned that he was taking the kid to the house. When Mike got back, he told me he had to split. He had an urgent call from his mother who was in an accident."

"Mike?" Aimee's concern doubled. "What was Mike's last name?"

"Mike Morten." The answer came from the foreman.

"No!" The unease of earlier returned with a vengeance eating away at her calm exterior. "Tom, that's Debra Sue's ex. We've got to call the police. He's kidnapped Mikey."

"Whoa, just a minute, little lady." Mr. Atterman scrutinized Aimee as if she were crazy. "How do you know this Mike Morten is the same man?"

"It's him." She motioned to Tom. "Do you have your cell phone?"

"Sure." Tom pulled it out handing it to Aimee. "How long has Mike Morten worked for you?"

"I just hired him. He came by when we were unloading material this morning and asked if I could use another hand. He said he'd put up fence before and was in between jobs and could sure use the work."

Mr. Atterman looked at Tom uneasily. "You said you were in a hurry to get this fence up, so I hired him. When he said he'd done some surveying, I teamed him up with Steve thinking the work would go faster with someone who knew the signals and all." He shook his head. "I'm sure sorry. I didn't know. I've never had anything like this happen before."

When dispatch answered, Aimee turned away from the men walking toward Tom's truck. "This is Aimee Hamilton at Paradise Found. We have a kidnapping in progress." She gave them all the information she knew. "Let me give the phone to Charlie Atterman, he can give you a description of the man and the type of vehicle." She handed the phone to the foreman, impatient to get back to the house and see if Debra Sue had heard anything.

When Atterman was through talking with the police, she motioned for Tom to take her back to the house.

"If Mike Morten comes back, hold him." He aimed his words at all the men. "Do not let him leave under any circumstances."

"Will do."

Devastated with the turn of events, Aimee wasn't sure how to tell Debra Sue.

"This Mike guy, will he hurt Mikey?" Tom looked straight ahead at the house.

Her head snapped up. "I don't know. I pray not. But when this type of man is angry enough with his ex, there's no telling what he'll do. They become unreasonable, unstable. Anything can happen." Blame and incompetency ate away at her confidence.

When Tom parked at the house, the screen door opened. Debra Sue and a couple of the other women came out on the porch looking hopeful, expectant. The other two children hovered close to their mother.

Stepping down out of the truck, Aimee nearly crumbled. Her farm was supposed to be a place of safety, protection for those who wanted freedom from abuse. How had Debra Sue's ex found them?

"Did you find him? Was he up there?"

Debra Sue strained to see if Mikey was in the truck. Her face changed from expectant to worry when Mikey didn't get out of the truck. She put her hands over her mouth to keep from crying out.

Aimee walked up to the porch. "Let's go inside." She motioned for Kay. "Would you mind taking the kids to the barn and find something fun for them to do?"

"Sounds like a plan to me." Kay smiled down brightly at Shelly and Stevie who acted reluctant to leave their mother's side. "If you can beat me to the barn door, I have a surprise I'll give you."

"What." Both kids asked excitedly.

"It's sweet, and you can blow bubbles with it." Kay winked. "And that's all I'm going to say."

Both kids looked up at their mother for permission.

"Go on. I'll be inside with Maggie and Aimee."

"All right." Kay clapped her hands. "Ready, set, go!"

The kids scrambled off the porch leaving Kay in their dust.

"Where's Mikey? Is he hurt?" Debra Sue's voice wobbled.

Aimee put her arm around the woman, leading her into the house. "Let's go inside."

When they were seated, Aimee glanced at Tom who stood just inside the doorway looking uneasy. "We believe your ex-husband may have taken Mikey."

"No." The word was ripped from Debra Sue's throat as if she were going to die. She doubled over, her arms cradling her middle.

Maggie rushed to her side and gathered the young mother in her arms and began to console her.

Tears running down her cheeks, Debra Sue looked at Aimee. "How do you know it's Mike. Maybe Mikey is still out back and he's hiding."

Aimee explained what little she knew.

"Has anyone called the police? Are they looking for Mike or my son?"

"Yes, the sheriff is on his way here to get a picture of Mikey and gather more information from you." The sound of a vehicle driving up and stopping outside the house had Aimee standing. "That's probably the sheriff now."

Tom waved her off. "I'll bring him in."

The sheriff knew a call from her would be critical and was to be taken seriously. When he came into the kitchen, his face filled with compassion. He handled Debra Sue with kindness, yet gently probed to make sure he got all the facts as to her husband's character, where he lived, and if she thought he would hurt his own son. When he asked where the most likely place he'd take the child, she shook her head.

"I haven't a clue. We've been gone for four months now." Debra Sue rubbed her hands together nervously. "His mother died last year, and he doesn't have any kinfolk around here, so I don't know where he'd go."

When Debra Sue left the room to get a photo of Mikey, Sheriff Randall pulled Aimee and Tom aside.

"Too often these cases don't turn out well. Either the child is spirited away and only found due to a slip up, or he's never heard of again. There's even a small chance the father will take his anger out on the child. But more likely, this is a get even ploy — *you've taken him, now I've got him, and you'll never see him again* type thing. Let's just hope we find him quickly."

He dug inside his pocket, pulled out a card and handed it to Aimee. "If he does contact the mother, give this number a call immediately. A team will be here within the hour to deal with the man."

A haunted Debra Sue walked back into the kitchen. She handed the Sheriff two pictures. "This is my ex-husband taken two years ago. He may have changed some." She ran her finger over Mikey's picture. "I have sole custody of my children, and have a restraining order against him because of abuse. He's in violation of court orders by taking my son. This is my boy. Please. Please, you've got to find him."

Chapter 28

Saturday dawned dark and brooding. The earth rumbled and lightning dashed across the sky as the heavens opened releasing a heavy downpour. Maggie fixed a quick but simple breakfast for everyone.

With each gust of wind and lightning strike, the women would jump, the kids would scream and huddle close to their mother. Figuring everyone would feel more secure from the threat of a tornado, Aimee sent them to the safe room in the barn but she stayed behind just in case the police called.

Aimee had built the underground shelter, not so much for the weather but, to protect the women in case one of the husbands learned of their whereabouts. This morning it served double duty by keeping the occupants safe while the storm raged outside.

A healthy amount of food and games were carried into the shelter to while away the time until the storm passed. Maggie wanted to stay in the house with Aimee, but she convinced her friend to go along with the other women to help keep them calm.

A strike of lightning, to close for comfort, caused the lights to flicker. A rumble of thunder shook the windowpanes. Aimee stood at the kitchen sink, a cup of warm tea in her hand, staring out the window. She set her cup aside and wrapped her arms around her middle, unease eating at her gut. For some inexplicable reason she had an eerie feeling someone watched, but she scoffed at the idea. Who in their right mind would be out on a morning like this lurking in the shadows when the rain was too intense to see more than two feet away?

The swirling, chaotic wind hammered her house with angry sheets of rain. She shivered, hunching her shoulders forward, a chill filling her insides. Normally, she enjoyed a good storm, but this morning she took no pleasure in nature's antics.

She had called Frank earlier, right after she'd woke to the rumbling outside, and suggested his men should wait out the storm inside her house instead of being drenched by the rain. He'd declined. Saying his men were stationed in their trucks and used to this type of detail rain or shine.

Aimee rubbed her arm to dispel the chill that crept across her skin. The feeling that something wasn't quite right, they had missed something where Mikey's abduction was concerned, had her pacing the floor.

They hadn't heard a word from Mikey's father, which the Sheriff said wasn't all that unusual. No one had seen them either. It was as if Mikey and his dad had vanished. Thankfully, there was no sign of Rick either.

As surely as the sun rose and set, she knew he'd come sooner or later.

What had they missed? What missing piece of the puzzle had they not found?

The screen door on the front porch began banging. The noise startled her enough to get her pulse racing. When the incessant hammering became annoying, she moved to the front door, unlocked and opened it, and then grabbed the handle to the screen. The wind nearly jerked the handle from her fingers.

Within seconds the rain had blown through the opening, saturating her jeans and her stocking feet. She closed the front door, driving the bolt home. Puddles of water had formed on the hardwood floor.

Aimee ran to the bathroom and gathered towels to sop up the water.

Her arms full of wet bath towels, she rounded the corner heading for the washroom. A vice-like grip on her arm pulled her up short. The towels flew from her hands, scattering across the floor. She was jerked around to face a man she didn't know.

Fingers bit into Aimee's skin as he shoved her up against the wall. He leaned in, his forearm pressing into her throat cutting off her oxygen. The cold steel of a gun was pressed against her temple. The rain from his dripping clothes soaked Aimee even more.

"Where is she?" The words were ground out harsh and hateful, his eyes wild with rage.

The sickly smell of alcohol had Aimee traveling back in time and inwardly shrinking from his touch. She hadn't experienced this kind of horrific fear since Rick.

The man, unshaven, hair unkempt and hanging in oily strands on his shoulders, looked demented. Gagging over the stench of his unwashed body, she willed her mind to calm down and relax. She wouldn't give into her fear. If she did, she'd be finished.

He pulled his arm back just enough from her throat so she could breathe.

"I said, where is she? I know she's here, so don't lie to me."

"I don't know who you're looking for. No one lives here but me."

His forearm pressed against her throat again, harder this time. She thought she was going to black out from lack of oxygen.

"You can either tell me, or I can kill you now and search for her myself." He shoved harder against her windpipe for emphasis then released her and stepped back.

Leaning forward, hands on her knees, Aimee drew in a choking breath.

The man yanked her up by her hair, a pistol pointed in her face.

Her life could end here and now. Yet she'd left so much unsaid, so many things undone. *God, help me.*

"There's no one here but me." She looked him in the eyes hoping he'd see the truth in her words. "Who are you looking for?"

"My wife. The slut's holed up here somewhere with my other two kids, and I want her out here now ... else I'll kill you."

Relief flooded over her knowing her assailant was none other than Mike Morten and not someone Rick had sent. At least she had a chance with Mike. All he wanted was his wife and kids, not her. A coldblooded killer wouldn't back down, but she might be able to reason with Mike.

His wild-eyed scrutiny had her heart pumping frantically. If he wasn't insane, the difference between sanity and madness was so minuscule it wouldn't be worth measuring.

"You must have the wrong house. Your wife isn't here. This is my home."

"She's here, I tell ya'."

Aimee shook her head. "No. I'm the only one here." She made a sweeping gesture with her arm. "Look for yourself. You won't find anyone. But I know just about everyone in these parts. I might know your wife and where you can find her."

Stepping back, he motioned for her to move to the table.

Careful not to do anything to set him off, she pulled out a chair and sat down facing him.

His left hand fished into his back pocket, pulled out a piece of crumpled paper, holding it out in front of him, keeping his eye on her. There was something written on the back. But what interested him most was on front.

He looked back and forth from the paper to her several times. After slapping it down on the table, he backed away again.

"Is that you? Is it? You better not lie to me." He pointed to the crumpled photo.

Aimee reached out for the snapshot doing her best to keep her expression bland, her emotions in check, and her hand from shaking.

She recognized the woman. Looking up at her from the picture was Jennifer Stanley, aka, Aimee Hamilton.

Her appearances had changed drastically since that picture was taken. At one time, she was married into affluence and money. She barely remembered the woman staring back at her with her blonde stylish hair, a politician's wife's smile, clothes from Neiman Marcus. In the photo, the bleak reality of her existence showed in her eyes. And though only a few year's since that photo was taken, Aimee felt she'd aged in spirit and soul, and looked nothing like Jennifer Stanley.

Everything was all twisted and out of whack. Had Rick sent Mike Morten to kill her?

That didn't make sense. How would Rick know Mike? How had her ex known Debra Sue was living here?

Aimee heard the swoosh of air a nanosecond before she felt the blow to her cheek. His backhand smack nearly robbed her of her senses.

"Look lady, I don't want to hurt you, but you asked for it. If you don't want more of the same then you better start talking, telling me the truth." He pointed at the picture in her hand. "Is that you?"

Chapter 29

Lightning lit Tom's room along with a clap of thunder so strong it rumbled the windows. The crack sounded as if the strike had hit right outside his bedroom wall.

He rubbed his hand cross the back of his neck, kneading out the knot collected there. The bad weather had sparked a reoccurrence of his fiendish nightmares. Only this time, Aimee was somehow in the mix, causing him to wake up in a foul mood, concerned for her safety.

No doubt, the combination of the storm and today's anniversary of his buddies' deaths had a lot to do with his foul mood. At the moment, with the rain still falling, he felt like a caged animal. He rammed a hand through his hair and then turned and left the room.

In the kitchen, he set the coffee to brew and then began pacing the length of the living room. He'd never meant to become so involved with Aimee and her little compound of women. Yet the ties were there, strong, binding him like steel.

Clyde whined, hitting his tail against the floor as he watched his master.

Stopping in the kitchen, Tom filled his cup, took a sip, and then set it down rather roughly. He felt like the walls were moving in on him and he wanted to strike out at his prison.

Clyde padded up to him, nudged his leg, giving off a soft whine.

"Sit."

Clyde sat, looking up at him expectantly.

"Good Boy." He gave the dog a generous scratching and several pats on the head.

"I know boy. We both want to get out of here. As soon as the storm lets up some, you can go out and run. How does that sound?"

A soft *woof* was the dog's answer.

Tom reached into Clyde's container and got a treat, holding it out to him.

The dog nimbly took the biscuit from Tom's fingers and then carried it over to his mat to lie down, content for the moment.

With the speed of a mortar round, Tom realized the true crux of his problem and the unsettling inside him. It wasn't the storm or the rain pouring down outside. It wasn't even the reminder of the anniversary. It was Aimee.

He needed to know she was safe, to see her beautiful smile, to smell the light fragrance of flowers that always hung in her hair. He needed to touch her and know that she was all right.

Man, he had it bad.

Lunchtime was a long time away. He needed an excuse, any excuse to see her.

He smiled. He'd use the storm and the need to check out how they fared. He knew his pretext was lame at best, but he didn't care.

For the first time since returning stateside, he felt something other than guilt and anger. Before Aimee came along, all he wanted was to be left alone so he could wallow in self-pity. Her gentle spirit had changed him.

He laughed over the *gentle*. Most times she was anything but gentle, at least with him.

Aimee's arrival into his life was like Patton's invasion of Normandy — unexpected, unwanted, but well planned out. The end result, she had stormed his defenses and captured his heart.

And though he hadn't asked for or wanted her intrusion, the woman was as tenacious as a bulldog. Once she got a hold of him, she wouldn't let go. Come to think of it, he hadn't had a peaceful day since he'd met her. Yet, if he were truthful, he'd have it no other way. She kept things interesting and enjoyable with her zany, carefree spirit. He would rather be with her more than anyone on this earth.

Aimee had the ability to make him laugh, even make him angry. She taught him bad things do happen to good people and it's no one's fault, especially not God's when evil seems to triumph.

He remembered how she had dimpled up at him the day she told him what he could do if he didn't like her explanation of why ... *take it up with Adam and Eve, because they're the ones who started this whole sin business in the first place.*

The wound from the loss of his friends was healing, becoming less severe, and all because of her.

She'd helped him stop blaming God. And the women who Aimee took in … he'd learned what it was to face real adversity and live in spite of the pain and continued threat.

Fortunate for him, when Aimee had come along, she wouldn't take no for an answer. Otherwise, he wouldn't have experienced the happiness of the last few months. She had given him all that and so much more.

Once again he had purpose. There were so many things he wanted to do.

He wanted to find Mikey and bring him home to his mother.

He wanted this Rick business over and done with so Aimee could stop looking around corners or over her shoulder.

And he wanted Aimee to become his wife.

Whoa! Where did that come from?

He wasn't certain Aimee loved him let alone would marry him. How had he gone from an old grouch without hope to this guy who thought he owned the world?

He smiled.

Now. How to convince Aimee to say yes to his proposal, because he was seriously in love with the woman?

Chapter 30

Aimee's face throbbed from Mike's backhand. The punishing blow had her reeling and trying to right herself. All the abuse she'd suffered from Rick came rushing back with a vengeance and almost had her cowering.

Alcohol and a gun were a bad combination. At any time, she could do or say something that could set him off, causing him to pull the trigger. Aimee knew her only hope was to convince Mike she wasn't Jennifer and that she didn't know where his wife and children were living. But could she pull it off?

"Are you deaf or just plain dumb, lady?" Again Mike waved the gun in her face. "I said is that you? Or do you need me to jar your memory some more."

Good. He was still uncertain of her identity. Maybe his doubt would work in her favor.

She shook her head. "That's not me. I don't know the woman."

Mike picked up the photo staring at it intently. "You certain? It kinda looks like you?" He did a double take several more times as if he couldn't make up his mind. He swayed on his feet, giving Aimee hope he'd pass out before killing her.

She pointed at the photo. "That woman has short, designer blonde hair, and looks to be worth a million bucks. Me, I have long curly red hair, and worth about fifty cents." She let loose a nervous chuckle. "I've lived here for quite a while now and I don't remember seeing anyone who even remotely resembles her."

If Mike's brain hadn't been so muddled with drink, he probably would have seen the likeness right off and known it was Aimee.

"Hey, look, if you give me her name I could call a few of my friends around town and see if they've heard of this woman." She worked to keep her tone even and her body from trembling. "If she lives in these parts, surely someone has seen her or maybe even knows her."

"Yeah. I just bet you'd like to call your friends. I'm not that stupid, lady." He crunched his brows together. "Shut up. I can't think with you yammering all the time." He weaved while rubbing his eyes with the back of his arm, then angled the gun at her again.

"I think you are her." He squinted in Aimee's direction then at the picture again.

She motioned at the room. "Do you think I would live here if I were that woman? I told you, my name is Aimee, not"—she looked up at him—"what did you say her name was?"

"Jennifer. Jennifer Stanley." He practically screamed the name.

Fear eating at her gut, she managed to shake her head. "Please, listen to me. I'm not her. Can't you see, you have the wrong person."

The banging sound of a car door shutting and then heavy quick steps on her back porch had Mike yanking Aimee out of her chair, his arm around her throat, gun to her temple. The loud knock on the back door startled them both.

He pushed Aimee in the direction of the mudroom, his face up next to her ear. The stench of alcohol strong.

"Get rid of whoever's out there. If you don't, I'll shoot both of you." His drunken puffs of breath fanned several small hairs across her cheek. She thought about jabbing him but figured he may get a shot off and maybe kill whoever was outside.

"If I don't answer, they'll just go away."

The pounding got louder and more insistent. "Aimee. It's Tom."

Her heart stopped. She couldn't allow this madman to harm him, regardless what he did to her.

"Answer it and get rid of him." His angry whispers sounded like screams to her ears.

"I'll try but—"

"You better do more than try if you don't want *Tom* to come up dead."

Mike poked the gun in her ribs as he shifted behind the door, out of sight.

After partially opening the door, she peeked out, the toe of her shoe acting like a stopper.

When Tom started to advance into the house, she waved him off. "Sorry I can't invite you in, Tom. I'm not feeling well. In fact, I was on my way to bed. Some kind of flu bug or something. Not quite sure."

Tom looked at her oddly as if weighing her words. "Where's Maggie—"

"Edom to visit friends." She gave a weak smile hoping he wouldn't mention any other names, particularly Debra Sue. Maybe he would take her words at face value. "I was too sick to go."

"If you're sick, you shouldn't be here by yourself. I could stay with you just in case you need help or get sicker." Tom scraped his feet on the porch mat before pushing on the door. He frowned when he met resistance.

"No, please. I'd rather be left alone. I don't want you to catch what I have. And I wouldn't rest with someone in my house. But thanks for the offer."

"Is something wrong? You're acting odd."

She felt the nudge of the barrel. "No. Nothing's wrong. I'm just sick, that's all. I really need to get back in bed."

"Well, if you're sure. Give me a call if you get worse or need anything."

"I will. Thanks for stopping by." Before she shut the door, she said, "Oh, would you do me a favor and tell Frank I found what he was looking for yesterday. Tell him if he drops by later when Maggie's home he can pick it up. I'll leave it in the kitchen."

Tilting his head, he stared at her oddly, narrowing his eyelids. "Sure, I'll tell him. Are you sure—"

"Thanks for coming by. Hopefully, I'll feel better by this afternoon." She closed the door.

The soft click of the door shutting nudged her memory. She hadn't locked the door earlier when the women left for the storm shelter. That was probably how Mike got in without her hearing him. How foolish of her.

Tom's retreating steps had her wanting to yell out to him, call him back, but she didn't. She knew she couldn't put him in danger. Maybe between Frank and Tom they would put two and two together and come up with the notion there was someone in her house who wasn't supposed to be there. But what could they do?

The wincing pain of Mike jabbing the gun hard in her ribs had her focusing on the problem at hand. He pushed her back into the kitchen. She stumbled and fell to her knees. Mike yanked her up by her hair, pulled her around, before shoving her into the chair again.

Her scalp tingled from the rough treatment. She kept her mouth shut, not wanting to give Mike the satisfaction of knowing he'd hurt her. If he were anything like Rick, her cries would fuel him to inflict more pain.

Looking crazed, Mike glanced around the room. His brooding gaze fell on her once again. "Who's this Maggie he was asking about? And what do you have for this Frank?"

"Maggie's a friend that lives with me. And unlike what I told Tom, she will be back anytime now. So if you don't want to get caught, you'd better leave now."

"You think you're a smart one, don't you." He sneered at her. "I don't plan on leaving here 'til I get what I came for."

"Which is?"

"My wife and kids and ... you."

His hateful sneer had Aimee cringing.

"You see, I was paid good money to come here. He hired me to kill you. My wife and kids are the bonus. If you give me much grief, I'll kill you here and now."

He motioned at her. "You women are all alike. Think you can run out on us and we won't find you. You shouldn't have taken my wife in. She belongs to me." He pointed at his chest.

"I don't know your wife. The only one who lives here beside myself is Maggie ... Maggie Dunn. She rents a room from me. Maggie is in her late forties with a scar that runs from her cheek to chin. Is she the one you're looking for?"

When he shook his head, she added, "Whoever informed you that your wife was here, gave you the wrong information."

He looked uncertain, as if he'd made a mistake and didn't know how to fix the problem.

"Please. You don't want to hurt me. I'm not the one you're looking for."

"I found Mikey up by the road, he was coming from the direction of this house. You have to be the one hiding my wife and kids." He jerked her up rather roughly, pushing her toward the living room. "Come on, you're going with me to check out the rest of the house. And don't try anything because at this point lady, I'd just as soon shoot you as listen to you."

Chapter 31

Tom hated leaving Aimee alone, but she had insisted. His gut, which was rarely wrong, told him there was something more than sickness going on with her.

He pulled up next to Frank's truck, rolled down his window, waiting for Frank to do the same.

"When I passed by earlier, you told me everything was peaceful down below. You said no one in or out, right?"

"Yeah. What's up?"

"There's something strange going on down at the house." He didn't want to put his fear in words, nor mention his gut feeling, but if Aimee was in trouble...

"What do you mean?" The PI studied him.

"Aimee said she was sick and that the others went into Edom to visit a friend. You didn't mention they had left earlier."

"No one has come past me." Frank narrowed his gaze.

Tom shook his head. "And another thing. Aimee asked me to deliver a message to you. Said to tell you she found what you were looking for yesterday.

When you come to pick it up, you'll find it in the kitchen." Tom stared at Frank. "What do you make of it?"

"The only thing I was searching for yesterday was Mikey. Why wouldn't she just come out and say she'd found the boy?"

"My thoughts exactly." Tom's insides were on fire. The uneasy feeling rumbled more inside him.

"You think someone is down there holding them hostage?"

"That's exactly what I think."

"I'll leave one of my men here to guard the gate, and get the other one to come with us."

Tom's worry increased a hundred hold. "How do you want to play this out?"

Frank scratched his jaw. "We need the element of surprise on our side."

"The front door is always locked. Our best chance will be the back door. And I didn't hear Aimee lock the back door after closing it." Tom hoped he was right on his assumption. If so, they could enter undetected.

"I'll position one man at the front of the house just in case. You and I will go in through the back."

Frank called the other men over to explain the plan. He also called the sheriff's office and told them to make their arrival a silent siren.

Strategy in place, they drove half the distance to the house then parked. Fortunately, the rain had stopped, making it easier to go the rest of the way on foot.

While on active duty, Tom and his men had run this type of reconnaissance often. Numerous times, they had entered homes and businesses undetected to rescue hostages and they had always come away unscathed.

This time, the stakes were high. It was Aimee inside, not some unknown. And he wasn't absolutely sure someone was with her. He could be batting at the wind.

Positioned to enter the house through the back door, Frank and he stopped when they heard a noise come from behind them. They swung around. Maggie and the other women, along with the children, were walking out of the barn.

"I'll stay here." Frank motioned at the women. "Get them quiet and back inside the barn. Tell them not to come out until someone comes to get them. Once they're back in the barn, we'll make our move."

Tom met the women before they crossed the road to the house, motioning them to silence and back to the barn.

Maggie's smile fell when she saw the gun in his hand.

"What's going on?" She glanced toward the house. "Where's Aimee?"

He saw the panic in Maggie's eyes but he didn't have the time to alleviate her fears.

"I need everyone to go back inside and lock the door. And Maggie, don't open that door for anyone until Frank or I tell you it's OK to come out. Do you understand?"

She nodded, worry imbedded deep in her frightened gaze.

He could see her concern. But like one of his soldiers, trained to act without clarification, Maggie turned and began silently shooing everyone back inside the barn.

He turned, his mind was already concentrating on one thing, and one thing only. Getting Aimee out of the house alive.

When he got back to the porch where Frank was waiting, he whispered, "Maggie said Aimee sent them all to the shelter when the storm started, but she stayed behind in the house. I'm thinking Debra Sue's ex is in that house and maybe even little Mikey."

"It'll make it tougher if the boy is with him. We'll just have to be careful and make sure no one gets hurt." He nodded toward the door. "Try it, see if it's unlocked."

Tom quietly opened the screen door, unhooked the spring so it wouldn't screech or snap back on them, and shoved the screen door against the wall. Next, he reached for the handle, turned it slowly a full half-turn. Relief flooded him when he met no resistance. Once the door was open, Tom held up his hand, staying Frank while he poked his head in and listened.

It was quiet. Too quiet. He stepped inside the mudroom, moved over by the kitchen door, and heard the creak of the floorboards overhead. Motioning to Frank that someone was upstairs, Tom led the way into Aimee's kitchen. He glanced around the great room for a sign of Aimee but didn't see anyone.

Voices and footsteps came from the stairwell.

Tom signaled Frank to take position along the wall next to the stairwell and out of sight, while Tom moved to the other side, sliding into the hall leading to Aimee's office.

"I told you, Maggie and I are the only ones who live here. And, furthermore, I've never heard of this woman Jennifer or your wife."

"No matter, you're coming with me until I figure this out."

"Please, I understand why you broke into my house. But if you take me out of here by gunpoint you'll be committing a federal crime, kidnapping. So, please, just walk away. I don't know who you are. No one's been hurt. I won't press charges."

"You must think I'm some kind of idiot."

Tom saw Aimee move her foot off the bottom rung of the step. His heart stopped. Her face pinched, a nine-millimeter gun was jabbed between her shoulder blades. If they took the man down now, he'd probably get one shot off. Most likely the bullet would end up in Aimee. But if they allowed him to take Aimee and walk out of here, she was as good as dead.

Aimee moved from the stairwell toward the kitchen. The man was right behind her

Frank signaled Tom.

They rushed the guy.

Frank tackled the man from behind as Tom hit him from the side.

A gunshot rang out.

Aimee screamed as she flew forward, her body slamming against the floor.

The gun was knocked from the man's hand. Frank and Tom tussled him to the ground before pinning his arms behind his back. Frank's man came running into the house from the back and grabbed the gun. He helped Frank subdue the guy.

Tom rushed to Aimee's motionless body, her blood already pooling on the floor. He dropped to his knees, gently turned and held her in his arms. Blood soaked her shirt, growing larger by the second. He looked around for something to press against the wound to stop the flow of blood.

"Get me some towels from the kitchen drawer, quick." His heart felt like it had been torn from his chest. This should have been him, not Aimee.

Frank shoved several towels in his hand, pulled out his phone, and then called 9-1-1.

Pulling Aimee's shirt back, Tom found the hole where the bullet had made its exit. He applied pressure with the towel over the wound. He leaned her over his arm, and applied a cloth to her back. Carefully, he pulled her back up tight against his chest trying his best to apply pressure to both wounds.

Tom glanced at the man lying face down, quiet, arms secured by a nylon tie. The overwhelming desire to kill him had him trembling. Aimee's moan had him shoving all thoughts of revenge aside and concentrating on her.

Never one much for praying, he figured God had a better use of His time and wouldn't care to hear from him. But now, holding Aimee in his arms, trying to stop the flow of blood that could mean life or death, he couldn't stop the cry from his heart, nor did he want to.

"God, please." Unashamed of the tears falling down his cheeks, Tom continued. "Aimee doesn't deserve this. Spare her life. Please God."

Tom felt Aimee stir. He glanced down.

Her eyes flickered opened. She looked at him, lifted her hand to his cheek, and smiled. "Thank you." The breathy sound was almost inaudible.

"Aimee, love."

She closed her eyes. Her breathing, labored and shallow, worried him.

He knew if she were to die, they might as well bury him right next to her because she was part of him and had been for some time now. To lose her when he'd just found her ... no he couldn't.

Please, God, you know I'm not one to bargain. But please spare her life. Take mine instead.

Chapter 32

Tom glared at the horrible contraption the hospital called a recliner. His neck hurt. Every joint in his body was stiff and achy. The pain was worth it though, as long as he could be with Aimee.

While she was unconscious he refused to leave her bedside. He didn't want her waking up in a strange place without seeing someone familiar.

He even had to lie and say he was her fiancé and the closest thing to family she had left, otherwise, they would have thrown him out of her room. After the first lie, the others came easier. The story they were to be married this coming month brought about a great amount of sympathy.

Uncertain if Aimee had health coverage—most likely not—he pulled out his credit card and told them he would take care of any and all of her medical bills. That move had ingratiated him all the more with the staff.

His falsehoods had bought him easy access to learn about her prognosis and care. But he figured if Aimee knew, she would chew him out right proper.

The nurse did her best to run him out of Aimee's room last night. He told them it would take more men and women than they had readily available to drag him away from her bedside.

He thought the hospital staff was being overly nice seeing to his comfort. Instead, they got even. They brought in a torture chamber in the guise of a recliner.

He glared at the ugly, brown thing again, torn faux leather and all. It looked to be a throwback to the fifties that should have been hauled off to the trash heap years ago. But he'd endure the contraption just to be near her for as long as she was unconscious.

Outside the window, the early dawn was turning the sky from inky black to dark blue. His mind traveled back to yesterday, a day he never wanted to relive.

The ETM picked Aimee up from the house and Tom followed in his truck, sticking to the ambulance like they were connected at the bumper. He shook his head over the close calls and near misses he'd had while racing down the highway and through the town of Tyler.

The whole time, he pleaded with God to spare Aimee's life. And He thankfully had.

Though Aimee lost a lot of blood, fortunately, the bullet past straight through her body, but barely missed her heart.

For a brief moment last night around nine, Aimee regained consciousness, agitated and frightened. When she saw him standing by her bedside holding her hand, she calmed down and smiled before closing her eyes.

He rubbed the back of his neck trying to work out the kinks. The sun eased up into the sky erasing the ugliness of yesterday, bringing with it a fresh start of a new day. He envisioned Aimee outdoors with her paints and easel, maybe down by the pond, a soft mist rising from the water. She shouldn't be here struggling for her life.

When this was all over, he'd convince her to marry him. If she agreed, he'd make sure she didn't have to worry about money or any lowlifes for the rest of her days.

His hand stroked his stubbly chin. In the mirror he looked like he'd been on a two-day's reconnaissance across the dessert. And though the odor hadn't reached his nose yet, he figured he had to be fairly ripe-smelling by now. He certainly felt grimy enough. If it hadn't been for the change of clothes stashed in his truck, he would have looked a whole lot worse.

When she woke up, he'd go home, get cleaned up, and then come back. But he wasn't budging until she opened her eyes again. He needed to see her smile, to know she was on the mend.

A groan brought him around to her bedside. He clasped her hand and found her fingers were like ice.

She opened her eyes, blinked, and then as if confused blinked again crunching her brow together.

"Tom?" Her word was more like a croak, but music to his heart.

"Yes." He gave her a tentative smile, hoping she wasn't in pain, hoping she wouldn't blame him for what happened.

Her eyes grew big with alarm. Her heart monitor bleeped double time across the screen. "Where—"

"Shhh. You're OK. You're in Tyler at Mother Francis Hospital."

"Thank you." She smiled, closed her eyes, and her breathing became steady again as her fingers curled around his palm, holding on tight.

A nurse walked in heading to Aimee's monitors. She looked at him questioningly.

"She woke up for just a few seconds. Spoke a few words, then—" The words stuck in his throat as he lifted his shoulders then let them drop back in place. "Is she ...?"

"That's a good sign. She's fine." The nurse adjusted Aimee's drip. "I've increased her pain med so she can rest comfortably." She glanced at him briefly. "This would be a good time for you to go home, clean up, and come back later. This afternoon we will begin lowering her dosage and she'll be more alert."

Aimee's hand relaxed from around his as she had slipped beyond his reach once again. He leaned over the bed railing and kissed her forehead before whispering in her ear, "I love you, Aimee. And when you wake up, I plan on telling you every day of your life just how much."

He moved back and watched as the nurse worked on Aimee. His heart constricted seeing her so helpless and unresponsive. It should have been him in that bed, not her.

How had he allowed Aimee to become so important? Before he knew what was happening, she'd captured his heart with her sassy disposition and moxie persistence.

"I think I'll take your advice to go home and clean up. But I'll be back in a couple of hours." His gaze remained on Aimee. "You have my cellphone number if you need me."

The nurse looked at her chart and then rattled off his number.

"That's it. If there's a change in her status call me immediately."

"I will. But don't worry. Her vitals are already better." The woman gave him a stern look. "Go home. Take a shower. Get some sleep. When you're rested, come back. She'll be ready to see you then. You don't want her seeing you looking like something the cat drug in, do you?"

"No, ma'am." He gave Aimee one last, longing look before walking out of the room.

The claustrophobic ride in the elevator was almost his undoing. When the doors opened, instead of running like he felt like doing, he made his long legs take even, quick strides toward the front door.

Stepping outside into the morning sunshine, he breathed in deeply, filling his lungs with fresh air. He exhaled, purging the medicinal smell of the hospital that clung to him.

After spending one month in a foreign hospital hanging between life and death, and then another five months in stateside facilities, he'd developed an aversion to hospitals. However, for Aimee, he was more than willing to fight his personal demons and spend whatever time he could by her bedside. She needed to know she was loved.

He needed to know she was receiving the best care money could buy. She'd had enough hate and violence in her short lifespan.

All the way home and even while he was cleaning up, his heart and thoughts were back at the hospital with Aimee. He shoved his toiletries and some clothes in his knapsack and then stored it in the backseat of his truck. Since his sister lived in Tyler, he figured he could spend his time at the hospital and then go to her place to clean up each morning.

His patience wore thin while he took care of business around his place. He packed his computer thinking he'd keep his mind occupied with some business and trading while at the hospital.

After making sure Frank and his men were still staked out at Aimee's front gate, the women at Paradise Found were all right, and that someone would take care of Clyde, he sped back to Tyler.

His comfort level for leaving the hospital without anyone there to watch over Aimee was so low it was scraping bottom. He shoved the accelerator to the floor needing to eat up the miles separating her from him.

If this was what they called an obsession, then he was obsessed with Aimee—he loved her beyond distraction.

Frank and Maggie would laugh if they knew how the delays to get back to Aimee had him on a short fuse. For some reason he couldn't shake the feeling she needed him. More the case, he needed her.

He'd never felt this way about anyone before. Not even his once-upon-a-time fiancée Linda could provoke these strong feelings Aimee seemed to draw from him.

To him, Aimee was what sunshine was to light, or what air was to breath. He didn't want to imagine life without her.

He knew he wasn't much of a catch with his broken body and all his issues from the war, but he was mending thanks to Aimee's help and prodding. And somewhere in all this he'd taken time to make his peace with God.

He was still a work in progress with a ways to go before he'd be completely healed. Yet, he no longer blamed God for the loss of his men.

Whatever it took to make Aimee's life comfortable and bring her happiness, he'd do. All he needed ... all he wanted was for her to get well and say *yes* to his proposal.

Yet, he'd wait until she was home from the hospital before asking her to marry him. Hopefully, her reaction to his proposal would be positive.

Come to think of it, she might be more easily enticed to marry him if he got her ex to back down and leave her alone.

Once Aimee was doing better, he'd make a trip to Austin to meet with Stanley. He'd let the man know that under no uncertain terms his pursuit of Aimee was over.

Whatever it took for Stanley to back down, he'd do it. The man wouldn't be dealing with Aimee any longer. From here on out, Stanley would deal with him.

Chapter 33

Aimee's chest was on fire. She wanted the pain to go away, but it wouldn't stop. Opening her eyes was more of a chore than she cared to accomplish. Yet, something tugged at her mind just out of reach. Something pesky. Something important. She needed to run, but she had no place to hide.

Alerted by a noise she knew she wasn't alone. The terror building inside her filled her with the urgency to defend herself. She forced her eyelids to open and search for the threat.

The light was blinding and cast a shadow over a man standing in front of the window, his back to her. A blinding pain in her head forced her to close her eyes again.

In those split seconds, she realized several things as her heartbeat slowed to a steady beat.

This wasn't her room. And though she couldn't make out the man by her window, she knew he wasn't a threat. The imminent danger was over.

"Hey, sleepyhead. How do you feel?"

She smiled. The sweet, familiar voice brought a calm to her world.

"Tom?" Her eyes focused on the dark shadow facing her.

"He moved next to her bed. "How do you feel?"

"Like a Mack truck ran over me, backed up, and then did it again."

His rumble of laughter sounded good to her ears.

She patted the mattress on her right side. "Please, this side. The light is too bright and doesn't help my headache."

"Are you in pain? Should I ring for the nurse? Maybe shut the blinds?"

"No, I'm fine. Please." She patted the bed again.

Her gaze followed him as he moved around the foot of her bed to the other side. He reached over the railing and picked up her hand, concern in his eyes.

"You gave me ..." He cleared his throat. "All of us quite a scare."

Fuzzy and a little lightheaded, Aimee tried to make sense of the fractured images in her brain. Then it all came back.

"Is Mikey OK? His father, did you catch him?"

"Hold on." Three adorable lines bunched up tight between his brows as he softly rubbed her hand. "Not so fast. I'll answer your questions, but I don't want you getting all worked up."

His show of concern for her welfare made her love him all the more. She just didn't know if he felt the same.

"Mikey is fine. While his father was in the house torturing you, Mikey was a little ways down the road asleep in the truck. And as to why you're here?

Mikey's father shot you when we jumped him. In my opinion, the man is doing a lot better than he should be after the way he treated you. If I'd had my way—"

She squeezed his hand. "I'm OK and it's over now."

"If you call being shot in the chest and barely surviving OK, well, then I beg to differ with you. He could have killed you."

"But he didn't."

The door opened. A nurse entered the room pushing a cart holding a laptop computer.

Tom stepped back silently watching every move the woman made.

"You're awake." She smiled as she moved about the room checking the different devices hooked up to Aimee. "I'm Thelma, your nurse today. How do you feel?"

Thelma pulled out a device and slid it across Aimee's forehead then entered her findings into the computer.

"I have a headache. My chest hurts some, but other than that ..."

"On a scale from one to ten, how would you rate the pain in your chest?"

"A five, maybe a six."

The nurse continued entering information. "Not bad for what you've been through. But you're on the mend now."

"How soon can I be released?" Aimee was afraid to tell the nurse she didn't have insurance or hardly a penny to her name.

"I would think a couple of days. But your doctor will discuss your release with you when he makes his rounds later this afternoon." Thelma adjusted the I.V.

Hospitals weren't cheap and she didn't have a clue how she'd pay for her medical bills. A payment plan maybe? What could they do, hold her hostage for non-payment? Not likely.

She'd figure something out, but her first step was to be released today if possible.

When the nurse left, Tom moved up beside the bed again. "I'm going to leave to let you get some rest. But I'll be back later this afternoon. Is there anything you need?"

"Please don't leave yet. I want to know how everyone is doing. What about Mikey? Is he OK? What will they do with his dad? How are the women—?"

"*Whoa.* Slow down. For once, you need to think about yourself. This isn't the time for you to worry about others." He reached over and gently ran his hand over her forehead and down her cheek.

His gaze spoke love, or was she imagining it?

"Mikey is doing great. The kid's tough. He bounced back quickly. It didn't appear that his father hurt him in any way. And they made sure that none of the kids saw the police haul their father off in handcuffs."

"I'm glad they spared them. They've gone through enough."

"And as far as the other women, they are all doing fine. Maggie will probably come to visit you tomorrow." His eyes got all misty as he leaned over the railing. He tipped her chin up. "You gave me quite a scare. I thought I was going to lose you before I could tell you." He stopped to search her face.

"What? Tell me what?" Surely, no one else had been hurt.

Tom wore a silly grin but his eyes were dead serious. "This may not be the proper time or place but ... Aimee Hamilton aka Jennifer Stanley, I love you. And I don't want to lose you." He sealed his words with a light kiss on her lips. "So get well. I can't wait to see what's in store for our future together."

Aimee wasn't sure if it was Tom's kiss, his avowal of love, or the meds that had her body zinging.

She started to speak.

Tom placed his index finger over her mouth. "Shhh. Don't talk. We'll continue this discussion later. Now get some rest. I'll be right over there reading." He gave her another light kiss before moving to a chair and sitting down.

She raised her hand to touch her lips, still feeling the imprint of his kiss. He hadn't only branded her lips, he'd branded her heart.

Chapter 34

Tom arrived early to drive Aimee home from the hospital. And like the last few days, he was being considerate and attentive, seeing to her every need. Yet there was something off. She didn't know what, but she could feel it in her bones.

Was he having second thoughts?

After his kiss and his declaration of love, he hadn't kissed her again or even mentioned their future together.

During the wait for her discharge, lifting her into his truck, and even buckling her in, he'd hardly said a word. Aimee, as she was prone to do when anxious or nervous, chattered away, excited to be on her way home and with Tom, even if all he did was smile and nod.

Her gaze roamed over Tom's unreadable profile. She studied the sharp angles and planes of his face, tiny scars, even chicken pox marks left behind from childhood, things she'd never noticed before. Each tiny imperfection made up the man she loved.

Refusing to worry over his silence, she closed her eyes and leaned her head against the headrest. His image etched on her mind.

She couldn't deny her love for Tom. How could she? She loved him more with each passing day, if that were possible.

Besides his initial brief couple of kisses and saying he wanted to speak to her about their future … nothing. If he didn't speak up soon, she would. She wasn't much for waiting.

"Are you comfortable? Are you hurting?" His hand covered hers.

Aimee opened her eyes, thrilled by the warmth of his touch. He watched her closely as his gaze swept back and forth between the road and her.

"No, just resting my eyes."

"I thought they should have kept you another day instead of releasing you."

His stormy features had her smiling.

"I told them money was no object."

"Which I'm grateful for all you've done. And I mean to pay you back with—"

"Yeah, I know … with interest." He grinned, then sobered, removing his hand to place it back on the steering wheel. "I'm not taking your money regardless what you say. So give it a rest."

"I can't let you pay my medical bills. They must be in the thousands. That's too—"

"Like I said, give it a rest. End of discussion."

Head back, eyes closed again, Aimee asked, "What's going on, Tom?" She huffed out a weary breath then opened her eyes, watching him wanting to know the truth.

"What do you mean?"

She gave another exasperated sigh. "Don't give me that. The other day, when I came to, you talked about love and our future. Since then, you seemed to have forgotten you wanted one with me. Why? Change your mind?"

"No." He slipped on the blinker, took a right onto a dirt road and then parked before turning toward her. "I haven't changed my mind. I'm afraid I spoke too soon."

"What do you mean by that?"

"I really don't know how you feel about me ... us. And I should have prevented what happened to you. I didn't keep you safe."

"And how could you or anyone have known what the man was up to or what he was capable of doing? Don't talk such nonsense. You did what was best for the situation." She unsnapped her seatbelt so she could turn in the seat to see him better without craning her neck.

"He was determined to find Debra Sue and the kids. And, even drunk, he was a whole lot craftier than I gave him credit for. I stood in his way."

"But you don't understand. I was trained to protect and was good at it too until the bomb. Now it appears I can't even keep the woman I love safe."

"Would you like to say that again?" Her heart soared with his declaration.

"I was trained to pro—"

"No. Not that part. The other part about the woman you love. I hope you were talking about me." She gave him a mischievous grin.

The slap of Tom's seatbelt against the door echoed in the truck. He leaned toward her, a hair's breadth dividing them.

"You know, good'n'well, that I meant you. I certainly didn't mean Maggie or one of the others, though I love them too, but in a different way. I love you—only you."

"Good. I'm glad we got that settled." She faced the front.

"Aimee." He touched her chin turning her head toward him. "Surely you know what you mean to me. I go crazy when I think how close I came to losing you."

"But you didn't lose me." She tenderly stroked his cheek.

She leaned the short distance for their lips to meet, wincing inwardly from the pain.

He gently slid his fingers under her hair along her neck, prolonging the kiss, increasing her desire. Too quickly he released her.

Sitting back, he raked a hand through his spiky buzz cut as he stared out the window almost angry-like. "You drive me crazy."

"Well, *excuuuse* me. I'm sorry." She yanked her seatbelt around her, excited that she could make Tom Branigan react out of character.

He stopped her from buckling the belt. "You're not sorry." He chuckled while holding her hand. "You love pushing my buttons and being a real pain." He cocked a brow. "Admit it."

She shrugged. "What can I say? It's fun to know I get under your skin." She glanced down at their entwined fingers. "But would it ease your mind if I told you I love you."

He shook his head, rolling his eyes skyward. "Heaven help me. You're going to drive me crazy."

He leaned in again for another kiss but stopped short when he saw her wince.

"You're in pain. Enough of this. You need to be home and in bed, and that's where I plan on taking you."

"Stop right there, Tom Branigan." She crooked her finger at him. "You owe me one kiss."

"I do, do I. What makes you think that?"

"Because you were going to kiss me and then stopped without following through."

"Well, then we better fix that right now."

He leaned in, giving her a sweet gentle kiss that tilted her world and left her trembling, loving him all the more, if that were possible.

Grabbing her seatbelt, he fastened it in place, then did the same to his. After making a U-turn, Tom got back on the highway heading for home.

"Want to know what I love about you?"

"My magnetic personality?" He chuckled.

She looked at him sideways grinning. "Well, there is that too. But what I love most about you is you are all tough on the outside, but soft as a kitten on the inside."

Grunting, he ignored her. "Lean back, close your eyes, and quit talking nonsense. I'll have you home in a few minutes."

She leaned back but couldn't relax. The warmth of his lips remained with her, reminding her the guy next to her was one special man and he belonged to her. She knew this blissful, euphoric moment would only last until she arrived home. Her friends would demand her attention, relegating Tom to the back burner until they were alone once again.

"Aimee?"

"Hmm?"

"Don't ever say I'm as soft as a kitten, or you just might release the tiger in me. And it won't be a pretty site."

She chuckled. "That might be worth seeing." Placing her hand on his arm, Aimee waited until she'd gained his attention. "You would never hurt me."

"You've got that right. But understand this..." He paused, as if picking his words carefully. "If anyone ever lays a hand on you again, he won't live long enough to gloat. I'll kill him." His words came out more like a vicious growl.

Catching a glimpse of her man when riled, a shiver coiled around her spine. Unlike her ex she knew his anger would never be directed at her. But she knew he wouldn't give the same consideration to Rick or anyone else who dared harm her.

Now, if only Rick would stay in Austin and not send anyone after her, Tom and she could live in peace.

Well ... as good as peaceful gets while taking in and helping abused women whose husbands are seeking revenge.

Chapter 35

The warm fuzzy feeling knowing Tom loved her lasted up until they parked outside her backdoor.

Maggie and the others came rushing out of the house and began fussing over her, asking questions, and practically carrying her to her bedroom. Her bed was already turned down, the drapes were closed blocking out light from the windows, and there was a glass of water on the nightstand.

When they started to undress her, Tom cleared his throat. "I think this is my cue to leave." His gaze spoke volumes. "I'll set your things right here." He dropped her bags by the door.

"Thanks for everything." Aimee wanted to say more but she didn't want to embarrass him in front of the women.

"I'll be back later for-ah-to pick up my dinner, and to make sure you're doing OK."

"I'd like that."

"I'll have your dinner waiting on you and the other men as usual," Maggie answered. "Tonight is beef barley soup and cornbread. I figured that would be easy for Aimee to digest."

"Sounds good." He smiled, but his loving gaze strayed to Aimee. "Rest well. I'll see you later."

He was gone and part of her went with him.

"Here, come on." Maggie gained her attention by gently shoving her toward the bed. "Let's get you into your pajamas so you can lie down and rest properly."

"I am a little tired. Thanks."

"I wouldn't wonder with just now coming from the hospital. And there'll be no more thanks coming from you. We're the ones who should be saying thanks. Where would any of us be without you?" Maggie's voice cracked. She cleared her throat, looking away. "Just don't go givin' us any more scares like this again, ya' hear."

"I'll do my best to stay out of trouble." She smiled.

"Humph. That's like asking the sun to shine on a rainy day."

"You may be right on that score." Aimee had missed being home with her friends.

Debra Sue stood back by the door apprehensive, head tucked.

"Come in." Aimee motioned her into the room. "How are you and the children doing?"

The woman slowly made her way to where Aimee sat on the edge of the bed.

"Everyone's doing fine. I didn't tell them what their father did to you." She looked down at her hands. "I'm so sorry."

"You're not to be sorry. And I think you did the right thing about not telling them. They don't need to know." Aimee reached out and took Debra Sue's hand. "And you aren't responsible for his actions. So, I'll hear no more about it."

Debra Sue wouldn't look at Aimee.

"Here, would you help me take off my top."

"Oh, yes." Debra Sue took special care not to hurt Aimee, unbuttoning her blouse and gently tugging on the sleeve. She cringed when she saw the dressing.

"Does it hurt?" Debra Sue gently pulled her arm through her pajama top.

"Not so much. Just uncomfortable." She wasn't about to tell her it was all she could do to keep from crying. The woman had suffered enough over her ex's actions.

"Sure, tell that to someone who believes you." Maggie grunted.

"Well, thankfully, the bullet went straight through, otherwise, I wouldn't be here for you to scold." She gave Maggie a saucy grin.

"Be that as it may, you'll be getting plenty of rest." Maggie pulled back the covers allowing Amy to slip into the bed.

"Just the sheet. If I need more I can pull it over."

After tucking Aimee in, Maggie looked at her. "I put a bell here on your night stand. If you need anything, ring it." The older woman plopped her fists on her waist. "And don't you dare get up without me or one of the others here to help."

"I'm not—"

Maggie raised her brow. "Do you want me to sit with you?"

"No."

"Then you better do as I tell you, you hear?"

Laughing, Aimee said, "All right. I'll ring."

"I thought so."

Everyone left the room, but Maggie gave her one last penetrating stare before closing the door slightly.

"You're a mother hen."

"I heard that."

Aimee chuckled, realizing she was more tired than she thought. Closing her eyes, she allowed sleep to work its magic. Somewhere between the point of groggy and *la-la-land*, her eyes snapped open as her heart began to race. What she'd been trying to remember since she'd regained consciousness came back with a vengeance.

Reaching for her cell phone on her nightstand, she dialed Frank's number. She knew Tom would be angry with her for not telling him, but she didn't want him to go to jail for killing Rick.

Maybe her ex hadn't hired Mike. It could have been one of the other husbands and she was collateral damage. *But why my photo? And why the name, Jennifer Stanley?*

"Frank."

"Hi, Tom said you were home. You're not supposed to be calling me. You should be resting. What's up?"

"Please don't mention this to Tom because I'm afraid he'll go ballistic on me."

"That bad, huh?"

"Afraid so. I just happened to remember something Mike said while he was holding me hostage." She hesitated. "I don't mean to throw the alarm switch, but I think Rick, my ex, hired Mike to kill me."

"What makes you say that?"

"Mike showed me my picture. Of course, I look nothing like that photo now. But needless to say, he asked if I was Jennifer Stanley. When I told him no, he said he didn't believe me. Then he said he was hired to kill me and as a bonus he would get his wife and kids back." Her indecisive headache became full blown.

"The police learned as much by cutting Mike a deal. When they went to arrest Rick, he had skipped town. But there's an APB out on him. I don't believe he'll be stupid enough to come within five miles of this place. But if he does, my men and I are ready, and so is Tom."

"I was afraid you'd say that." Aimee worried her bottom lip with her teeth. "If you think Mike was shrewd in his method of getting past your men, Rick is ten times more so. He wants me. And no manner of protection you put around me, it won't stop him. Rick won't let anyone stand in his way, even if he has to kill everyone to get to me."

She rubbed the spot where her head ached the worse.

"Yes. But he doesn't know, we're waiting for him. I have a man posted inside your house and will be there until Rick is caught. So you see, he'll have a tough time getting to you. But right now you need to stop worrying about what might happen and concentrate on mending and getting your strength back."

"Thanks, Frank, I'll try."

His assurances didn't make Aimee feel any safer. A man, if he were trained like Frank or Tom just might keep most men out. But unlike Frank, Aimee didn't have the confidence in their ability to stop her ex.

He was ruthless, coldblooded, and had nothing to lose if the authorities were already looking for him. Of a certainty, Rick was on his way here.

There was nothing she could do now but wait for him to show.

Chapter 36

If normal meant having a man follow her around 24/7, then Aimee couldn't wait for normal to be over and done with. The only places her guards weren't allowed were her bedroom and bathroom. Even then, that didn't stop them from searching the two areas first before they would allow her to enter.

How could they conceivably think someone would be lurking in the closet, under the bed, or in the shower, was beyond her.

Aimee understood their caution but her frustration level had reached breaking point. If something didn't happen soon, she was going to pitch one grand hissy fit and throw everyone out of her house.

For the last two weeks, Tom and she had hardly had a minute together alone without someone popping in to check on her. She wanted Rick caught, her old life back, and her freedom to go about living once again.

The guards weren't only here to protect Aimee, they were watchful of the others also. With no sign of

Rick, Aimee wondered if her ex was trying to lull them into a false sense of security so they would let down their guard.

Fortunately, the fence was completed four days after she got home from the hospital, practically making her place a fortress. But Aimee blew a gasket when she found out Tom had paid extra for the quick service.

Though far from the norm, everyone around her little compound had developed a semi-daily routine. The men ate all their meals at the house but at odd times. They also came and went without a set schedule. Frank reasoned he didn't want anyone who might be watching see a pattern to the guards coming and going, which would allow their defense of Aimee and the women to be weakened.

Tom continued to train the women while Aimee sat on the sidelines and watched. Sometimes Frank would help with the training, and sometimes he'd sit with Aimee on the porch. She noticed the days Frank would sit with her, Tom always cut the training short to join them.

Maggie had a good time at Tom's expense. She'd make some type of comment—he was protecting his turf or there must be a fox in the henhouse and Tom's protecting his chick—then she'd laugh at her own joke.

Tom would good-naturedly let her comments roll right off.

Thankfully, the women were becoming less frightened of the men. Even with the potential threat still out there, they seemed to be even more motivated than before the Mike incident.

Aimee felt blessed to have such good friends. Yet, Friday, the day Debra Sue and her kids would be leaving, was coming too soon. The pain of losing them weighed heavy on her heart. She would miss them dearly.

Already, the shelter had called and said they would be sending two new women on Monday. One young woman had a three-month-old, the other — no children. At least getting their new members settled would keep Aimee busy and her mind off the loss of Debra Sue and her children.

Aimee sat on the porch enjoying the unseasonably cooler weather. And though her wounds were healing nicely, she still had to take it easy.

The screen door squeaked drawing Aimee's attention. Maggie held out a tall glass of iced tea, then set another glass on the table at the opposite end of the bench.

"Thanks, are you joining me?"

"No. Tom just called and said he's on his way. This one's for him. With him acting shadow, I figured he'd want to sit out here with you and spout poetry or somethin'." Maggie snorted, a sparkle in her eyes.

"You're incorrigible." There were no secrets in her household. Everyone had seen Tom's protectiveness and figured he'd declared himself.

"Say what you will, but that man's got it bad." Maggie cocked her brow. "The only one here that has it worse than him is you." She looked up the road, shielding her eyes. "Here he comes now." Turning to open the screen door she smiled at Aimee. "I'll leave you two lovebirds alone. Maybe today's the day he'll come up to scratch and have the nerve to ask you to marry him."

Aimee made a *tisk-tisking* sound shaking her head. "Would you like me to tell Tom you think he's Chicken Liver?"

Maggie's answer was her laughter trailing behind as she went inside.

Tom parked his truck and then sat looking at Aimee through his window, a silly grin in place. He finally opened the door and headed in her direction.

"Hey, gorgeous."

"Hey, yourself. I was beginning to wonder if you were going to sit there in your truck just looking." She smiled up at him. "I'm glad you decided to join me."

Tom stooped over and planted a hungry kiss on her lips, then pulled back to stare at her. "I was enjoying the view." His grin was teasing. "Have I told you lately that I love you?"

Playing along, she answered, "No, not lately."

He kissed her again. "Well, then, let me remedy that. I love you Aimee Hamilton more than life itself. And if we didn't have a bunch of snoopy eyes watching us, I'd show you just how much."

"We don't want to scandalize our audience." Chuckling, she patted the bench beside her.

Scooting in beside her, he put his arm around her shoulder and gently pulled her head to his chest, inhaling deeply.

"I love you."

"I know you do." He pulled back gazing into her eyes then took hold of her hands. "This may not be the time or place, but I have something to ask you."

Aimee's heart began racing. She tried to keep it light. "Ask away."

"I've gotta do it right." He pulled something out of his pocket, and then fell to one knee, still holding her hand, love shining in his face. "Will you marry me?"

Her throat tightened as tears of joy filled her eyes. "Yes."

He slipped a diamond the size of a goose egg onto her finger, or at least that's how it looked through the tears gathered in her eyes as the diamond winked up at her.

"I promise to protect, honor, and cherish you all the days of my life. I love you and I always will."

Speechless, Aimee reached out and touched his cheek. She never believed she could love someone as much as she loved Tom, but she did.

Tom leaned in, gathered her gently in his arm, pulling her to her feet. "You have made me the happiest man in the world."

His arms slipped around her waist, drawing her close, as his head dipped toward hers. When their lips met, his kiss was filled with so much love she thought her heart would burst.

The squeak of the screen had Tom pulling back as Maggie and the others rushed out the door.

"Well, it's about time." Maggie pounded him on the back. "I was beginning to wonder if I was gonna have to give you some pointers on how to get it done."

Everyone laughed.

"Well, let us see." Kim motioned for Aimee to show the ring.

"Oooeee. That's some rock he gave you." Maggie looked up at Tom. "You have my approval."

"Thanks." Tom winked at Maggie. "It's good to know I did something right, since I didn't move as fast as you thought I should."

"That rock makes up for your slowness." Maggie threw him a challenging look. "Now let's see how long it takes you to tie the knot."

"Maggie!" Aimee's face did a slow burn.

"I'm just saying." The woman shrugged. "I don't want to be old and gray before I see you walk down the aisle. So please do it somewhere in the near future."

"I'll tell you what, Maggie, if I can talk Aimee into walking with me down to the dock, we'll see if we can come back with a date."

Maggie began shooing the other women back into the house. "Go along, get out of here. I'd like a date settled so I can start planning."

"You're hopeless. But I love you anyway." Aimee hugged the woman.

"I know you do. Now go on." Maggie made a shooing sound motioning them off the porch before going back inside.

Tom linked Aimee's arm through his, leading her toward the pond.

"Well, do you have an idea when you would like to get married, because if you leave it up to me, I'll say tomorrow."

Aimee shook her head. "We need to discuss a few things before I can come to a decision." She chuckled. "But ... it won't be tomorrow."

He raised his brows. "Day after then?"

"Be serious." She punched him in the ribs with her elbow

"*Oowwh.*" He feigned injury, then gave her a hug. "I am serious. And the sooner we get married the better, as far as I'm concerned."

They reached the deck and Tom helped her into her seat, then he pulled a chair around so he could face her.

"I love you, Tom. And I want to marry you, but I have responsibilities."

"I know what you're going to say, and that's what took me so long to ask you to marry me. I wanted everything worked out in my mind before I asked. I knew you would be concerned about the women and Paradise Found."

"You did?" Aimee couldn't imagine a more thoughtful or loving man. Most men wouldn't have been concerned about her being committed to help other battered women.

"Yes. You once said that if I prayed, I'd see that God had sent me here to help you. I've come to the same conclusion. If it weren't for the women, I would have never met you. I'd still be filled with misery. But now ..." Tom held up his hand gesturing back at the house. "Those women brought us together, and I'm not going anywhere. I'm here for the long haul. I'll help you any way that I can. And I'll train every frightened stray that is shipped our way."

Tom's poignant, crooked grin was beautiful. Her heart was full to bursting. "What will we do with the two houses?"

He leaned forward in his chair, his face mere inches from hers. Resting his elbow on his knees, he clasped her hands, looking at her thoughtfully.

"Except for being my wife and sleeping together"—he raised his brows suggestively—"nothing much will change. Here's what I propose.

"During the day, you will do what you do now. You'll work here at Paradise Found and paint, if that's what you still want to do. But let me interject, I have enough money where you won't have to paint to run the place."

"I can't take your money."

"We'll be married. What's mine is yours. We will fund Paradise Found together. "

"I couldn't let you do that."

"Aimee, I love you. Everything I own is yours. So whatever you want or need to do for the women you'll be able to do without hesitation."

The thought of not having to worry about how to pay the bills or buy food was almost too huge to imagine.

"I'm not bragging when I say I'm good at earning money."

She teased him, "That's good to know. At least we won't be paupers."

He kissed her fingers, his eyes telling her he'd like to do more but would wait.

"Where was I? Ah, yes, we can eat with the women or cook at our place, your choice. Then at night, you'll come home to me." He smiled enticingly.

"Maggie and Kim are both strong and resourceful enough to take on the added responsibility of handling the women while you're at home. And, if something comes up, we are only a call away. So what do you think? Shall we set the date?"

Chapter 37

Together, Tom and Aimee talked with Maggie and Kim to propose the new ideas and arrangement once they were married. Aimee was afraid the women wouldn't take to the new plan.

"Would I have to quit my job at The Forge?" Kim looked worried.

Tom nodded at Aimee to answer. "Not unless you want to. But Tom has generously offered to pay — "

"We will pay you ..." He gave Aimee a meaningful look.

This was all so new. It was hard to grasp everything Tom owned would be theirs together.

"Right. W-we will pay you for working here at Paradise or you can continue to work at The Forge, your choice."

She looked at Maggie. "Tom — "

He cleared his throat.

She smiled and shrugged. "We will be paying you a salary also for helping to run Paradise Found. I'll only be here during the day once we're married."

Maggie grunted. "Well I'd hope so." She gave a nod at Kim. "I don't know about Kim, but I'll be more than willing to help run this place and you don't have to pay me."

"Oh, but we do. You will be having more responsibility, more work."

"I'd like to help too. I'd much rather work here than to wait tables." Kim looked ecstatic over her newfound role.

"So when's the wedding?" Maggie watched them expectantly.

"Believe it or not, Aimee wouldn't set a date until after we'd talked with the two of you. So since she has, and you have both agreed to work for us" — he turned his gaze on her — "when will it be Aimee?"

Tom gave her a look that caused her stomach to clinch and every sane thought to fly out of her head.

"Tomorrow?" He smiled

That brought her out of her stupor. "No. As much as I'd like to, it takes longer than that to get a marriage license. And ..." She hoped Tom would be in agreement. "I would like for my family to come and meet you and hopefully attend our wedding. So how will next month work?"

"If meeting your family is what it will take to make you mine, then next month it will be. But I'm telling you right now, I'm not too keen on this waiting business."

When they were through talking with Maggie and Kim, Tom coaxed Aimee into calling her father.

Picking up the phone and calling her dad wasn't easy, but once Aimee got over the initial tears and explanation for her disappearance, they had a good talk.

Her father was livid with Rick for what he'd cost his family.

She was relieved to know they hadn't heard from Rick and that her sister had broken it off with him two months ago.

"We want to come see your place and meet Tom." Her father sounded emphatic.

"He wants to meet you too." She squeezed Tom's hand. Knowing they'd be saying goodbye to Debra Sue and the kids, she didn't want the added tears she'd be shedding at her family's reunion.

"I have a family leaving us this Friday and then a couple of new women moving in. How does a week from this Saturday sound?"

"That'll work."

Her father's excited voice pleased her.

"Next month we're getting married in a small wedding chapel in Ben Wheeler. Will you come to the wedding?"

"We wouldn't miss it. Give us the date and time and we'll be there."

"It'll be small. Just a few close friends and Tom's family. We're keeping it low key because of the compound."

"I understand. But we want to pay for all of your wedding expenses. It'll be our gift to you. Just send me the information." The line went quiet. "What about Rick. Is he still a threat?"

Aimee couldn't lie. Evasion was best. "He's been taken care of. The Sheriff has been alerted. And I have a friend who is a PI looking for Rick. So I don't believe we'll have to worry about him."

"Good. Then we'll see you a week from Saturday."

When she finished talking with her father, Tom gave her a hug.

"That's my girl. See that wasn't so bad was it?"

"No. And they'll be coming to the wedding. He wants to pay for everything, his gift to us."

They were sitting on the front porch and Aimee looked around her place, wondering what the coming years would bring. She hoped children—something they'd never talked about.

"We've never discussed ..."

Tom gave her a puzzled look. "What? You can discuss anything with me."

She bit her lower lip, wondering how best to put the words.

"Aimee?"

"Children." She glanced up hoping to not see disgust.

His brilliant smile erased the worry.

"I'd like as many as you're willing to have, especially if they are all like you."

Shaking her head, she said, "You're impossible. But four or five kids would be nice. But I want a couple of them to be boys. Spitting images of their father."

She stood beaming down at him. "Now, I've got to start planning."

Tom pulled her onto his lap. "Not before you give me a proper kiss."

After he had thoroughly kissed her, he released her and took her hand. She walked him out to his truck.

"Are you sure you want to take on all this?" She moved her hand in a full sweep.

"I'm not taking on anything but loving you to distraction. The rest is just part of you."

"Thanks. I love you."

She watched Tom until he had backed away and headed up the road before going inside.

"Well, is it all settled?" Maggie turned from the stove.

"Yes. My family is coming to meet Tom next week. And they will be attending the wedding."

"Good. I already have the cake picked out for your reception. Will we be having it here?"

Aimee wrinkled her brow. "I don't know. Maybe Tom's place, since it's bigger and can hold more people."

"Then I suggest you get to planning. Because the wedding will be here before you know it."

~ ~ ~

Over the next several days, Aimee had a lot to keep her busy with Debra moving out on Friday, her wedding happening in three weeks, and her folks coming next Saturday. Yet, a constant at the back of her mind — Rick hadn't been seen or heard from. She knew he hadn't given up. He'd come for her, which worried her even more with all that was going on around her.

On Thursday, Tom drove Aimee to Leah's shop to deliver two paintings. When she went inside the gallery, Leah's assistant told them Leah was in bed sick with the flu.

"Tom, if you don't mind, I'll just pop up and see how's she's doing."

"All right. I'll be waiting out in the truck."

Instead of knocking on Leah's door, Aimee walked inside and found Leah in bed.

"Hey, what's going on? Do you think you can just lay around in bed and be waited on?" Aimee brushed an errant curl from Leah's brow. Her friend was flushed and felt warm to the touch.

"Aimee, you shouldn't be here. I don't want you to catch what I have."

"I'm not staying long. Tom is down in the truck waiting on me, but I had to look in on you and see how you were doing."

"I feel like dirt that's been trampled by a herd of cattle." Leah closed her eyes for a brief moment.

"I'm so sorry. I hope you get to feeling better."

"You're not the only one." Leah gave a wry chuckle then moaned.

"Is there anything I can do for you?"

Leah shook her head. "I'll be fine. Just need to rest."

"Then I'll let you get back to sleep. I'll send Tom back with some of Maggie's chicken soup."

"Thanks."

"When you're feeling better, give me a call."

"I will."

Aimee slipped out the door and down to the truck.

"How's she doing?"

"She felt hot to me, and wasn't feeling well at all." She frowned. "I wanted to tell her our news, but she wasn't up to it. I'll tell her when she's feeling better."

"It'll keep." He smiled.

~ ~ ~

The van to pick up Debra Sue and the kids arrived at eight, too soon as far as Aimee was concerned. Everyone helped load the little odds and ends that amounted to no more than three boxes full and the kids' backpacks stuffed to running over.

Tears were plenty, goodbyes were prolonged until the driver cleared his throat and said they had to get on the road. Keisha, Kim, Maggie, and Aimee stood watching the van drive up the road and out of sight.

"I sure am going to miss Debra Sue and those little ones." Maggie used her apron to wipe her cheeks.

"I will too." Aimee swiped the moisture from her cheeks. Feeling anything but happy, she smiled. "However, by Monday we'll have another little one we can spoil. Only this one will be a little more hands-on than Debra Sue's three."

"Well, I've got pies to bake and they won't bake on their own." Maggie opened the screen door.

"Yes, and I've got to get around for work." Kim brushed her hair to one side behind her ear. "With the Ben Wheeler music festival this weekend, business will be heavier than normal." She raised her brow. "But the tips should be good."

Aimee listened to the women talk but didn't feel like contributing. Her head was pounding and she was beginning to feel achy all over. Maybe because

Debra Sue's departure, but more likely she was coming down with whatever Leah had caught.

"What's wrong with you?" Maggie studied her.

"I'm not sure. I think I must have caught what Leah had yesterday." She turned toward her room. "I believe I'll go lie down for a while and see if that won't help."

"You go straight to bed. I'll bring you a couple of aspirins and some water."

She had too much to do to be sick. There were the wedding plans, the new arrivals on Monday, and her family in a week.

Feeling much like a limp rag doll with every bone in her body throbbing and her head feeling way beyond the normal size. Aimee sat on the bed to undress and slipped into her PJs.

She crawled beneath the covers, and was barely able to open her eyes enough to take the two pills and water from Maggie. She fell back against the pillow nestling her head in its softness praying for oblivion.

Drifting from consciousness, Aimee tried to open her eyes as her heart raced uncontrollably. She had to reach Tom and tell him Rick was here.

The smell of his sickly cologne was on her pillow.

Chapter 38

Dark. Blistering hot. She had to be in Hell.

Aimee's groggy mind knew better. But if not Hell, where was she?

The urgency to get away from the heat and the imminent danger had her heart thundering against her chest. Where was Tom?

Her room dark, the house quiet, the necessity to find Tom had her pushing up out of bed. It took all her strength to stand and then her legs didn't seem to want to work. Her heart raced as if she were running a marathon. She prayed she wouldn't fall flat on her face. Swaying, she steadied herself against the nightstand then shoved off for the door.

Grabbing hold, Aimee leaned against the doorframe for a few seconds hoping to regain her footing. She took a jerky step out into the hall. An arm wrapped around her throat as a hand covered her mouth choking off her scream.

"Ahh, Jennifer, my love, you should have known better than to run. You knew I would find you. Now we'll even the score."

The cloying scent of Rick's cologne wrapped around her calling up the old memories. The beatings, the pain, even his repentance afterward that lasted only until the next beating. She cringed from his touch, expecting the worst. In her present condition, she knew she was no match for him.

Where was Tom? Had he been on guard? She couldn't remember.

Had Rick killed Tom? Her mind screamed against the thought as she struggled to get free. The blow from Rick's fist caused her to pitch forward into darkness.

~ ~ ~

Aimee clawed her way up out of the haze that held her captive. The damp cold seeped in, making her bones ache. Muddled and confused, she rolled into a ball for warmth as heavy tremors shook her body and her chest burned like it was on fire.

The musty smell of dirt mixed with the stench of rodents caused her to become sharply aware of her surroundings. Yet, the dense darkness that met her gaze struck her with terror but gave her no satisfaction of where she might be. The urgency to move had her leaning up on her elbow. She shook her head to clear the fog. Where was she and how did she get there?

Like a small hole in a dam that grows larger and larger and soon tears down the wall, the events flooded into her mind.

Rick's breathe on her cheek. The repugnant smell of his cologne. The sneer of his voice in her ear as he slid his hand over her mouth roughly pulling her up next to him. And then like other times when they were married, he'd knocked her out cold.

Repulsed and shaking, she attuned her ears to the room, listening for Rick or the odd, out-of-place noise. Was he here playing a sick joke on her? Or had he dumped her somewhere so he could return later to finish her off?

Though she didn't detect any movement, she figured she needed to get out of there as soon as possible.

Aimee pushed upward into a sitting position, clamping her mouth shut against the pain bombarding her body. Grit stabbed her hands from the dirt floor as nausea struck her stomach. She swallowed hoping to calm her stomach as she allowed herself time to adjust and get accustomed to the pain.

The dirt floor added to the mystery of where she was being held. Yet, more importantly, where was Rick?

The need to escape before he returned had Aimee on all fours, her pain almost doubling her over. Again, she waited for the sickness to pass before attempting to stand. The shivers of earlier were replaced by a fine coating of moisture as beads of sweat trickled down her face, dripping onto the dirt. She shoved to her feet then swayed, nearly falling back to the ground.

Moving slowly, she stretched out her hands feeling for a wall, bench, anything for support, or to give her a hint of where she might be. Her toe connected with something hard.

Stairs. They were leading up. Was she on the ground floor?

She fumbled around for a light switch and found dirt walls and a board with bare wiring. A cellar. But whose? Had Rick locked her in and left her here to die?

With labored steps, she climbed the rickety stairs testing each rung for soundness before moving up. Her labored breath and aching bones caused her ascent to be slow and strenuous. At the top landing, she found the door was closed and jammed or stuck at the bottom.

Feeling woozy, Aimee knew she had only enough strength to slam her body against the door once. If it didn't open on the first try, it would be doubtful she could try again.

Taking a deep breath, she braced herself for the pain and then rammed her shoulder against the wood. The door swung open, tumbling her out on the ground into the cool night air. Lying on her back, she caught her breath.

She could either stay here in the prone position staring at the stars and wait for Rick to catch her, or she could get up and get as far away from this place as possible.

Aimee got to her knees and then stumbled to her feet. She glanced around to get her bearings and recognized the place. The dark, gaping hole she had escaped from was a little ways from a small ramshackle house at the back portion of her property. The house and the cellar belonged to her.

The building was one she'd neglected to tear down when she bought the property. However, if she got out of this mess alive, getting rid of the house and filling the cellar with dirt would be her first priority.

When she heard someone thrashing through the weeds, Aimee squelched the instinct to yell for help. Instead, she moved silently into the shadows. She headed toward the abandoned house and away from the sound and the cellar.

Bracing her body against the outside wall, she felt the rough, splintered wood bite into her skin and snag her clothes. She hugged the wall and silently moved around out of sight. She waited and listened, praying she wouldn't be detected.

Questions spun in her head as she heard the footsteps come closer. Was it Rick? Had he come back to kill her? Did he kill the others? Where was Tom? Frank?

Until she knew who or what was out there, she would keep silent and out of sight. Whoever they were, they didn't seem to care if they were detected. She prayed the person would move on without finding her.

Rick's curse rent the air.

She trembled, placing her hand over her mouth. Now she knew, Rick was back to finish her off.

"Jennifer, darling, I just want to talk to you. I miss you. I want you to come home."

His compassionate, almost loving voice, had her heart quaking. She waited, listening to the silence wondering where he was and what he was up to?

Another curse pierced the night. "Jennifer, you can run, but you can't hide. I'll find you like I did earlier."

This time his voice was much like all the other times when he would beat her almost senseless. The true Richard Stanley.

A flash of light blazed across the brush then disappeared.

Aimee took that moment to slink deeper into the darkness.

He moved toward the house, closer to where she stood, exposed and vulnerable. She held her breath, making herself as small as possible, trying to blend into the shadows, hoping he wouldn't see her.

More foul words shattered the darkness. "When I find you, Jennifer, I'll make you wish you had never run from me. You do remember what it was like, don't you, darling? You remember all the pain I'm able to inflict? So, Jennifer dear, come out, come out wherever you are. Come out, come out ... I have something for you."

His sing-song mocking voice shattered her nerves. She set her resolve not to be caught.

He yelled her name several more times before entering the abandoned house. She heard his thundering footsteps as he walked around inside and she saw his light flashing.

Glad for his distraction and noise he was making inside, Aimee darted in the direction of home. She hoped she could reach the house before Rick. She took a different path than he had just used, and tried to keep her noise to a minimum.

Stumbling through the tall brush, thorns and branches tore at her skin and the pajamas she still wore. The pain she ignored. She knew her only chance to survive was to reach her house before Rick. The thought spurred her to run faster.

The thunder of feet and thrashing of brush had Aimee deviating off the path. She stopped to hide behind a huge oak tree and quieted her breathing, listening for Rick's advancing steps.

The sound came closer, but she didn't dare look from around the tree for fear he would see her.

Rick sprinted past where she was hiding, heading toward her house, his flashlight making long, searching arcs back and forth as he ran.

She waited until she didn't hear him, then waited several seconds more before starting out again. This time she veered to the left, knowing a shortcut, but not sure she would reach her destination before Rick. If she did, she could get her shotgun and maybe hold him until the police came.

Seeing the barn straight ahead, she knew she was almost there. She kept moving, darting from tree to tree searching the area for any sign of her ex.

Could she have beaten him back to the house? She couldn't know for sure, but she had to take a chance. The shotgun was her only hope of survival.

Sweat ran off her brow and dripped into her eyes, stinging. She swiped to clear her vision then started again. Hanging in the shadows, she looked around for him again. When she saw her back porch was within sprinting distance she held back, giving her body the needed rest before going the short distance to her back porch.

Her chest burned like fire, her breathing labored and rugged. Yet, the pain tearing at her body was nothing compared to the pain Rick would inflict if he caught her.

She judged the distance to her porch to be forty feet or less. Could she make it?

Maybe, but she was uncertain if she had enough stamina to run the distance and then get inside the house to her gun. If she made it inside could she even handle her shotgun? The way her hands and arms shook from exertion was doubtful.

Leaning her back against a tree, Aimee slid down the side of the bark, her rear resting on the gnarled protruding tree roots. She kept her ears attuned to the night sounds around her, wondering if she had the strength to rise again.

She peered around the tree. Seeing no sign of Rick, Aimee forced herself to stand. In her present condition, she couldn't run. She took another look around and then crouching, she crept across the small expanse of backyard. Doing her best to stay within the shadows she made it to the side of the porch. One more quick glance around, she pulled herself up the steps and reached for the screen door.

Aimee heard him, but couldn't react soon enough. His arm snaked around her waist, pulling her back, pinning her against his rock-hard body. His other forearm was around her neck, choking off her air.

"Ahh, darling, I see you made it back, and just in time too."

Like all the other times when they were married, his sadistic laughter froze her reaction. She wanted to curl up into a ball and ward off his attack.

"I've been waiting for you to come out of hiding. And now here you are." He loosened his chokehold.

Rick's familiar cloying scent, one she used to love but learned to hate, filled her nostrils as he planted a kiss on her neck causing her insides to revolt. Why hadn't she seen him?

"I was afraid you might have wandered off and died, cutting short the pleasure of my company one last time."

Loathing coursed through her body. She kicked back hoping to hit his shin but missed, costing her dearly as pain shot through her.

His laughter rang in her ears as he slammed her hard, front first, against the porch post. The blow to her head and body made her knees buckle as her stomach lurched and her head exploded with pain. He used the flat of his hand and punched her back, holding in place. The moon overhead glinted off a steel blade as Rick brought the knife around to her neck, pricking her throat.

"Have you missed me, Sweetheart?"

His endearment sickened her. "Not hardly." She jerked and did her best to kick back at him again.

He easily sidestepped her effort. Yanking her back by the collar of her shirt, slamming her harder up against the post again, causing a momentary blackout.

Regaining her wits, in her weakened condition, she knew she was no match for him. She didn't know how much longer she could hold out before she collapsed at his feet. The best chance to survive Rick and his beatings was to play docile and obedient. Maybe if she held on long enough, someone would come to her rescue, or she might possibly find a way to fight him off.

"You thought if you changed your name and got lost in this dump of a backwater town, I would never find you. Well, sweetheart, you should have known better. I never give up what's mine. You belong to me, not that stupid commando sniffing around your heels."

His laughter chilled her. Had he killed Tom?

"I must say he's not much of a man if he can't even protect you." He pulled her back from the post and pushed her toward the backdoor. "Shall we go inside? I think we have some unfinished business to take care of before I kill you."

When he let up on his hold, she swung her elbow back hard into Rick's solar plexus and was rewarded with a grunt and a slight loosening of his grip. With a swiftness that belied her battered state, she pushed out with her arms bursting free of his hold. She pivoted to face him and rammed her palm up under his chin, knocking him back.

He stumbled off the porch backwards.

Turning around, she grabbed the screen handle pulling it open and twisted the knob pushing the door back.

Rick's hand snagged her hair, yanking her head back, forcing her to her knees.

She clamped her lips closed to keep from crying out. That's what he wanted and liked most—to hear her beg, scream, and writhe in pain. She wouldn't give him the satisfaction regardless how much she felt like giving up.

Panting from the couple of well-placed jabs she gave him, Rick moved in front of her, the knife to her juggler.

"I have every intention of killing you, Jen." His words were cold, calculated, and without emotion. "But now I'm going to do it slow and painful. By the time I'm done with you, you'll beg me to finish the job." He slid a caressing finger down the side of her cheek, trailing down her neck to the V of her top.

"However, before I do ..." His leering gaze followed the path his finger traveled as his hand continued down to her cleavage then stopped. "I want to show you how much you're going miss. And when I'm done, you'll experience the pain and humiliation I have endured from your disappearance. What do you think about that?"

The same hand that seconds ago caressed her, dug into her flesh, his nails cutting into her skin as he yanked her up brutally tight against his body. His breath fanned her cheek. With the hand that held the knife, he forced her chin up, his lips a hairsbreadth from hers.

She was unable to hold back her repulsion.

He noticed and squeezed her tighter making it difficult for her to breathe.

"You don't deserve me. You never did." He leaned back, hatred in his glare. "Look at you. You're nothing more than trash I pulled off the streets."

His hard, calculated stare chilled her to the bone. She'd seen Rick's cruel vindictive side many times before. Yet this time something was different.

He released her and just as quickly, the back of his hand slammed against her jaw making her head fly back from the force. She staggered, trying to stay upright as white sparks of light filled her eyes.

Before when Rick beat her, she'd crawl inside her head, divorcing herself from her surroundings and Rick to endure the pain. Always before, she prayed to lose consciousness, hoping maybe then he'd leave her alone.

No more.

She pulled her shoulders back, stood as tall as her battered body would allow, and then stared him in the eye.

"I used to think you beat me because it was my fault. Maybe something I'd said or done." She shook her head. "I know differently now. It was never about me. It was all about you. You're sick and you need help. But you don't want help, do you?"

"Help?" His face twisted, revealing the ugliness in his soul. "Look around you, Jennifer. I think you're the one that needs help."

Rick turned her to face the door. His arm wound around her chest, the knife at her throat.

"You wanted to be free of me. Well, sweetheart, you soon will be ... for eternity. And then I'll pick up with your sister where I left off with you."

Aimee fought like the very demons of Hell had taken hold of her. She didn't want Rick anywhere near Melissa. Her sister could never withstand his abuse.

He resisted her efforts, shoving her forward. Her head hit the doorframe as she felt a sting to her throat. Warmth surrounded her as her knees gave way and she tumbled downward.

Now she would never get to tell Tom ...

Chapter 39

Aimee's screams rent the air as she fought the hands that held her.

"Shhh. It's all right. Aimee, it's me."

"No." She struggled more, lashing out until strong arms encircled her, holding her firm.

"Baby, it's me, Tom. You're safe now."

Blinking several times to clear her vision and the nightmare from her mind, she glanced around to confirm Tom wasn't a hallucination.

She was in her bedroom, in her own bed. Tom had her legs penned beneath his, holding her in his arms. Aimee was clad in her pale turquoise PJs. The brightly colored granny square afghan Debra Sue had crocheted for Aimee's birthday last year was thrown off to the side.

Her gaze connected with Tom's. She'd never seen a more welcoming or endearing sight. His troubled look brightened when Aimee ran her hand across his rough, stubble cheek, then touched a purple bruise.

"Does it hurt?"

"No."

Love shined deep from his eyes. "How about you? Are you in pain?"

"Not much." The croaky voice didn't sound like hers. "Especially, with you holding me. But I'd feel more comfortable if you would move your legs."

"Sorry about that." He repositioned Aimee in his arms, straightening his long legs out on the bed. "You were kicking and I was afraid you would hurt yourself or ... me." He grinned. "You carry one powerful wallop and your legs, when flailing around, are lethal.

"I couldn't have been in my right mind. Did I do that?" She touched his bruise again.

"No."

"Good." She closed her eyes and burrowed deeper in his arms as she felt every joint in her body protest.

He chuckled as he brushed his hand across her brow, moving some wayward hair from her face.

She snuggled deeper into his embrace. Her head felt like a bunch of tiny men were running loose batting tennis balls around in her skull. To say she ached from head to toe would be a misnomer, but she wasn't about to tell Tom. She didn't want him to leave.

All of it came crashing in—the cellar, running, hiding, the knife, Rick. She tried to sit up but Tom held her back.

"Shhh. Lay still. Rest."

She stayed put like he asked but she wasn't about to rest until she had answers.

"Did he hurt anyone—Maggie?" She stirred again trying to sit up. Tom made her stay put. "Is she all right?"

"That woman's been worrying and fussing over you like there's no tomorrow. But other than that, yes, she's fine." He chuckled. "A freight train could have come through the house and Maggie would have slept right through it"

Aimee smiled and then worried again. "What about Phil, the guard? He wasn't ..."

Tom shifted slightly. "No. He has a knot the size of a melon where Rick tried to bash his head in. Other than that, he's fine and a little embarrassed for Rick sneaking up on him like that." Tom smoothed her hair back from her cheek. "Rick was inside the house, apparently hiding somewhere waiting for everyone to settle down for the night before he put his plan into action. No one knew he was here. He tied up the guard and gagged him so he couldn't alert anyone."

Aimee shivered. To think Rick was here all the time almost made her sick.

Turning to look up at Tom, she said, "I remember something. When I went to bed, I smelled his cologne on my pillow." She cringed. "He must have been in my room the whole time I was sick and sleeping."

Glancing up, she asked, "Who caught him?"

"I did. Knowing you were sick, I had an uneasy feeling about you. I came up to the house to check to see if you were all right. That's when I found him bashing your head against the doorframe. I could have killed him."

Aimee felt Tom's body tense and knew he was reliving the awful scene. She squeezed his hand. "I'm glad you didn't, even if he did deserve it."

Relaxing against Tom she jerked to attention. "What did you do to him? Is he in jail?"

"No. He's in the hospital under police guard. But he won't be going anywhere soon."

"Oh?"

"Yeah, he lost the use of both arms and one leg, at least for a while anyway. Come to think of it, his other leg is in pretty bad shape also. And ... he'll be drinking from a straw for a month or two. Other than that, the man's in fine shape."

Aimee smiled. Not that she wanted Rick dead or hurt, but she figured it had taken a lot of restraint on Tom's part to keep from killing him.

"Was it your doing?"

"Well ..." Tom looked down at her, a sparkle in his eyes. "Mainly my doing. The butt of my rifle caused him to stumble over the bench on the back porch, breaking his left arm. But then when I pulled him up to stand, he took a swing at me. That's when my fist connected with his chin and broke his jaw."

"Is that all?" Aimee began chuckling and had to wrap her free arm around her chest to keep it from hurting.

"No." He shook his head. "I thought for sure the man was down for the count. But, that guy just doesn't know when to say uncle." He shrugged. "Which was fine with me." He looked at her oddly a twinkle in his eyes. "By the way, I guess I owe you a potted plant."

"Why did he hit you with the pot?"

He gave her an indignant look. "Are you kidding? That guy is a horrible shot. He picked up one of those pretty potted plants you had on your porch railings, threw it at me, but missed by a long shot. I'm afraid the pot didn't survive though."

His smug grin was adorable.

"It smashed to smithereens on the ground, and the flowers are in little pieces all over the lawn."

She loved the sound of Tom's voice and didn't want him to stop talking. "What happened then?"

"Well, that's when I punched the guy in the gut." He paused. "I guess I owe you for one painted milk can too."

"You do? Why?"

"You remember the old milk can on your back porch that you painted all pretty like with flowers and leaves?"

"Yeah. I worked hard and long on that can. It was my favorite. Don't tell me you broke it too." She tried her best to look stern but failed miserably when she chuckled.

"Hey, don't blame me. It was that ex of yours. When I punched him, he fell on top of that pretty little milk can of yours." He gave her a quirky grin. "I think that's when he broke his right arm and cracked a few ribs." He shrugged glancing around the room. "And ... I believe the milk can is a goner."

Holding her ribs, Aimee sputtered out, "Stop, you're hurting me."

"I'm sorry. I can finish tomorrow when you're feeling better."

Tom tried to scoot her over, out of his arms. He would have gotten away with his ruse, if she hadn't seen that little devilish glint in his eyes.

She stayed put, threatening him to move.

"Don't you dare. You're not budging until I know exactly what happened, and why you have this huge bruise on your face." She loved touching his cheek, feeling the late afternoon stubble, sensing their hearts beat as one.

"Not much more to tell."

She narrowed her eyes, staring him down. "I counted one broken jaw, two broken arms, a few broken ribs, but as of yet you haven't said how Rick got the broken leg."

"Oh, yeah. Come to think of it, I guess I owe you for some back porch railing too."

"Railing?" She tried to sit up but stayed put groaning.

"You OK?"

"Yes, but don't try to sidestep my question."

"Oh, yeah, as to the railing, I'm afraid I don't know my own strength. I knocked the man plumb through it. When he landed out in the yard, his leg was twisted at an odd angle. Nasty break." He wrinkled his nose. "Must have broke it when he fell. Or ..."

There was that twinkle again.

"Could be it got broken when I kick him in the knee before punching him through the railing. Can't be sure." Tom's face showed satisfaction. His grin was the biggest ever. "His other leg suffered some when I stomped on it for good measure."

"Tom, you shouldn't have." She couldn't hide the laughter in her voice.

He sobered. "He got nothing less than he deserved. In fact, if I could I — "

She placed her fingers over his lips. "Shhh. No. As long as he's in jail for a very long, long time where he can't hurt me or anyone else, I'll be satisfied. "

He kissed her hand. His touch brought excitement as his gaze spoke of things to come.

"I love you, you know that don't you?" His words were earnest, no teasing glint, just pure love shining through.

"Yes. And I love you and always will."

"And you know I would never lay a hand on you in anger, don't you?"

"Yes. That's why I chose to love you. Why are you asking such a foolish question?"

"Good. I'm glad we've got that settled. You can trust me. Tell me anything. I'll keep your secrets and do my best to never disappoint you."

Aimee reached up, pulling his head toward hers. "You, Tom Branigan, could never disappoint me. And … I trust you with my life."

Their lips met and sealed all their promises to last a lifetime and more.

Chapter 40

The parking lot of the small white wedding chapel was full of cars. Inside, every seat was taken. Somehow the wedding list had grown out of proportion, from a small gathering in front of family and close friends to include Roni and her husband, and many more of her sorority sisters and spouses, a couple of Tom's Special Ops buddies, and the few in town who knew Aimee and Tom's secret of Paradise Found.

Given the signal that Aimee had arrived, Pastor Jennings leaned toward Tom. "Are you ready, son?"

Tom looked at the man as if he were nuts.

Frank, who had been asked to stand up with Tom to be his best man, chuckled. "I believe he was ready from the day he first laid eyes on Aimee."

"I wouldn't say the first day, but definitely the second." Tom grinned. "But yes, I've been ready for a long time. The sooner you say the words, the better, as far as I'm concerned." He cracked a smile. "It's like a reconnaissance mission."

"How so?"

Frank laughed and shook his head. "Here we go."

"It's like this. I've seen the lay of the land, fell hard for the woman I rescued, and now I want to get home and start the rest of the mission. Live happily ever after with Aimee by my side."

Pastor Jennings laughed while slapping Tom on the back. "Then I say ... let's get this marriage tied up right and proper."

"I'm with you there." Tom opened the side door and motioned for the pastor to proceed. He couldn't wait to call Aimee his wife.

When he turned to face the crowd his knees knocked. He tugged at his shirt and necktie that felt like a noose. *Why hadn't he talked Aimee into standing before the judge?*

"It's just family and friends, Tom. Take a deep breath and don't you dare faint on me."

Frank's joke at Tom's expense pulled him out of his stupor. "Whatever possessed me to ask you to be my best man?"

"As to that, you wanted to rub it in because you won the gal. And ... you can't help but like me."

The music started cutting off all further conversation as Tom strained for a look at his bride. Melissa, the maid of honor, stood at the back of the chapel smiling and then started walking down the aisle.

When Melissa stood in place opposite of Tom and Frank, the music changed into the wedding march. Everyone stood and then turned to look back at the door.

At first, he couldn't see her, and then his breath snagged in his chest. He almost forgot to breathe as he caught his first glimpse of Aimee standing by her father at the back of the building.

She smiled at him and then began walking slowly down the aisle toward him.

It wasn't the knee-length, off-white dress she wore, or the veil hanging around her shoulders concealing her auburn hair with specks of gold, nor the beautiful bouquet she carried. What snagged his attention most was the pure joy and love shining from her eyes. Her gaze never strayed from his.

Tom knew he would never forget this moment for as long as he lived. It would be forever etched into the memory of his mind. As sure as God was his Light in the darkness, Aimee was his heart and soul.

~ ~ ~

Aimee made sure Leah, Maggie, Kim, and Keisha, along with the two new members of their family, Sara and Tina, sat in the family section when they arrived at the chapel.

On Monday before the wedding, Maggie cried when Aimee drove her and the others to town to buy each of them a dress and shoes to wear to the occasion.

Tom had insisted on paying for their outfits, saying they were his responsibility now.

His sister, Mary Ann, and Bob insisted on furnishing the flowers for the church, saying it was the least they could. Aimee accepted graciously, happy for the opportunity to get to know her future sister-in-law and family better.

MaryAnn was much like her brother in looks, except she smiled all the time. Her two boys, Josh 3 and Max 5, kept Aimee in stitches with their antics — always playing jokes on their mother.

Maggie and the other women had fussed all week long preparing food for the reception. Even when Tom said he'd hire some help, Maggie flat refused. So she wouldn't get her feelings hurt, Tom accepted Maggie's offer, but put his foot down when it came to the wedding and reception.

He told her, she and the others could prepare the food and cake. However, he wouldn't allow Maggie or any of the other women to serve. They were to enjoy the wedding and reception like everyone else, because they were family.

When Aimee's father told Maggie her cake was a masterpiece, the woman nearly busted out crying.

Tom found a catering company to handle the set up and serving on the day of the wedding.

The long hand on the clock drug as delays and the necessary chore of preparations prevented Aimee from seeing Tom.

Maggie and the others had fussed over her, helping her dress, making sure she had everything just right, so much so, she wanted to tell them to back off, then felt ashamed. They were doing it out of love, so she could be patient a little longer.

Her father and stepmother along with Melissa had come up from Houston yesterday and stayed the night for the Saturday eleven o'clock morning wedding. Fortunately, Tom and her father had hit it off from the very first. They were even planning a hunt together on Tom's and her property in November.

For the last several days she'd had very little time alone with Tom, which had soured her mood, making her irritable and ill-tempered. She should have just told Tom's family and hers to meet them at the Justice of the Peace. It would have been a lot less stress and a lot easier on the nerves.

Standing with her father and Melissa on the porch of the chapel waiting for the music to start, she tapped her foot, while shifting and twisting her bouquet. Melissa shook her head and smiled.

Her father watched, a smug smile in place. "I don't believe I've ever seen you this anxious before. Not even when you were worried about being accepted into the University of Texas. Are you sure you love him and he loves you?"

Aimee stopped her fidgeting and gave her full attention to her father.

"I'm not anxious about marrying Tom. I'm in a hurry to begin my life with him. And though I haven't known Tom all that long, he's everything I have ever wanted in a man and the complete opposite of Rick.

"Oh, daddy, if you knew him like I do, you would see that he's gentle, warm hearted, and generous. Tom's the epitome of kindness and concern. And even though he tries to hide his caring side, he is all those things and more.

He would do anything for me even to his detriment. Tom is the other half of me. He completes me. He's the breath I breathe, the air I need to live.

And I trust him implicitly." She smiled at her father. "And he loves me."

Her father gave her a hug, then held her by the shoulders. "That's all I wanted to hear." He smiled. "Let's get inside and get you hitched."

She dabbed at the tears in her eyes before leaning up to give her father a kiss on his cheek. Taking her finger, she wiped the small smudge of lipstick she'd left behind, and then adjusted the flower in his boutonniere.

Melissa gave her a hug. "I love you big sister. And one day I want to grow up to be just like you."

"Thank you. That means so much to me."

Her sister opened the door, stepped inside, and then glided down the aisle.

Aimee's pulse quickened, impatient for a glimpse of Tom. Her father held the door, allowing her to walk through then took her arm. The strains coming from the string quartet played Mendelssohn's "A Midsummer Night's Dream" and filled the small chapel as the audience stood and turned to look at Aimee and her father.

Her heart sped up and she searched for the one man who could make her world spin on its axis. Her gaze landed on Tom and her heart leapt with joy. She kept her eyes on him as she moved up the aisle. How could she love one man so much and feel lost without him?

When they reached the front, Tom stepped forward.

Her father placed her hand in Tom's. "I give you my daughter."

"I will cherish her above all else. She is my heart and soul." Tom's voice rang strong with conviction.

Aimee could hardly see him for the tears filling her eyes. She wanted to cry, wanted to shout for joy, wanted to say I do. But most of all she wanted to hear the minister say you may kiss the bride because then she would truly be one with Tom.

Instead, she stood, her hand in Tom's feeling the warmth of his love seep into her soul.

They exchanged their vows looking into each other's eyes. They professed their love before their family and friends, and just when Aimee thought the ceremony would never end she smiled ...

"By the power vested in me, I now pronounce you husband and wife. You may kiss your bride."

Tom's head descended, sealing their vows as their lips met and Aimee's heart soared with ecstasy for what was yet to come. The moment Aimee had been waiting for was finally a reality.

"Mrs. Branigan, thank you for marrying me. You've made me the happiest man alive. Now if we could just take off and leave all these people behind – " He stared at her hopefully.

Aimee gave Tom a saucy smile. "Why Tom Branigan, whatever do you mean. Are you propositioning me in front of God and everyone?"

Tom's laughter rang out as the string quartet began to play the "Wedding March" by Mendelssohn.

"You betcha."

"Why *sirrah*, I do believe that's our cue to walk down the aisle and get this show on the road." Her words dripped warm and syrupy. She batted her lashes like a coy southern belle, while all the time wishing they could do what her husband had suggested.

"Why do I get the feeling you're going to run circles around me?" Tom raised his brow.

He bent down and kissed her thoroughly, leaving her stunned in a good way.

When she came to her senses she asked, "Why *sirrah*, whatever do you mean?" Her continued drawl drew another laugh.

"I love you." He winked at her. "And as you suggested, let's get this show on the road"

"I'm ready, lead the way."

Tom shocked her by picking her up in his arms, carrying her down the aisle and out the door while the audience laughed and clapped, accompanied by a few wolf whistles.

Aimee looked up into Tom's eyes and saw the promise of a lifetime of love. She knew in her heart, whether there were good times or bad, theirs was a love that would stand the test of time.

Dear Reader,

Thanks for reading *Run ... You Can't Hide.* If you enjoyed the book, please <u>drop me a line</u>. I would love to hear from you.

Authors survive on reviews. So please post one if you like this book. Also, you can help promote clean, entertaining reads by doing the following:

1. Leave your comments, ratings, and likes at <u>Amazon.com</u>
2. Tell your friends and family about my <u>books</u>.
3. Post a comment on your social medias or on my <u>Facebook</u> page.
4. And last but not least, I would love for you to join my Reader's Club. Sign up at <u>www.JaniceOlson.com.</u> By joining my RC, you will receive periodic updates of my latest releases, newsletters, and notifications for periodic giveaways.

As always, if you find errors in this book, please email me at: <u>Janice@JaniceOlson.com</u> so that I may improve the quality of my books for you and other readers like you.

And in the spirit of Texas, *y'all come back now, ya' hear.*

Janice Olson

For Other Books by Janice Olson

Romantic Suspense:

The Texas Sorority Sisters ~ Independent Series

Serenity's Deception
Lethal Intent
Chameleon
Run … You Can't Hide
'Tis the Season … for Justice (Christmas 2015)

Romance with a twist of humor:

The Texas Serendipity ~ Independent Series

Mr. What's-His-Name
A Plus-One Christmas (Christmas 2015)
Singletude (2016)

A note from Janice:

Domestic abuse is a huge problem around the world that affects women, men, and children while destroying lives.

In view of the story you have just read, and though my novel *Run ... You Can't Hide* is purely fictional, domestic abuse is real and takes place every day.

To help better understand domestic violence, I have listed just a few of the statistics from the "Domestic Violence Statistics," found on their Website at:
www.domesticviolencestatistics.or/domestic-violence-statistices/

- Every 9 seconds in the US a woman is assaulted or beaten.
- Around the world, at least one in every three women has been beaten, coerced into sex, or otherwise abused during her lifetime. Most often, the abuser is a member of her own family.
- Domestic violence is the leading cause of injury to women—more than car accidents, muggings, and rapes combined.
- Studies suggest that up to 10 million children witness some form of domestic violence annually.
- Nearly 1 in 5 teenage girls who have been in a relationship said a boyfriend threatened violence or self-harm if presented with a breakup.
- Every day in the US, more than three women are murdered by their husbands or boyfriends.
- Men who as children witnessed their parents' domestic violence were twice as likely to abuse their own wives than sons of nonviolent parents.

As reported by Alanna Vagianos on 10/23/2014, on Website of the Huffington Post, www.huffingtonpost.com/2014/10/23/domestic-violence-statistics-n-5959776.html, Alanna gives a dim view of domestic abuse:

- 38,028,000 – The number of women who have experienced physical intimate partner violence in their lifetimes
- 4,774,000 – The number of women in the U.S. who experience physical violence by an intimate partner every year.
- 1,509 – The number of women murdered by men they knew in 2011. Of the 1,509 women murdered, 926 women were killed by an intimate partner, and 264 of those were killed by an intimate partner during an argument.
- 1 in 4 – The number of women who will be victims of severe violence by an intimate partner in their lifetimes.
- 1 in 7 – The number of men who will be victims of severe violence by an intimate partner in their lifetimes.

These are horrible statistics that ultimately affect us all.

Perhaps you have been touched by domestic violence, you can find help and stop the abuse. If you know someone who is being abused, please encourage them to seek help. You can find aid online or ask your clergy, hospital, or police precinct for information concerning help for domestic abuse.

Together, we can take a stand and stamp out domestic violence!

Janice Olson